TRAVIS McGEE

An astute and outspoken commentator on 20th-century life . . . a man of intelligence, wit, and compassion . . . a modern-day philosopher whose observations chronicle a changing world. With each book, McGee gets older, wiser, and more cynical . . . but always better at adapting himself to a world he both renounces and respects.

"MacDONALD'S BOOKS ARE NARCOTIC AND, ONCE HOOKED, A READER CAN'T KICK THE HABIT UNTIL THE SUPPLY RUNS OUT." *Chicago Tribune Book World*

"The author of the justly famous Travis McGee series . . . knows everything dangerous there is to know about people . . . in a John D. MacDonald novel, you learn how a lot of things work . . . Some of the lessons are not at all good for you, but they are as fascinating as staring at a cobra."
The New York Times

"One of MacDonald's most admirable qualities as a novelist is that he almost unfailingly manages to deliver precisely the pleasures that his readers anticipate . . . he has much to say, all of it interesting . . . believable and occasionally breathtaking." *The Washington Post Book World*

"TRAVIS McGEE IS ONE OF THE MOST ENDURING AND UNUSUAL HEROES IN DETECTIVE FICTION." *The Baltimore Sun*

Get to know one of fiction's most enduring heroes by reading the twenty Travis McGee novels in order . . . right up to his latest smash best seller, *Cinnamon Skin*.

JOHN D. MacDONALD

Bright Orange

for the

Shroud

FAWCETT GOLD MEDAL • NEW YORK

A Fawcett Gold Medal Book

Published by Ballantine Books

Copyright © 1965 by John D. MacDonald Publishing, Inc.

A condensation of this novel appeared in COSMOPOLITAN Magazine.

ISBN 0-449-12988-8

Manufactured in the United States of America

First Fawcett Gold Medal Edition: September 1965
First Ballantine Books Edition: August 1983
Fourth Printing: May 1985

ONE

ANOTHER SEASON was ending. The mid-May sun had a tropic sting against my bare shoulders. Sweat ran into my eyes. I had discovered an ugly little pocket of dry rot in the windshield corner of the panel of the topside controls on my houseboat, and after trying not to think about it for a week, I had dug out the tools, picked up some pieces of prime mahogany, and excised the area of infection with a saber saw.

Cutting and sanding the new pieces to fit was a finicky chore. Sawdust stuck to my sweaty chest and arms. I was sustained by an awareness of the cool dark bottles of Dos Equis beer in the stainless steel box below, and by the anticipation of trudging from Bahia Mar over to the public beach where a mild wind from the east was capping the deep blue swells with white.

Also I was sustained by the determination that this would be a slob summer for McGee. It wouldn't be a gaudy summer. There wasn't enough bread for that. But a careful husbanding of funds would see me through, leaving the emergency fund untapped, ready to finance some kind of an operation in the fall.

I needed a slob summer. The machine was abused. Softness at the waist. Tremor of the hands. Bad tastes in the morning. A heaviness of muscle and bone, a tendency to sigh. Each time you wonder, Can you get it back? The good toughness and bounce and tirelessness, the weight down to a rawhide two oh five, a nasty tendency to sing during the morning shower, the conviction each day will contain wondrous things?

And I wanted it to be a loner summer. There'd been too much damned yat-a-ta-yak, fervid conversations, midnight plots, and dirty little violences for which I had been all too unprepared. The pink weal six inches below my armpit was a reminder of luck. If my foot hadn't slipped exactly when it did. . . .

A knife blade grating along a rib bone is a sound so ugly and so personal it can come right into your sleep and wake you up ten nights running.

I got a good fit on the biggest piece, drilled it, and was setting the long bronze screws home when I heard a tentative and hollow call from dockside.

"Trav? Hey, Trav? Hey, McGee?"

I turned and walked to the aft end of my sun deck and looked down at the dock. A tall, frail, sallow-looking fellow in a wrinkled tan suit too large for him stared up at me with an anxious little smile that came and went—a mendicant smile, like dogs wear in the countries where they kick dogs.

"How are you, Trav?" he said.

And just as I was about to ask him who he was, I realized, with considerable shock, that it was Arthur Wilkinson, dreadfully changed.

"Hello, Arthur."

"Can I . . . may I come aboard?"

"Certainly. Why ask?"

The gangplank chain was down. He came across, stepped onto the afterdeck, tottered, tried to smile up at me, grabbed at emptiness and collapsed onto the teak deck with a knobbly thud. I got down there in two jumps, rolled him over. He'd abraded the unhealthy flesh under one eye in the fall. I felt the pulse in his throat. It was slow and steady. Two fat teenage girls came and stared from the dock, snickering. See the funny drunk, like on television.

I opened the aft door to the lounge, gathered Arthur up and toted him in. It was like picking up a sack of feather-dry two-by-fours. He smelled stale. I took him all the way through and put him down on the bed in the guest stateroom. The air-conditioning was chill against my bare sweat. I felt Arthur's head. He didn't seem to have a fever. I had never seen a man so changed by one year of life.

His mouth worked, and he opened his eyes and tried to sit up. I pushed him back. "You sick, Arthur?"

"Just weak, I guess. I guess I just fainted. I'm sorry. I don't want to be . . ."

"A burden? A nuisance? Skip the social graces, Arthur."

I guess you always look for a little spirit, a little glint of the fang on even the most humble dog in town.

"I'm very polite," he said listlessly. "You know that, Trav. A very polite man." He looked away. "Even . . . even when

6

he was killing me, I think I was probably very, very polite."

He faded away then, like a puff of steam, quickly gone, his eyes not quite closed. I put my fingertips against the side of his throat—the pulse was still there.

As I was wondering just what the hell to do next, he came floating back up, frowned at me. "I can't cope with people like that. She must have known that. Right from the start she must have known about me."

"Who tried to kill you?"

"I guess it really doesn't matter very much. If it hadn't been him, it would have been the next one, or the one after that. Let me rest a little while and then I'll go. There wasn't any point in coming to you. I should have known that too."

Suddenly I recognized a part of that stale smell about him. It was a little bit like freshly baked bread, but not as pleasant. It's the distinctive smell of starvation, the effluvium of the sweat ducts when the body has begun to feed on itself.

"Shut up, Arthur. When did you eat last?"

"I'm not real sure. I think . . . I don't know."

"Stay where you are," I told him. I went to my stainless steel galley, looked in a locker, picked out a tin of clear, rich British broth, poured it into a pan and turned the burner on high. As it heated I looked in on him again. He gave me that reappearing nervous smile. He had a facial tic. His eyes filled with tears, and I went back to the broth. I poured it into a mug, hesitated, then tapped the liquor locker and added a fair jolt of Irish whiskey.

After I helped him get propped up, I saw he could hold it all right in both hands and sip it.

"Good."

"Take it slow, Arthur. I'll be right back."

I sluiced the sawdust and sweat off in a fast shower in the huge stall the original owner had built aboard *The Busted Flush*, put on denims and a T-shirt and checked him again. The mug was empty. He was slightly flushed. I opened the promised bottle of dark beer and went back in and sat on the foot of the bed.

"What the hell have you done to yourself, Arthur?"

His voice blurred. "Too much, maybe."

"Maybe I asked it the wrong way. What has Wilma done to you?"

Again the tears of weakness. "Oh Christ, Trav, I . . ."

"We'll go into it later, boy. You get out of the clothes

7

and into a hot shower. Then you eat some eggs. Then you sleep. Okay?"

"I don't want to be a . . ."

"Arthur, you could begin to bore me. Shut up."

After he was asleep, I took a good look at his arms. Big H could pull a man down quickly. No needle marks. But it didn't have to mean anything. Only the eyedropper group, the ones who pick the big vein open with a pin, acquire scars. Any tidy soul with a decent hypo and enough sense to use an alcohol swab afterward can go unmarked indefinitely, as any urban cop can tell you. He was still a little grimy. It was going to take more than one shower, or two. The beard stubble didn't help either. I checked through his clothes. They had been cheap originally. The labels were from Naples, Florida. He had a flat cigarette package with three one-inch butts carefully stowed therein. He had a match folder from Red's Diner in Homestead. He had two pennies and some lint. I rolled his shoes up in the clothing, carried the bundle out at arm's length and dropped it into the trash bin on the dock. Then washed my hands.

The sun was going down. I went topside. The cockpit cocktail hour, with music and girl-laughter from neighbor cruisers. As I drove the remaining screws home without working up a sweat, I kept thinking of Arthur Wilkinson as I had seen him last, over a year ago.

A big fellow, big as I am, but not the same physical type. Slow, awkward, uncoordinated—a mild and rather pedantic guy. I could remember coming across a few of the same breed way back in high school basketball days. Coaches would hustle them on the basis of size alone. They were very earnest, but they had no balance. You could catch them just right, with the hip, and they would go blundering and crashing off the court. For them, high school was the final experience in any body-contact sport.

Arthur Wilkinson had been a member of the group for a few months. I met him when he was trying to decide whether or not to invest some money in a marina enterprise. He was going around, talking earnestly to boat people. He surveyed me at drinking time, and stayed, and came back other times—came back once too often, perhaps, that time somebody had brought Wilma around.

He had told me about himself. Upstate New York boy. Little Falls. Department store family. Got a degree from Hamilton College. Went to work in the store. Became en-

8

gaged to a doctor's daughter. Didn't particularly like or dislike the department store trade. Future all lined out, nailed down. Then it all fell apart, one piece at a time, beginning with the death of his widower father, then his girl marrying another guy, until, restless, irritable, unhappy, he had sold out his controlling interest to a chain, liquidated other properties and headed for Florida.

He got along fine with the group. He was amiable and very decent. We felt protective about him. He had been schooled for survival in Little Falls, and might indeed have been formidably adapted to that environment, but away from it there was something displaced about him. He was perfectly frank about his problem. He had left, after taxes, almost a quarter of a million dollars. It was in good solid securities, bringing in, after personal income taxes, nearly nine thousand a year. But he felt it shameful to squat on it. He wanted to move it around, put some work with it, make it produce. Some of the genes of his great granddaddy kept prodding him.

The group changes; the flavor remains the same. When he was in the pack, he was the gatherer of driftwood for the beach picnics, the one who drove drunks home, the one who didn't forget the beer, the understanding listener who gets girl-tears on his beach coat, the pigeon good for the small loan, the patsy who comes calling and ends up painting the fence. All groups seem to have one. He had a fair complexion, blushed readily. He always looked scrubbed. He laughed at all the jokes, nearly always at the right place, even though he had heard them before. In short, a very nice guy, that Arthur Wilkinson. Part of the group, but nobody got really close to him. He had that little streak of reserve, of keeping the ultimate secrets. Liquor might have unlocked him except for one thing. When he took one over his limit, he fell smilingly, placidly, irrevocably asleep. And smiled in his sleep.

I could remember that for a little while Arthur and Chookie McCall had something going. She had just finished a dancing engagement at the Bahama Room at the Mile O'Beach. She's big, beautifully proportioned, vastly healthy, a dynamo brunette with a stern and striking face. Chook had fought with Frank Durkin and he had taken off and she was rebounding, and certainly Arthur was a better deal than Frank. Without a dime, Arthur would have been worth nine Frank Durkins. Why do so many great gals latch onto a Frank Durkin to mess up their lives? When she got a three-week gig up at Daytona Beach perhaps Arthur could have gone with her, but he didn't make the right moves. Then Wilma Ferner moved in when Chook was away. . . .

There are a lot more Arthur Wilkinsons in the world than there are Wilma Ferners. And this Wilma was a classic example of the type. Little, but with a bone structure so delicate she made a hundred and five pounds look like a lush abundance. Fine white-blonde hair always in that initial state of disarray which creates the urge to mess it up completely. Husky theatrical voice which covered about two octaves in what was, for her, normal conversation. Lots of anecdotes, in which she played every part, face as mobile as a clown's, making lots of gestures, flinging herself around, the gestures seemingly awkward at times until one noticed that they kept that ripe little body in a constant state of animation and display, a project given a continuous assist by her wardrobe. There were little traces of accent in her normal speech, when she wasn't imitating someone, but it seemed to vary from day to day. Hold a small clear wineglass of Harvey's Bristol Milk up to the light and it is pretty close to the color of her eyes. And, once you got past all the crinkling and sparkling and winking, her eyes had just about as much expression as still wine.

She came in on a big Huckins out of Savannah, amid boat guests in various conditions of disrepair, much of the damage evidently being accomplished by people beating people in the face with their fists. She moved into a hotel room ashore, in the Yankee Clipper, and after the cruiser took off without her, she somehow managed to affix herself to our group, saying that the lovely people on the Huckins were going to pick her up on their way back from Nassau, and she had begged off because she could not *endure* Nassau one more *stinking* time.

In that venerable and useful show biz expression, she was always on. The gals seemed to have an instinctive wariness of her. The men were intrigued. She claimed to have been born in Calcutta, mentioned the tragic death of a father in the Australian diplomatic service, mentioned directly and obliquely her own careers as set designer in Italy, fashion coordinator in Brussels, photographer's model in Johannesburg, society and fashion editor on a newspaper in Cairo, private secretary to the wife of one of the presidents of Guatemala. As she cooed, twisted, bounced, exclaimed, imitated, chuckled, I must admit that I had a few moments

10

of very steamy curiosity. But there were too many warning flags up. The pointed nails curved too extremely over the soft tips of the little fingers. The poses and pauses were too carefully timed. And there was just a bit too much effervescence and charm. Perhaps if she had come along a few years earlier—before I had seen and learned all kinds of con, before I had found some of the sicknesses no clinic can identify . . .

So we wondered who would nail it. Or vice versa. She was carrying a weapon at port arms, waiting for a target of opportunity.

I remember a very late night when I sat alone with my hairy economist friend named Meyer in the cockpit of his small cruiser which he christened *The John Maynard Keynes*, after a beach time when Wilma had been so totally on she had sparkled like the moonlit surf.

"Wonder how old she is?" I asked idly.

"My friend, I have kept meticulous track of all pertinent incidents. To have done what she claims to have done, she is somewhere between one hundred and five and one hundred and seven. I added five more years tonight."

"Psychopathic liar, Meyer?"

"An inexact science uses inexact terms. I spit on parlor expertise, Travis."

"Sure. I have one suspicion, though. There is so much merchandise in the showcase there's nothing left back in the storeroom."

"I wouldn't gamble on that either."

"What the hell would you gamble on, Meyer?"

"A man with no trace of the feminine in him, with no duality at all, is a man without tenderness, sympathy, gentleness, kindness, responsiveness. He is brute-mean, a hammer, a fist. McGee, what is a woman with no trace of the masculine in her makeup?"

"Mmm. Merciless in a different way?"

"You show promise, McGee. The empathy of kindness is a result of the duality, not of the feminine trace. Our strange friend, the Alabama Tiger, is maneuvering the lady just right. And she resents it. He moves in with a forked stick, and he'll pin her head to the ground and then pick her up in such a way she can't get her fangs into him. Maybe women are the only things in the world he knows so well."

I told Meyer he was crazy, that anybody could see that the Alabama Tiger and Wilma Ferner had disliked each other on sight. Meyer wouldn't argue it. On the adjoining

11

deck, in a big rich Wheeler, the Alabama Tiger maintains what is by now the longest floating houseparty in the world. He is a huge, sloppy guy, once a murderous All-American tackle, who later made a pot of money and decided to spend it on boats, booze and broads. He stays blandly, cheerfully tight during all waking hours. He has a face like crude stone sculpture, carved into a mild grin. In forty seconds he can make you feel as if you are the most interesting person he has ever met, and you will feel as if you never met anyone more understanding. He could charm tenement landlords, post office employees, circus dwarfs and tax assessors.

When Wilma finally took aim, Arthur Wilkinson was the hapless target, and there was not one damn thing any of us could do about it. He had less chance than a lovely wench when the Goths came to town. His eyes glazed over. A broad fatuous grin was permanently in place. She was at his elbow, steering him, to keep him from walking into immovable objects. He thought her junebug cute, delicate and dear, infinitely valuable. He felt humble to be so favored, to be awarded this rare prize. Any hint that the junebug might be a scorpion didn't offend him. He just couldn't hear what was said to him. He laughed, thinking it some kind of a joke. After the minimum waiting time, they were married late one afternoon at the court house, and left in a new white Pontiac convertible, the back seat stacked with her matched luggage, her smile as brilliant as a brand new vermin trap ordered from Herter's catalogue. I had kissed the dear little cheek of the junebug bride. She'd smelled soapy clean. She called me a dear boy. My present was a six pack—Metaxa, Fundador, Plymouth gin, Chivas Regal, Old Crow and a Piper Heidsieck '59. For the expendable marriage, you give the expendable gift. She left a message for the yacht that wouldn't be back to pick her up. And I knew the two of them would not come back to Lauderdale as long as she was in command. She had sensed the appraisal of the group, and would require a more gullible environment.

Three days after they left, we all knew something was wrong with the Alabama Tiger. Instead of his benign and placid condition of mild alcoholic euphoria, he swung between morose sobriety and wild, reckless, dangerous drunks. The permanent houseparty began to dwindle. It was Meyer who dug the reason out of him after finding the Tiger sitting lumpily on the beach at dawn with a loaded 38 tucked inside his shirt. And because he wanted a little help in keeping an eye on him, Meyer told me the story.

Wilma had secretly invited the Tiger over to headquarters at the hotel one morning. With a deftness, Meyer said, more common in the Far East than in our less ancient cultures, she had quickly learned how to turn him on and off, as if he were a construction kit she had wired herself. Then, with a dreadful control, she had taken him right to the edge and hung him up there, incapable of either release or retreat.

"In his own deathless words," Meyer said, "whooflin' and shakin' like an ol' hawg hung on the charger wires. He honestly began to believe it was going to kill him. He could feel his heart beginning to burst. And she was laughing at him, he said, her face like a spook. Then suddenly, without release or warning, he felt dead. He heard her singing in her shower. After she was dressed, she kissed him on the forehead, patted his cheek and left. He thought of killing her as she bent over to kiss him, but even that seemed too unimportant for the effort involved. Suddenly he had become an old man. She had accepted the tension between them, the contest of wills, and had taken a little time out to whip him before leaving. It might interest you, McGee, to know that it happened last Thursday morning."

She had married Arthur Thursday afternoon.

"There could be a little heart damage," Meyer said. "There certainly seems to be plenty of emotional damage."

Monday night, late, I walked over to the Tiger's big flushdeck Wheeler and from fifty feet away I decided, with that sense of loss you have when a legend ends, that the oldest permanent floating houseparty in the world had finally ended. One small light glowed. But from twenty feet I picked up the tempo of Hawaiian music on his record player system, turned very low. Approaching, I made out a girl-shape in the glow of dock-lights, dancing alone slowly on the after deck under the striped canvas canopy, highlights glinting on the glass in her hand as she turned.

She saw me and angled her dance toward the rail, and I saw that it was one of the Ching sisters, Mary Li or Mary Lo, the identical twins who sing-and-dance at the Roundabout, closed Mondays. She was involved in a variant of the dance forms of her native Hawaii. It is impossible to tell the twins apart. Almost impossible. I had heard that Mary Lo is distinguished by a tiny vivid gem-like tattoo of a good luck ladybug, but so intimately located that by the time one

13

encounters it, any thought of choice has long since been obviated.

Her hair swayed dark and heavy as she turned, and her smile was white in duskiness. "Hey you, McGee," she said in a low tone. "Long as one little thing keeps swinging, Poppa Tiger's bash is still alive. You haul aboard, make yourself a cup there."

As I made my drink she said, "We running a fox roster, man, the chicks who swung good here, keeping him braced up."

"How is he making it, Mary?"

"Now he smiled some tonight, and he cried just a little time because he said he was done for good and all, but a little time back my sister came topside all tuckered and said he made out, and now they sacked out like death itself, and this here is the party, McGee man, down to just me. And now you, but Frannie coming by after she gets off work at two, bringing that bongo cat, and I say things pick up from here, pick up good. A swinger boat, with booze like a convention, you got to brace the management when he's down."

"The only reason, Mary?"

She stopped her dance eye to eye, a handspan away.

"Like that dirty-mind cop wants to close us down, Poppa Tiger goes way upstairs and has the clout to mend his ways. Like our nephew needed the school letter that time, Poppa Tiger writes pretty. I just want to keep the free booze coming man, and tap that locker full of prime beef, and get the boat kicks."

"I knew better. I thought it would be nice to hear you say it, Mary."

"Brace up this dead drink for me, on the house. It's fat vodka, one cube and a smitch from the little cranberry juice can."

"Gah."

"Don't drink it, just make it."

We had some drinks, and I watched her dance, and we had some laughs because the old bear was on the mend. Frannie brought along some other kids from the club she was working. And as an unexpected by-product of celebration, I learned beyond any chance of confusion that the night dancer had been Mary Lo. Selections from the Tiger pack are not my usual type, as it tends to be too casual and mechanical for the ornamented romanticism of the McGee, who always wants a scarf in token to tie to the crest of the cut-rate helmet, wants the soul-torn glance, the tremors of

14

the heart, the sense—or the illusion—of both choice and importance. But Mary Lo left no bad taste. She made it like a game for kids, chuckling and crooning her pleasures, and it did indeed pleasantly blur the use Wilma made of the same game. After they have strangled the king with boiling wine, it is therapeutic to get a little tipsy on a more palatable brand.

TWO

ARTHUR FELL BACK into my life on that Tuesday afternoon. Acquaintance rather than friend. The dividing line is communication, I think. A friend is someone to whom you can say any jackass thing that enters your mind. With acquaintances, you are forever aware of their slightly unreal image of you, and to keep them content, you edit yourself to fit. Many marriages are between acquaintances. You can be with a person for three hours of your life and have a friend. Another one will remain an acquaintance for thirty years.

While he slept I dug into the more remote lockers in the bow section until I found the small ragged suitcase I remembered. Girl-bought clothes for a version of McGee of long ago, when I hid out and they hunted me, and I was afraid the stink of my rotting leg would clue them in. Killed the two of them while in delirium. No memory of how she got me to the hospital. Heard later how she managed to keep them from taking the leg off. Now there is that crooked pale arroyo, long down the right thigh, deep into muscle tissue. Function unimpaired. But a chancy time, deep there in fevers, seeing the pearly gleam of the gates, talking to the dead brother, sometimes looking up out of a well at the professional faces bending over the bed.

These were the clothes she brought me, the clothes in which I was wheeled out into the vivid unreal world, clothes in which I first tottered about, ten feet tall and two inches wide, certain that if I fell off the crutches I would break like a glass stork. They would fit Arthur nicely in his dwindled condition and were only slightly musty from long storage. In a housewifely mood, I hung them out to air, thinking of the money the dead ones had stolen, quite legally, from the

15

dead brother and how, quite illegally, the girl and I had stolen it back, cut it down the middle.

While Arthur slept, I wondered how the hell to get rid of him. That was the extent of my Christian charity. I could accept being an aid station but not a convalescent clinic. I went over the composition of the group as Arthur had known it, looking for a substitute pigeon. I had my slob summer all planned. Immediately after the dry rot surgery and a few other maintenance matters, I wanted to take *The Busted Flush* down to Dinner Key, get her hauled and get the bottom scraped and painted, and then chug at my stately 6+ knots—with a six-hundred mile range on the two 58 hp Hercules Diesels—over to the Bahamas on a dead calm day. The 52-foot barge-type houseboat can take pretty rough weather if forced to, but she rolls so badly she tends to bust up the little servomechanisms aboard which make life lush. I had been mentally composing a guest list, limited to those random salty souls who can get away, hold their liquor, endure sunshine, make good talk, swim the reefs, navigate, handle the lines, slay food fish and appreciate the therapeutic value of silence. It is the McGee version of being a loner—merely having some people about to whom you don't have to constantly react. Arthur did not fit that specification closely enough.

When darkness came, I took the aired clothes below and put them on a chair in the guest stateroom. He was snoring in a muted way. I closed his door, fixed myself a Plymouth gin on the rocks, closed the lounge curtains, looked up Chookie McCall's number. No answer. I hadn't seen her or heard anything about her in two months. I tried Hal, the bartender at the Mile O'Beach who keeps good track of our gypsy contingent of entertainers. Hal said she'd been working at Bernie's East up to May first when they closed the Brimstone Room, and as far as he knew all she was doing was a Saturday morning one-hour show of dance instruction on KLAK-TV. But he had it on good authority she was all set to regroup her six pack and open back at the Mile O'Beach in the Bahama Room come November 15th.

"Hal, is Frank Durkin back yet?"

"Back yet! Don't sit on your hands until he gets back. Dint you hear what they got him on?"

"Only that he took a fall."

"It was assault with intent to kill, or felonious assault or whatever the hell they call it. Three to five up in Raiford, and you can bet Frankie will get smartass with those screws

16

up there and they will keep him for the five. Chook goes up to see him once a month. She'll be making a lot of trips. All that woman could find something better, McGee, and you know it. She don't get any younger."

"Younger? Hell, she's only twenty-five at the most."

"Ten years in the entertainment business, and thirty when they turn Frankie Durkin loose. It adds up, Trav. If I was trying to locate her tonight, I think maybe Muriel Hess would be a good bet. She's in the book. They've been working together on material for when she starts up here in the fall."

I thanked him and tried the number. Chook was there. "What's on your mind, stranger?"

"Buying a steak for the dancing girl."

"Plural?"

"Not if you can help it."

There was a long palm-over-the-mouthpiece silence, and then she said, "What kind of a place, Trav?"

"The Open Range?"

"Yum! I'll have to go back to my place and change. How about coming over for a drink? Forty minutes?"

I shaved and changed, and left a note for Arthur in case he woke up. Because of all the boat errands, I had Miss Agnes parked nearby, my electric blue Rolls pickup truck, an amateur conversion accomplished by some desperate idiot during her checkered past. She is not yet old enough to vote. But almost. She started with a touch, and I went along the beach to where Miss McCall lives in the back end of a motel so elderly it has long since been converted from transient to permanent residence. She's in what used to be two units. Wrapped in a robe, smelling of steam and soap, she gave me a sisterly kiss, told me to fix her a bourbon and water. I handed it in to her.

In a reasonably short time she came out in high heels and a pale green-gray dress. "McGee, I think I say yes because how many guys I go out with can I wear heels with?" She inspected me. "You're too heavy."

"Thanks. I feel too heavy."

"Are you going to do anything about it?"

"I've started."

"With booze in your hand?"

"I'm starting a little slow, but I'm one of those who lose it with exercise. Not enough lately. But a lot more coming up. Chook, you are *not* too heavy."

"Because I work at it *all* the time."

She was indeed something, All that woman, as Hal had

17

said. Five ten, maybe 136 pounds, maybe 39-25-39, and every inch glossy, firm, pneumatic—intensely alive, perfectly conditioned as are only the dedicated professional dancers, circus flyers, tumblers, and combat rangers. Close up you can hear their motors humming. Heart beat in repose is in the fifties. Lung capacity extraordinary. Whites of the eyes a blue-white.

Not a pretty woman. Features too vital and heavy. Brows heavy. Hair harsh and black and glossy, like a racing mare. Indian-black eyes, bold nose, big broad mouth. A handsome, striking human being. When she was five years old they had started her on ballet. When she was twelve she had grown too big to be accepted in any company. When she was fifteen, claiming nineteen, she was in the chorus of a Broadway musical.

While I freshened the drinks she told me what she was working out with Muriel, a New Nations theme, researching the music and rhythms. She said it would give them some exotic stuff and some darling costumes and some sexy choreography. We sat to finish the drink. She said Wassener, the new manager, was considering a no-bra policy for the little troupe next season, and was sounding out the authorities to see how bad a beef he might get. She said she hoped it wouldn't work out, as it would mean either canceling out two good girls she already had lined up, or talking them into wax jobs. "Posing and blackouts and that stuff," she said, "it's a different thing. You just keep your chin up and you arch your back a little and tighten your shoulders back, but I've been trying to tell Mr. Wassener dancing is something else. MiGod, a time step in fast tempo, and all of a sudden it could look like a comedy routine, you know what I mean. If he thinks it'll draw, what he should get is a couple of big dumb ponies and just let them stand upstage on pedestals maybe, in baby spots and turn slow."

After I agreed, there was a last inch of the drink silence, and I knew I had to say something about Frank Durkin. Like being forced to discuss ointment with somebody with an incurable skin rash.

"Sorry to hear Frank took such a long count."

She sprang to her feet and gave me a look Custer must have gotten very tired of before they chopped him up. "It wasn't *fair*, goddam it! The guy was being very smartass, and Frankie didn't owe him any fifty dollars. It was a mistake. When he followed him out into the parking lot, all Frankie was going to do was scare him. But he jumped the wrong way and Frankie ran over him. What they did, Travis, believe me, they judged him on the other times he's been in trouble. And that's unconstitutional, isn't it? Isn't it?"

"I don't know."

"He has that terrible temper. Right in court he tried to get his hands on the judge. Believe me, he's his own worst enemy. But this isn't fair at all."

What could anyone tell her? To forget him? She'd swing from the floor and loosen your teeth. The only times she ever tried to forget him was after their savage quarrels. She was a very fine woman, and Frankie Durkin was no damned good. Sponged off her. Kept her on the hook with promises of marriage. Fancied himself crafty and managed to out-smart himself in most deals. Then cursed his luck. I would have said his luck was excellent—because he would have long since been caged or fried as a murderer if, in several known instances, he'd achieved his heart's desire. I saw him in his fury once. His pale blue eyes turned white as milk. His underprivileged face went slack as taffy. And, grunting with each breath, he began to try to kill a friend of mine. Could have made it if they'd been alone. As he wasn't worth breaking any hand bones on, I took the billy I kill toothy fish with and bounced it off his skull. After three lumps he was still trying to crawl toward Mack's throat, but the fourth one pacified him. When he woke up he seemed unfocused, like a man after a hard fever. And had no hard feelings at all.

"How is he taking it?"

"Real hard, Trav. He keeps telling me he can't stand it, he's got to do something." She sighed. "But there's nothing he can do. Maybe . . . when he gets out, he'll be ready to settle down. Let's get out of here."

Miss Agnes drifted us silently over to the mainland, to the Open Range, a place disfigured by mass production Texas folk art, steer horns, branding irons, saddle hardware, coiled lariats and bullwhips. But the booths are deep and padded, the lights low, the steaks prime and huge. Chook ordered hers so raw I was grateful for the low candlepower of the booth lamp. I invested some additional ditch-Arthur money in a bottle of burgundy. I have seen Chook under other circumstances do the social-eating routine. But with me she could follow her inclination and eat in the busy, dedicated, appreciative silence of a farmhand or roustabout, chugging her way deftly through tossed, baked and extra rare, and at

19

last leaning back from the emptiness to give me an absent, dreamy smile, and stifle a generous belch.

Judging I was at the exact moment, I said, "Small favor?"

"Anything at all, Trav darling."

"I'm cutting you in on a lame duck who showed up. In bad, bad shape. It would be sort of for old time's sake for you."

"Who?"

"Arthur Wilkinson."

I thought I saw a momentary softness in her eyes before they turned fierce. She leaned forward. "I tell you what I am not. I am not a trash basket. I am no place you can dump the leavings from that pig."

"Put your wheels down, Chookie. Who's the most naïve little chick in your troupe?"

"Huh? Well . . . Mary Lou King."

"She engaged?"

"Sort of. What is this, anyway?"

"Now suppose say . . . Rock Hudson came barreling in at her, all guns blazing. What would Mary Lou do?"

Chook giggled. "Gawd, she'd roll over like a dead bug."

"I'm under a handicap. I never did find out what status you reached with Arthur. He'd never volunteer that sort of information, as you well know. It was my guess it got pretty humid."

She studied her nails. "When Frankie took off that time, he busted my place up before he went. Everything. He even tore up my scrapbooks. He said I'd never lay eyes on him again as long as I lived. And I don't even know what it was we were fighting about. Okay, so I needed a gentle guy. Not for sex. I'm not cold—maybe I'm more the other way than I should be, but, hell, I can always put on old music and dig out old routines and a practice uniform, work hard for a few hours and sleep like a baby." She gave me a quick dark glance. "I guess I should be honest. Mostly it was to have somebody close, but that's no reason to knock the other part of it. And maybe I was trying to use him to tear loose from Frankie. At first I told him all my lousy troubles. And we took some walks. And then after one walk, we ended up in my bed. And if I left it entirely up to Arthur, we wouldn't have. I had to make it easy for him without letting him catch on to what I was doing. You know me, Trav. I'm not a pig. I suppose . . . if I taught third grade in Webster Falls, I wouldn't last too long. But in the business I'm in . . . I'm thought square. You know?"

"I know."

For just an instant I had a feeling of waste and loss. There was so much shrewdness, native intelligence, perception there. The awareness of self, undistorted, a virtue growing ever more rare in our times. It made you wonder what this creature of such vast vitality could have become if she had taken some other direction with her life. Too many of the good ones aren't being used up all the way.

But a little personal resonance got to me. Because I'd never found the right way of using myself up. So I had settled for a variation of the lush life, bumming along the golden strand until funds sagged too low, then venturing forth to clip the clip artists, wresting the stolen meat—legally stolen usually—out of the bandit jowls, then splitting the salvage down the middle with the victim—who, without the services of McGee, would have had to settle for nothing, which, as I have often pointed out, is considerably less than half.

It isn't a very respectable dedication. So just say it's a living. Sometimes I get a very faint echo of the knight errant psychosis. And try to make more out of it than is there. But everybody's hall closet is full of lances and shields and other tourney gear. The guy who sells you insurance gets singed by his own secret kind of dragon breath. And his own Maid Marian yoo-hoos him back to the castle tower.

Maybe, somewhere along the line, I could have gone the other route. But you get a taste for the hunt. You keep wondering how close the next one is going to get to you. And you have to see. And nothing can slow the reflexes like the weight of mortgages, withholding, connubial contentment, estate program, regular checkups and puttering around your own lawn.

But now they are phasing out the hunters. Within this big complex culture, full of diodes, paperclips, account numbers, they are earnestly boarding up the holes, sealing the conduits, installing bugs and alarms in every corridor. In a few years there'll be no room left for the likes of McGee. They'll grab him, carry him away and adjust him to reality, and put him to work at something useful in one of the little cubicles in the giant structure.

So who are you to think of a fuller life for Miss Chookie McCall?

"Could it have worked out with Arthur?" I asked her.

She shrugged those strong shoulders. "He's almost five years older, but he seemed kind of like a kid. I don't know.

21

So considerate and so . . . grateful. He was getting to be a better lover. It was like at first, getting him to think things were his idea. Trav, honest to God, what was I supposed to do? Ask him to please come to Jacksonville with me? I mean there's pride too. He wanted to. But he thought it wouldn't be right. I wanted him there. Maybe it was like putting up a wall, a little at a time, shutting out the hurt from Frankie. Maybe we could have made the wall thick enough and tall enough. Maybe not. Maybe when Frankie came back, it would have been the same for me, Arthur or no Arthur, Frankie crooking his finger and I crawl to him. I won't ever know, will I, because Arthur didn't go up to Jax with me, and so we didn't have that three weeks and we didn't have the four months back here before Frankie came back, broke and sick and mean as a basket of snakes. I came back and Wilma had Arthur skinned and nailed to the bar, and the son of a bitch shook hands with me as if he couldn't remember my name. Pride still counts with me. I am not going to be a damned rescue mission, Trav. Believe me. Go look for a little mother somewhere else. He made his lousy choice."

"Okay. I see your point. But just stop by the boat and take a look at him."

"No! You don't get clever with me. Once in Akron the dressing room was alive with mice, and I set a trap. All it did was maim one little bastard, and three weeks later, after I got him back on his feet, I turned him loose. He'd lick peanut butter off my fingertip. Trav, I wouldn't go anywhere near Arthur."

THREE

WHEN I GOT BACK to *The Busted Flush* with Chook, Arthur Wilkinson was as I had left him, the note still there. I put on the overhead light. I heard her suck air. Her strong cool fingers clamped on my hand. I looked at her thoughtful profile, saw her tanned forehead knotted into a frown, white teeth indenting her lower lip. I turned the light off and turned her, and we went back to the lounge, two closed doors between us and Arthur.

"You should get a doctor to look at him!" she said indignantly.

"Maybe. Later on. No fever. He passed out, as I told you, but he said he just felt faint. Malnutrition is my guess."

"Maybe you got a license to practice? Trav, he looks so horrible! Like a skull, like he was dying instead of sleeping. How do you know?"

"That he's sleeping? What else?"

"But what could have happened to him?"

"Chook, that was a very nice guy, and I don't think he had the survival drive you and I have. He's the victim type. Wilma was his mousetrap, and nobody cared if he got maimed. No peanut butter. We had one in Korea. A big gentle kid fresh out of the Hill School. Everybody from my platoon sergeant on down tried to get the green off him before he got nailed. But one rainy afternoon he got suckered by the fake screaming we'd gotten used to, and he went to help and got stitched throat to groin with a machine pistol. I heard about it and went over as they were sticking the litter onto a jeep. He died right then, and the look on his face was not pain or anger or regret. He just looked very puzzled, as if he was trying to fit this little incident into what he'd been taught at home and couldn't quite make it. It's the way some earnest people take a practical joke."

"Shouldn't we see if Arthur is really all right?"

"Let him get his sleep. Fix you a stinger?"

"I don't know. No. I mean yes. I'm going to take another look at him."

Five minutes later I tiptoed into the companionway beyond the head. The guest stateroom door was closed. I heard the tone of her voice, not the words. Gentleness. He coughed and answered her and coughed again.

Back in the lounge I locked the big tuner into WAEZ-FM, and fed it into the smaller speakers at low volume, too low to drive my big AR-3's. I stretched out on the curve of the big yellow couch, took small bites of the gin stinger, listened to a string quartet fit together the Chinese puzzle pieces of some ice-cold Bach, and smiled a fatuous egg-sucking smile at my prime solution to the Arthur problem.

In about twenty minutes she joined me, eyes red, smile shy, walking with less assurance than her custom. She sat on the end of the couch beyond my feet and said, "I fixed him some warm milk and he went right to sleep again."

"That's nice."

"I guess it's just being exhausted and half starved and heartsick, Trav."

"That was my guess."

"The poor dumb bastard."

"Outclassed."

I got her stinger out of the freezer and brought it to her. She sipped it. "There isn't anything else you can do, of course," she said.

"Beg your pardon?"

She looked at me and opened her eyes very wide. "Get it back, of course. They cleaned him clean. That's why he came to you."

I got up and went over to the tuner and killed Mr. Bach. I stood in front of Chook. "Now just one minute there, woman. Hold it. There's no . . ."

"For God's sake, stop looking as if you're going to bray like a wounded moose, McGee. We talked about you once."

"Make some sense."

"He wondered about you. You know. What you *do*. So I sort of told him."

"You sort of told him."

"Just how you step in when people get the wrong end of the stick, and you keep half of what you can recover. McGee, why in the world do you think he came right to you! Could anything be more obvious? Why do you think that poor whipped creature crawled across the state and fell on your doorstep? You can't *possibly* turn him down."

"I can give it a very good try, honey."

Silence. She finished the drink. She clacked the empty glass down. She came up off the couch, moved close, stood tall, fixed me with a poisonous stare, upslanted, fists on hips. "Did I do you a favor coming here?" she said in almost a whisper. "Do you owe me for that, and for one or two other small things I could name? Do you want me to go after them myself? I will, you know. I'm calling you on this one, you big ugly lazy jerk. They smashed him. They gutted him. And there's no other place he can turn." Giving emphasis to each word by rapping my chest with a hard knuckle, she said, "You-are-going-to-help-that-man."

"Now listen . . ."

"And I want a piece of the action, Travis."

"I have no intention of . . ."

"The first thing we have to do is get him on his feet, and pry every living piece of information out of him."

"How about that weekly television thing you . . ."

"I'm two tapes ahead, and I can go down there and do

24

three more in one day. Trav, they didn't leave him a *dime*! It was some kind of land development thing. Over near Naples."

"Maybe by fall . . ."

"Travis!"

By the following Saturday afternoon *The Busted Flush* was swinging on two hooks in Florida Bay, two miles off Candle Key, all larders stocked, five hundred gallons in the fresh water tanks. With alterations from time to time, I've tried to make the old barge-type houseboat ever more independent of shoreside services. Except when home at Bahia Mar, I like to avoid the boat basin togetherness. Under one hatch I have a whole area paved with husky batteries, enough of them so that I can stay at anchor and draw on them for four days before they begin to get a little feeble. When they're down, I can use them to start up an electric trickle-feed generator which can bring them back up in six hours. If I ever get careless enough to run them all the way down, I can break out the big 10 kw gasoline generator and use it to get the electric one started. At anchor I switch everything over to 32 V. I can't run the air-conditioning off the batteries, but I can run it off the gas generator. Then it is a decision as to which will be the most annoying, the heat or the noise.

The sun was heading for Hawaii. Just enough breeze for a pattycake sound against the hull. I was stretched out on the sun deck. A line of pelicans creaked by, beating and coasting, heading home to the rookery. What I had learned so far from Arthur didn't sound promising. But I comforted myself with thinking that while we were getting him in shape, I was doing myself some promised good. I was on cheese, meat and salad. No booze. No cigarettes. Just one big old pot pipe packed with Black Watch for the sunset hour. Due any time now.

Every muscle felt stretched, bruised and sore. We'd anchored at mid-morning. I'd spent a couple of hours in mask and fins, knocking and gouging some of the grass beards and corruption off the hull. After lunch I'd lain on the sundeck with my toes hooked under the rail and done about ten sets of situps. Chook had caught me at it and talked me into some of the exercises she prescribed for her dance group. One exercise was a bitch. She could do it effortlessly. You lift your left leg, grab the ankle with your right hand, and play one-legged jump rope with it, over and back. Then switch hands and ankles and jump on the other leg. After that we swam. I could win the sprints. In our distance events, she had a nasty habit of slowly drawing even, and then slowly pulling away, and an even nastier habit of smiling placidly at me while I wheezed and gasped.

I heard a sound and turned my head and saw her climb the ladderway to the sundeck. She looked concerned. She sat crosslegged beside me. In that old faded pink suit, dark hair in a salty tangle, no makeup, she looked magnificent.

"He feels kind of weak and dizzy," she said. "I think I let him get too much sun. It can sap your strength. I gave him a salt tablet, and it's making him nauseated."

"Want me to go take a look at him?"

"Not right now. He's trying to doze off. Gee, he's so damn grateful for every little thing. And it broke my heart, the way he looked in trunks, so scrawny and pathetic."

"He eats many lunches like today, it won't last long."

She inspected a pink scratch on a ripe brown calf. "Trav? How are you going to go about it? What are you going to try to do?"

"I wouldn't have the slightest idea."

"How long are we going to stay here?"

"Until he has the guts to want to go back, Chook."

"But why should he *have* to? I mean if he dreads it so."

"Because, dear girl, he is my reference library. He doesn't know what very small thing might turn out to be very important, so he doesn't think of it or mention it. Then when it's about to go off in my face, he can tell me where the fuse is, which is something he can't do from a hundred miles away."

She looked at me speculatively. "He wants to give up the whole idea."

"Okay. Sure."

"*Damn* you!"

"Sweetie, you can take a good and gentle horse, and you can start using a chain on it. Maybe you turn it into a killer. And maybe you break it right down to nothing, to a trembling hunk of meat. Then can you ever turn it back into a horse? Depends on the blood line. Sometimes you don't want the victim along. Sometime, like this time, you have the hunch you'll need him. I won't go into this without him. So he has to forget the chain. You're along to turn him back into a horse, Chook. You've got to prop him up. I don't want you in on any of the rest of it."

"Why not?"

"It sounds just a little too dirty so far."

"And I have just walked out the convent gates in my little white pinafore. Come *on*, Trav!"

"Miss McCall, the most dangerous animal in the world is not the professional killer. It's the amateur. When they sense that somebody is taking back what they went to so much effort to acquire, that's when they get violent. The essentially dishonest man is capable of truly murderous indignation. In this instance, the bitch will be looking on, heightening the performance, looking for blood. I don't think she'll relish losing."

I sensed mischief as she studied me. "I guess any man would find her pretty exciting."

"Hell, it's exciting to be pushed out a window. Or run over."

"And you didn't have the least little urge, darling? She did sort of have an eye on you."

"The scorpion is a very cute little brown bug, the way she plods along with that tail curled over her back. She's a living fossil, you know, unchanged in millions of years. It's imaginable that some bug-lover might want to pick one up and stroke her scaly little back."

Big brown girl in scanty pink, in Zen-pose on my splendid vinyl imitation of teak. It is real teak on the aft deck below, partially justifying such trickery. Staring dubiously at me. "Men aren't that bright about those."

"Arthur wasn't."

"And what have *you* got? Radar?"

"Alarm systems. Bachelor devices to detect poisonous types. One good way is to watch how the other women react. You and the others, when Wilma Ferner was around, all your mouths got a little tight, and you were very very polite to her. And you made no girl talk at all with her. No clothes talk. No date talk. No guided trips to the biff. No girl secrets. Just the way, honey, a woman should be damned wary of a man other men have no use for."

That was a little careless, and too close to home. Frankie gives most men the warm sweet urge to hit him heavily in the mouth. Chook's dark eyes became remote. "If the breeze dies it could get buggy here."

"The long-range forecast says we'll get more wind instead of less." I rose smartly to my feet. If I'd been alone, perhaps I would have crawled moaning to the sundeck rail and hauled myself up. Vanity is a miracle drug. I could count on three or four more days of torment before, I hoped, the limberness would come back, along with the hardened belly and lost pounds and unjangled nerves.

As I stretched and yawned, Chookie said, "Hey!" and came to me and in a very gingerly way touched, with one fingertip, the pink weal below my left armpit. "I didn't notice that. It's new, huh?"

"Aw, it's just a scratch."

"Knife?"

"Yup."

She swallowed and looked ill. "The idea of knives, it makes my stomach turn over. And it makes me think of Mary Lo Ching."

While I'd been away on this last one, the one that gave me the funds for a slob summer, an animal had gotten to Mary Lo with a knife. The twins had been working in Miami Beach, in March. They got him in a few hours by rounding up known sex offenders. They'd thought this one harmless. He'd been tucked away a few times for short falls. Peeping, indecent exposure. His profession was fry cook. All the time he was working himself up to a big one, and Mary Lo had been in just the wrong place at the wrong time. He hadn't been selective. Just the first one he could get to. They didn't count the wounds. They just said "more than fifty."

The psychiatrists call it a sickness. The cops call it a hell of a problem. The sociologists call it a product of our culture, our puritanical tendency to consider sex a delicious nastiness. Some of them escalate to the big violence. Others stay with a small kick, peering into bedrooms. You can't give a man life for that, nor even constructive psychiatric help during a short sentence. He cuts brush on the county gang, tormented by the other prisoners, driven further into his private madness. Then he comes out and cuts up Mary Lo, and at once everybody is an expert on how he should have been handled by the authorities, up to and including gelding the very first time he committed a nuisance in a public park.

"Anybody know anything about Mary Li?" I asked.

"Just that she went back to Hawaii." Chook stepped back a pace and looked at me from ears to heels as if examining one of the metal sculptures in the garden of the Museum of Modern Art. She shook her head sadly and said, "McGee, I swear, I never really noticed before how many times you've been torn up."

"This one here happened when I was three. My big

28

brother threw a hammer up into a tree to knock some apples down. The hammer came down too."

"Do you *like* being in a crazy kind of business that gets you so close to being killed?"

"I don't like to hurt. Every little nick makes me that much more careful. Maybe I'll get so careful I'll have to find some other line of work."

"Seriously?"

"Seriously. Miners get silicosis. Doctors get coronaries. Bankers get ulcers. Politicians get strokes. Remember about the alligators? Honey, if *nothing* happened to people, we'd all be ass-deep in people."

"And I should see what happened to the other guys. Okay, you can't be serious." She marched off, and went down the ladderway like a . . . a dancer going down a ladderway.

I could be serious in that particular area, but not on her terms. I'd had enough stitches to make a quilt, and had enjoyed not one of them at all, at all. And most floor nurses have a top sergeant syndrome. I went below and packed the promised pipe. Chook was in the stainless steel galley, banging pots. I went through to the guest stateroom where I had quartered myself. Chook had made that decision while we were provisioning the boat, when she brought her gear aboard. She had declared flatly that she wasn't going to mouse around. All three of us knew she'd slept with Arthur before his marriage, and the huge bed in the master stateroom—the bed that had been there when I'd won the boat—gave her a better chance to keep watch over him, and if he wanted to make something of it, then she was willing to be compliant on the basis of therapy, affection, old time's sake, morale—call it whatever the hell you feel like calling it, McGee.

I had told her I avoided putting names on things whenever possible, and I transferred my personal gear and went back to the hot greasy chore of smoothing out the port engine which, after too much idleness, was running hesitantly, fading when I gave it more throttle, complaining that it wanted its jets cleaned.

By mid-evening, Arthur Wilkinson felt better. It was a soft night. We sat in three deck chairs on the afterdeck, facing the long path of silver moonlight on the black water.

I overpowered his reluctance and made him go over some of the stuff he had already told me, interrupting him with questions to see if I could unlock other parts of his memory.

"Like I told you, Trav, I had the idea we were going to go farther away, maybe the southwest, but after we stayed overnight in Naples, she said maybe it would be nice to rent a beach house for a while. Because it was April we could probably find something nice. What she found was nice, all right. Isolated, and a big stretch of private beach, and a pool. It was seven hundred a month, plus utilities. That included the man who came twice a week to take care of the grounds, but then there was another two hundred and fifty for the woman who came in about noon every day but Sunday."

"Name?"

"What? Oh . . . Mildred. Mildred Mooney. Fifty, I'd guess. Heavy. She had a car and did the marketing and cooking and housework. She'd serve dinner and then leave and do the dishes when she came the next day. So it came to maybe twelve hundred a month for operating expenses. And about that much again for Wilma. Hairdresser and dressmaker, cosmetics, mail orders to Saks, Bonwits, places like that. Masseuse, a special wine she likes. And shoes. God, the shoes! So say in round figures there's twenty-five hundred a month going out, which would be thirty thousand a year, three times what was coming in. After wedding expenses, and trading for the convertible, I had five thousand cash aside from the securities, but it was melting away so fast it scared me. I estimated it would be gone before the end of June."

"You tried to make her understand?"

"Of course. Wilma would stare at me as if I was talking Urdu. She couldn't seem to comprehend. It made me feel cheap and small-minded. She said it wasn't any great problem. In a little while I could start looking around and find something where I could make all the money we'd ever need. I was worried—but it was all kind of indistinct. The only thing that really seemed to count was just . . . having her. In the beginning, it was so damned . . . wonderful."

"But it changed?"

"Yes. But I don't want to talk about that."

"Later?"

"Maybe. I don't know. It all turned into something . . . quite different. I don't want to try to explain it."

"If I left?" Chook said.

"No. Thanks, but that wouldn't make any difference."

"Get on with it then. When was the first contact with the land syndicate people?"

"Late May. She'd gone walking down the beach in the late afternoon, and she came back with Calvin Stebber. Some kid

30

had hooked a shark and as he was fighting it and beaching it with people watching him. That's how she got in casual conversation with him, and it turned out they knew a lot of the same people, so she brought him back for a drink. Short and heavy and very tan. Always smiling. I'd say he wasn't much over forty, but he looked older. And he seemed . . . important. They jabbered away about people I've read about. Onassis, Niarchos, people like that. He was very vague about what he was doing. He just said that he'd come down to work out a small project, but it was dragging on a lot longer than he'd estimated. He seemed . . . fond of Wilma. He wished us happiness.

"After he left, Wilma got quite excited. She told me that Calvin Stebber was enormously rich and went around making very successful investments in all kinds of things. She said that if we played our cards right, maybe he would let us in on whatever he was doing, and certainly the very least we could expect would be four times our money back, because he was never interested in smaller returns. To tell the truth, it seemed to me like a good way out, if she could swing it. With four times the capital I'd have enough income to keep her the way she wanted to live. Stebber was staying aboard a yacht at the Cutlass Yacht Club, and when he left he asked us to stop by for drinks the next day.

"The yacht was absolutely huge, maybe a hundred feet long, some kind of a converted naval vessel, I think."

"Name and registry?"

"*The Buccaneer*, out of Tampa, Florida. He said friends had loaned it to him. That's when I met the other three men in the syndicate."

I had to slow Arthur down so that I could get the other three men nailed down, made into separate and distinct people in my mind.

G. Harrison Gisik. The old one. The sick one. Tall and frail and old and quiet. Bad color. Moved slowly and with apparent great effort. From Montreal.

Like Stebber, G. Harrison Gisik had no woman with him. The other two each had one. The other two were each local.

Crane Watts. Local attorney. Dark, goodlooking, friendly. And unremarkable. He came equipped with wife. Vivian. Called Viv. Dark, sturdy, pretty—scored by sun and wind—an athlete. Tennis, sailing, golf, riding. She was, Arthur thought, a lady.

Boone Waxwell. The other local. From a local swamp, possibly. Sizable. Rough and hard and loud. An accent from way back in the mangroves. Black curly hair. Pale pale blue eyes. Sallowy face. Boone Waxwell, known as Boo. And he came equipped with a non-wife, a redhead of exceptional mammary dimension. Dilly Starr. As loud as good ol' Boo, and, as soon as she got tight, slightly more obscene. And she got tight quickly.

"So okay," I said. "The four members of the syndicate. Stebber, Gisik, Crane, Waxwell. And Stebber the only one living aboard. A party, with Boo and his broad making all you nicer folks a little edgy. So?"

"We sat around and had drinks. There was a man aboard who made drinks and passed things, a Cuban maybe. Mario, they called him. When Calvin Stebber had a chance, when Dilly was in the head and Boo had gone ashore to buy cigars, he explained to us that sometimes, in deals, you weren't able to pick your associates on the basis of their social graces. 'Waxwell is the key to this project,' he said."

"How soon did they let you in on it?" I asked him.

"Not right away. It was about two weeks. Wilma kept after him, and she kept telling me that he said there wasn't a chance, that there wasn't really enough to go around as it was. But she didn't give up hope. Finally one morning he phoned me from the yacht and asked me to stop by alone. He was alone too. He said I had a very persistent wife. Persistence alone wouldn't have been enough. But this deal had dragged on so long that one of the principals had backed out. He said he felt obligated to offer it to other associates, but as long as I was on the scene and because he was so fond of Wilma, he had talked Mr. Gisik into agreeing to let me in, with certain stipulations."

"Is that when he explained the deal to you?"

"Just in broad outline, Trav, not in detail. We were in the main lounge, and he spread the maps out on the chart table. What he called the Kippler Tract was marked off and tinted. Sixty-one thousand acres. It was a strange shape, beginning north of Marco and getting wider over east of Everglades City, and going practically to the Dade County line. The syndicate was negotiating the option of it on a two-year basis at thirty dollars an acre against a purchase price of a hundred and twenty an acre. As soon as they had a firm option, he and another group were setting up a development corporation to buy the tract from the syndicate for three hundred and eighty dollars an acre. It meant that, after taking off syndicate overhead and operating expenses, the members would end up with five dollars for every dollar invested in the option—which would come to one million eight hundred and thirty thousand just for the option. He showed me the prospectus of what Deltona was doing at Marco Island, where the Collier interests along with Canadian money were planning a community of thirty thousand people. He said his staff had investigated every aspect of the plan, projected growth, water resources and so on, and if we could just get the option, it couldn't miss.

"Then he told me that he was in for seven hundred thousand, Gisik for four hundred thousand, a New York associate for five hundred thousand. The remaining two hundred and thirty thousand was represented by Crane Watts and Boo Waxwell, one hundred even by Watts. He said those small pieces were a nuisance, but it was essential to have a bright young lawyer on the scene, and that Boo Waxwell was the one with the close association with the Kippler heirs and able, if anybody was, to talk them into the deal. The New York associate had bowed out and there was five hundred thousand open. He said my five hundred thousand would become three million, a net return of one million nine after taxes, and my investment back.

"I said I'd like one hundred thousand worth, and he looked at me as if I was a dog on the street and he rolled up the maps saying he hadn't realized he was wasting his time as well as mine, and thanks for stopping by. Wilma was furious. She said I'd blown the whole thing. She said she'd talk to Calvin Stebber again and see if there was any chance at all of his taking me in on the basis of two hundred thousand. I said it didn't seem smart to gamble the whole thing, and she said it wasn't a gamble."

"Then he let you in."

"Reluctantly. I sent an airmail special to my brokerage house to sell at current market and airmail me a certified check for two hundred thousand. We met on the yacht. I signed the syndicate agreement, and it was witnessed and notarized. It gave me 9 and 15/100ths shares in the syndicate."

"And you didn't have a lawyer of your own check it out."

"Travis . . . you can't understand how it was. They seemed so important. They were doing me a favor to let me in. Without Wilma, they would never have let me in. It was my chance to afford her. And from the moment I'd messed the deal up when I had the first chance, Wilma wouldn't let me near her. She'd hardly speak to me. She moved to a different bedroom in the beach house. And . . . they said it was a

33

standard agreement. It was about six pages, single-spaced, on legal size paper, and I had to sign four copies. Wilma stood with her hand on my shoulder as I signed, and gave me a big kiss when it was over."

"Stebber left soon after that?"

"A day or two later. About then Boo Waxwell began to hang around. He'd drop in without warning. It was obvious to me that he was attracted to Wilma. And she seemed too friendly toward him. When I complained to her, she said Calvin Stebber had said we had to be friendly to him. I tried to find out from Waxwell how things were going, but he'd just laugh and tell me not to sweat."

"When did they ask for more?"

"On August first I got a letter from Crane Watts. It referred to paragraph something, sub-paragraph something, and asked for my check in the amount of thirty-three thousand three hundred and thirty-three dollars and thirty-four cents at my earliest convenience. I was shocked. I dug out my copy and looked at the paragraph. It said that members of the syndicate could be assessed on the basis of participation to cover additional expenses. I went to see him right away. He wasn't as friendly as before. I hadn't seen his office before. It was north of the city on the Tamiami Trail, and it was just a cubicle in a roadside real estate office. He acted as if I was taking up valuable time. He said that negotiations had progressed to the point where the Kippler heirs had decided they wanted thirty-five dollars option money per acre, which meant the syndicate members had to come up with an additional three hundred and five thousand dollars, and simple mathematics showed that 9.15 percent of that was what he had requested by letter.

"I said that I didn't think I could make it, and that I guessed I'd just have to accept a proportional reduction of my share of the venture. He gave me a funny look and said he could understand my request, but if I had examined the sub-paragraph immediately following, certainly I'd realize it couldn't be done. I hadn't brought it. He got out an office copy and showed me the paragraph. It said, in effect, that if any participant failed to meet approved assessments, his share of the venture was forfeit, and would be divided among the remaining members in proportion to the interest they held at the time. He said it was perfectly legal, and the document had been signed, notarized and recorded.

"I went back to the beach house and it took me quite a while to get it through Wilma's head. Finally she understood that unless I came up with the additional money, we'd lose the two hundred thousand. She said it wasn't fair. She said she would phone Calvin Stebber and get it all straightened out. I don't know where she finally located him. She didn't want me in the room. She said I made her nervous. After she talked to him, she came out and told me that he'd said his hands were tied. If he made any special arrangement for me, the others would raise hell. She said she'd asked him if he'd buy my share out, but he said his cash position at the moment was too low even to consider it at that time. He recommended raising the money, saying it was undoubtedly the last assessment, and he was certain the deal would go through any day. Wilma was agitated for a long time, but finally we sat down and tried to work it all out. I had, at current market, about fifty-eight thousand left in just two stocks, Standard Oil of New Jersey and Continental Can. I was going to have to sell something anyway to meet current expenses, as we had five hundred in the bank and three thousand in unpaid bills. I left twenty thousand in stocks, paid Crane Watts and the bills and put three thousand in the checking account.

"On September first the option price went up to forty dollars an acre, and they asked for exactly the same amount again. By then I had four hundred in the bank and the twenty thousand. But I knew we *had* to raise it. I'd taken the agreement to another lawyer by then. He said it was iron-clad, and only a damn fool would have signed such a thing. That was the time Wilma really cooperated. I thought that she was really beginning to understand the value of money. We sat down together and put everything into the pot. The rest of my stock, the car, my cameras, her furs and jewels. She went over to Miami and sold her stuff. We were just able to get it all together, with about four hundred dollars over. We paid off, and gave up the beach house and moved to a cheap motel room five or six blocks north of the intersection of Fifth Avenue and the Trail, the Citrus Blossom it was called. We cooked on a grill in the room.

She kept asking what in the world we'd ever do if they asked for more. And she'd cry. It was her idea that I should make up a list of old friends who might come in on a good thing. She kept after me. I didn't want to do it. Finally I had a list of thirty-two reasonably successful people who might be willing to trust me. She rewrote my letter several times, making it sound like the greatest opportunity in the world, and we made up thirty-two originals on the motel typewriter and sent them off, asking for a minimum of one thousand

35

each, and any amount up to ten thousand they might want to put in. Then we waited. There were sixteen replies. Eight of them said they were sorry. Eight sent money. Four of them sent a thousand each. Two sent five hundred. One sent a hundred dollars and one sent fifty dollars. Fifty-one hundred and fifty that we put in the joint account. No letters came in the next week. I sent signed notes to the eight friends as I had promised in the original letter. Then I got a call at the motel from Crane Watts. Calvin Stebber was staying at the Three Crowns in Sarasota and he wanted us to come up and see him. Watts said it might be good news. Wilma had such a headache she said I better go alone. We had no car. I took a Trailways bus to Sarasota and got there at five o'clock, and at the desk they told me Mr. Stebber had checked out but he had left a message for a Mr. Wilkinson. I identified myself and they gave it to me. It merely said that it looked as if it might be another six months or so before the deal would go through, and probably before the time was up there would be another assessment, just a small one, for operating expenses. My share would probably not be over eight or ten thousand.

"I just sat there. I couldn't seem to think clearly. I took a bus back. I didn't get to the motel until a little after midnight. My key wouldn't work. I hammered on the door. Wilma didn't answer. I went to the office and the owner came to the door after I'd rung the night bell a long time. He said the lock had been changed and he hadn't been paid for two weeks, and he was holding onto my clothes and luggage until I paid up. I said there was some mistake, that my wife had paid him. He said she hadn't. I asked where she was, and he said that in the middle of the afternoon he'd seen her and some man carrying suitcases out to a car and driving away, and it made him think we were going to beat him out of the rent, so he had put my stuff in storage and changed the lock. He hadn't noticed the car particularly, just that it was a pale-colored car with Florida plates. She hadn't left any message for me. I walked around the rest of the night. When the bank opened I found out she'd cleaned out the account the previous morning, when I thought she'd gone grocery shopping and came home with that headache."

Toward the end of it his voice had grown dull and listless. Chook stirred and sighed. A gust of the freshening breeze swung the boat, and some predatory night bird went by, honking with anguish.

"But you found her again, later on," I said, to get him started.

"I'm pretty tired."

Chook reached and patted him. "You go to bed, honey. Want me to fix you anything?"

"No thanks," he murmured. He got up with an effort and went below, saying goodnight to us as the screened door hissed shut.

"Poor wounded bastard," Chook said in a half whisper.

"It was a very thorough job. They got everything except the clothes he had on. They even milked old friendships."

"He hasn't much resistance yet. Or much spirit."

"Both of those are up to you."

"Sure, but try to make it a little easier on him, Trav, huh?"

"She took off in late September. It's late May, Chook. The trail is eight months cold. Where are they, and how much do they have left? And just how smart are they? One thing seems obvious. Wilma was the bird dog. Rope a live one and bring him to Naples. Remember, she got booted off that cruiser out of Savannah. I think there was one on there a little too shrewd for her, so she took a long look at what we had around here. And picked Arthur. Marriage can lull suspicion, and she used sex as a whip, and when she had him completely tamed and sufficiently worried about money, she contacted Stebber to tell him the pigeon was ready for the pot. It was a professional job, honey. They made him ache to get in on it. They made him so eager he'd have signed his own death warrant without reading it."

"Was it all legal?"

"I don't know. At least legal enough so that you'd probably have a three-year court fight to prove it wasn't, and then it would be only a civil action to recover the funds. He can't finance that. He couldn't finance two cups of coffee."

"Can you do anything?"

"I could try. If you can prop him up a little, I can try."

She stood up and came over and gave me a quick hug, a kiss beside the eye, and told me I was a treasure. Long after she left, the treasure lifted a few score aches and sorenesses and went to bed.

FOUR

LATE SUNDAY AFTERNOON, up on the sundeck, I got the rest of the account from Arthur Wilkinson. Chook had him heavily oiled against additional burn. She was using the sundeck rail as a torture rack, and I was pleased to turn so that I could not see her. I had taken so much punishment all day, it hurt to watch her. But over Arthur's recital I could sometimes hear her little gasps of effort, a creak of a joint strained to the maximum, and even that was mildly upsetting.

Arthur had gotten absolutely no satisfaction from the young lawyer. He had offered to sell Watts his syndicate shares for twenty-five thousand. Crane Watts said he wasn't interested. Next, in a kind of bemused desperation, he had tried to find Boone Waxwell, had learned that Waxwell had a place at Goodland on Marco Island. With the last of the small amount of money he had taken on the Sarasota trip, he had taken a bus to the turnoff to Marco, had hitched a ride to the island bridge, and then had walked to Goodland. At a gas station they told him how to find Waxwell's cottage. He got there at sunset. It was an isolated place at the end of a dirt road, more shack than cottage. A pale gray sedan was parked in the yard. Country music was so loud over the radio they didn't hear him on the porch, and when he looked through the screen he saw Wilma sprawled naked, tousled and asleep on a couch, and with a particular vividness he remembered her pale blonde head resting on a souvenir pillow from Rock City. Boo Waxwell, in underwear shorts, sat slumped by the little radio, bottle on the floor between his feet, trying to play guitar chords along with the radio music. He saw Arthur and grinned at him, and came grinning to the screen door, opened it and pushed Arthur back, asking him what the hell he wanted. Arthur said he wanted to speak to Wilma. Waxwell said there wasn't much point in that on account of Wilma had gotten herself a temporary divorce, country-style.

Wilma had then appeared in the doorway beside Waxwell, light of the sunset against her face, a small and delicate face puffy with sleep and satiation, eyes drained empty by

38

bed and bottle, nestling in soiled housecoat into the hard curve of Boo Waxwell's arm, looking out at him with a placid and almost bovine indifference, outlined in that end-of-day glow against the room darkening behind her.

He said it was strange how vivid the little things were, the precise design in faded blue of an eagle clutching a bomb, wavering as the muscles of Waxwell's upper arm shifted under the tattooed hide. The irregular deep rose shade of a suck-mark on the side of Wilma's delicate throat. And tiny rainbow glintings from the diamonds of the watch on her wrist— the watch she had claimed she sold in Miami.

Then he knew that it had all been lies, all of it, with nothing left to believe. Like an anguished, oversized child, he had rushed at Waxwell to destroy him, had landed no blow, had been pummeled back, wedged into a corner of porch post and railing, felt all the grinding blows into gut and groin and, over Waxwell's diligent shoulder had seen the woman small in the doorway, hugging herself and watching, underlip sagging away from the small even teeth. Then the railing gave way and he fell backward into the yard. He got up at once and slowly walked back the way he had come, hunched, both forearms clamped across his belly. He had the feeling that it was the only thing holding him together. His legs felt feathery, floating him along with no effort. Somewhere along the dirt road to the cottage he had fallen. He could not get up. He felt as if something was shifting and flowing inside him, the life moving warmly out of him. He would have slept, except for mosquitoes so thick he breathed them in, snuffing them from his nose, blowing them from his lips. He squirmed to a tree and pulled himself upright and went on, trying all the time to straighten himself up a little more. By the time he got to the bridge he was almost straight. There was a pink glow left in the west. He began the long walk back to the trail and for a time he was all right, and then he began falling. He said it was very strange. He would find himself way out by the center line, and then when he went over to the shoulder, a dark bush would seem to leap up at him and he would land heavily, gasping.

An old pickup truck stopped as he was trying to get up, and they came and put a bright flashlight beam on him, and from far away he heard a man and woman discussing in casual nasal tones how drunk he was and from what.

Summoning the last of energy, he said very distinctly, "I'm not drunk. I've been beaten."

"Whar you want we should take you, mister?" the man asked.

"I've got no place to go."

When things came back into focus, he was between the man and the woman on the front seat of the pickup. They took him home. East on the Trail to the turnoff to Everglades City, through Everglades and across the causeway to Chokoloskee Island, and over to the far shore, where these people named Sam and Leafy Dunning lived with their five kids in a trailer and attached cottage and prefab garage. He learned later they had spent a picnic day over on Marco Beach, and when they had picked him up, the five kids and the picnic gear and beach gear were in the bed of the old pickup.

Sam Dunning, in season, operated a charter boat out of the Rod and Gun Club over at Everglades City. It was out of season, and he was netting commercial with a partner, even shares, using an old bay skiff.

For three days Arthur could hobble about like an old man. All he could keep down were the soups she fixed for him. He slept a great deal, sensing it was in part an aftermath of the beating, and partly the emotional exhaustion of what had happened to him. He slept by day in a string hammock in the side yard, and by night on a mattress in the garage, waking often to find the children staring solemnly at him.

Leafy borrowed old clothes from a neighbor, big enough to fit him, while she washed and cleaned and mended what he'd been wearing. He thought that it was the fourth day before she asked him any questions at all, came out into the yard when he was walking around in the afternoon, feeling a little steadier on his feet. There were pieces of old car and pieces of marine engine in the yard, coarse grass half hiding them. He sat in the shade of the live oak tree on an overturned dinghy, and Leafy leaned against the trunk, arms folded, head tilted, a wiry, faded, bright-eyed woman in khaki pants and a blue work shirt, visibly pregnant.

"Who did beat on you, Arthur?"

"Boone Waxwell."

"All them Waxwells are pure mean as moccasin snakes. You got folks to go to someplace?"

"No."

"What kind of work you do, mostly?"

"Well . . . in a store."

"Get yourself fired?"

"I quit."

40

"Clothes you had on were right good. Messed up, but good. And you talk nice, like you had good schooling, and you eat polite. Sam and me, we looked in your clothes, but you got no papers at all."

"There should be a wallet, with a license and cards and so on."

"And maybe a thousand dollars? If you had one, Arthur, you spilled it out falling all over that road. What we got to know, Sam and me, is if the police got some interest in you, because they can go hard on folks giving anybody house room."

"I'm not wanted for anything. Not for questioning or anything else."

She studied him and nodded to herself. "All right, then. What you got to have, I guess, is some kind of work to get some money to be on your way, and you can stay on here till you got it, paying me board when you start drawing pay. I guess there's some men got it in them to just roam. That's all right for kids, Arthur, but a grown man, it turns into something different, and without a steady woman you can grow old into a bum. You think on that some."

Sam had found him work on the maintenance crew readying the Rod and Gun Club for the season opening. He sent in the bureaucratic forms necessary to reassemble the paper affirmations of his identity, a replacement driver's license, a duplicate social security card. When he was laid off at the Club, he found a job as common labor on a development housing project over near the airport.

Sam Dunning partitioned a small corner of the garage, and Leafy fixed it up with a cot, chair, lamp, and packing box storage disguised by a piece of cotton drapery material thumbtacked to the top edge. He paid her twelve dollars a week for room and meals, after long earnest bargaining. She wanted ten. He wanted to give fifteen.

There on the sundeck, in a thoughtful voice, Arthur told us that it was a strange time in his life. He had never done manual labor. Until he acquired a few basic skills, the foreman came close to firing him several times for innate clumsiness. The skills pleased him—rough carpentry without owl eyes surrounding the nail heads, learning when the cement mix was the right consistency, learning how to trundle a wheelbarrow along a springy plank. He said it was as if he had turned half of himself off, settling into routine, speaking when spoken to, sitting with the Dunning kids when Sam and Leafy went out on Saturday nights. On days off he helped

Sam with boat maintenance, and sometimes crewed for him on a charter. He felt as if he was in hiding from every familiar thing, and, in the process, becoming someone else. He spent almost nothing, and accumulated money, without counting it. He could lay on his cot and keep his mind empty. When it would veer toward Wilma or toward the lost money, he would catch it quickly, return it to the comforting grayness, feeling only a swoop of dizziness at the narrowness of the escape. Sometimes he awoke from sleep to sense erotic dream-memories of Wilma fading quickly, leaving only some of the tastes of her on his mouth, textures of her on his hands.

Leafy had her child in January, her third boy. His present to her was an automatic washing machine, a used one in good condition. He and Sam got it tied into the water line and wired the day before Sam brought her home. She was ecstatic. Her attitude toward him warmed perceptibly, and soon, in the most obvious ways, she began to try to make a match between Arthur and a seventeen-year old girl down the road named Christine Canfield. Christine had run off to Crystal River with a stone crab fisherman and had come home alone at Christmas, slightly pregnant. She was the youngest of three daughters, the older two married and moved away, one to Fort Myers, the other to Homestead. Christine was a placid, pleasant, slow-moving child who smiled often and laughed readily. She was husky, brown-blonde, pretty in a childlike way.

"Nobody's in the place Cobb Canfield put up for his Lucy before Tommy got the good job in Fort Myers. You could fix it up right nice," Leafy said.

"Listen, she's only seventeen years old!"

"She's carrying proof she's a woman, and it hardly shows yet. She likes you fine, just fine, Arthur. She's healthy and she's a worker, and they're good stock. And she got the wild run out of her, and Cobb'd be so grateful to get it worked out, he'd do you good, believe me. Christine'd make you a good steady woman, not like some her age on the island."

"I should have told you before, Leafy. I'm married."

Her eyes narrowed as she accepted this new problem. "You plan on taking up again with your wife, Arthur?"

"No."

"She got cause to come looking for you?"

"No."

She nodded to herself. "The law doesn't pay it no mind unless somebody comes along to make a fuss. You just keep

42

your mouth shut about that wife. Cobb is too proud to let her set up any common law thing with you, so all you have to do is keep your mouth shut and marry her, and who does that hurt? Nobody, and does you both good, and gives that bush kitten she's carrying a daddy. Christine, she can make a garden bear the year round, and with a snitch hook she's good as you'll ever see, and it don't make for bad living having a young wife grateful to you."

Chook completed her series of tortures and came and sat by us, breathing deeply, brown body gleaming with perspiration, hair damp. "Surprised we ever saw you again, Arthur."

"Maybe you wouldn't have. I thought about it. She was as trusting and affectionate as a dog you bring in out of the rain. I could have stayed right there the rest of my life. But I kept remembering eight friends who had believed in me. Somehow that was worse than my money being gone, the way theirs went with it. I couldn't hide from that the rest of my life. And the pressure from Leafy and Christine merely made me more aware of it. So I told them I had something personal to take care of, and I'd be back as soon as I could, maybe in a few weeks. That was two months ago. I went back to Naples thinking I could try to recover enough just to pay back my friends."

He had gone to the Citrus Blossom Motel and found that his possessions had long since been sold, leaving a deficit of nine dollars on the room. He paid it out of the seven hundred he'd saved. He found another room. He bought the clothing I'd thrown in the dockside trash can. He went to see Crane Watts. Watts got the file out. There had been one additional assessment. When attempts to contact Mr. Wilkinson had failed, his participation was eliminated according to the terms of the agreement. As they had been unable to acquire an option on the Kippler Tract after lengthy negotiations, the syndicate had been dissolved and all monies remaining in the account had been divided on the basis of final participation. Arthur had demanded the addresses of Stebber and Gisik, and Watts had said that if he wished to write them, the letters could be sent to Watts' office for forwarding. Arthur told Watts, with some heat, that he felt he had been defrauded, and he was damned well going to stir up all the trouble he could for them, and if they wanted to settle, to avoid investigation, he would sign an unconditional release in return for a ten-thousand-dollar refund. Watts, Arthur told us, looked unkempt in beard stubble, soiled

43

sports shirt and bourbon breath at eleven o'clock that morning. Heartened by Watts' lack of assurance, Arthur had lied to him, saying that his attorney was preparing a detailed complaint to be filed with the Attorney General of the State of Florida, with a certified copy to the Bar Association. Watts, angered, said it was nonsense. There had been no illegality.

Arthur gave his temporary address, and said that somebody better get in touch with him, and damned soon, and bring the money.

He got a phone call at five that evening. A girl with a brisk voice said she was phoning at Crane Watts' request, to say that Calvin Stebber would like to have a drink with Mr. Wilkinson at the Piccadilly Pub on Fifth Avenue at six and discuss Mr. Wilkinson's problem.

Arthur was prompt. The tap room was luxurious and exceedingly dark. He sat on a stool at the padded bar, and when his eyes had adjusted, he searched the long bar and nearby tables and did not see Smiling Calvin. Soon a young woman appeared at his elbow, a trim and tailored girl, severe and pretty, who said she was Miss Brown, sent by Mr. Stebber who would be a little late, and would he come over to the table. He carried his drink over. Miss Brown parried his questions about Stebber with secretarial skill. She took microsips of a dry sherry. He was paged, went to the phone, found that it was a mistake. Someone wanted a Mr. Wilkerson, sales representative for Florida Builders Supply. Back at the table, suddenly the room tilted and he sprawled over against Miss Brown. She giggled at him. Then, in foggy memory, Miss Brown and a man in a red coat were helping him out to Miss Brown's car. He woke up in another county, in Palm County, in the drunk tank, without funds or identification, sick, weak and with a blinding headache. In the afternoon a sheriff's deputy, with a massive indifference, told him the score. He'd been picked up, stumbling around on a public beach, stinking and incoherent, brought in and booked as John Doe. They had a film strip of him. Standard procedure. He could plead guilty and take a thirty-day knock right now, or plead not guilty and go loose on two hundred dollars bail and wait for circuit court which would be about forty days from now. And he could make one call.

He could have called Leafy. Or Christine. He elected the thirty days for himself. After four days of lockup, he signed up for road work as the lesser of two evils, swung the brush hook in lazy tempo under the tolerant guards, always turned his face away from the glitter of the tourist cars staring

44

their way by, wore road gang twill too small for him. Out of tension, or despair, or aftereffects of whatever Miss Brown had dolloped his drink with, or the greasy texture of the rice and beans, he could keep little on his stomach. Road gang work gave him a fifty cents a day credit. He bought milk and white bread, and sometimes he kept it down and sometimes he didn't. Sun and effort dizzied him.

One bush to be chopped was Stebber, and the next was Watts, then G. Harrison Gisik, Boo Waxwell, Wilma, Miss Brown. As he began to fit the issue work clothes, in afternoon delirium he recalled what Chook had told him about me. And he knew that he'd be a fool to try anything else on his own. Maybe a fool to even ask for help. They gave him back his clothes and let him go, with a dollar thirty left from his work credit. He tried to hitch his way across the peninsula, but something was wrong, somehow, with the way he looked. They would slow down, some of them, then change their minds, roar on into the pavement mirages. Sudden rains soaked him. He bought sandwiches, had to abandon them after the first bite. He got a few short rides, found dry corners to sleep in, remembered very little of the last few days of it, then had the vivid memory of coming aboard *The Busted Flush*, and the deck swinging up at him, slapping him in the face as he tried to fend it off . . .

"Just enough to pay my friends back," he said. "I understand you take the expenses off the top and divide what else you can recover. If it wasn't for them, I'd give up, Trav. Maybe it's hopeless anyway. I had all that money, and now it's all unreal, as if I never really had it. My great grandfather barged a load of fabrics, furniture and hardware up from New York, rented a warehouse and sold the goods for enough to pay off the loan on the first load and buy a second free and clear. That's where the money started. Eighteen fifty-one. By nineteen hundred there was a great deal of money. My father wasn't good with money. It dwindled. I thought I was better. I thought I could make it grow. God!"

Chook reached and gave his oily shoulder an affectionate, comforting pat. "Some very smart people get terribly cheated, Arthur. And usually it happens far from home."

"I just . . . don't want to go back there," he said. "I dream that I'm there and I'm dead. I see myself dead on the sidewalk and people walking around me as they go by, nodding as if they knew all along."

Chook took my wrist and turned it to look at my watch. "Time for you to choke down another eggnog, Arthur old buddy. Nicely spiked to give you a big appetite for dinner."

After she left, Arthur said, "I guess the biggest part of the expense is feeding me."

I laughed more than it was worth. After all, it was his first mild joke. Sign of improvement. Other signs too. Stubble shaved clean. Hair neatly cropped by Chookie McCall, an unexpected talent. Sun burning away the pasty look. Pounds coming back. And Chook had him on some mild exercises, just enough to begin to restore muscle tone.

She came up with his eggnog and a list. Perishables were dwindling. Eggs, milk, butter, lettuce. Candle Key had a Handy-Dandy-Open-Nights-and-Sunday. The wind would make easy sailing in the dink. The little limey outboard runs like a gold watch. My shoulders felt as if they were webbed with hot wires. So, with an excess of character, I left sail and motor behind, climbed down into the dink, and headed across the two miles of bay, rowing with the miniature oars.

Coming back against the wind was almost as much fun as migraine, and it didn't help a bit to have the wind die the instant I clambered aboard and made the dinghy fast. Chook came and took the groceries. As she did so, and with a dull red sun sitting on the horizon line, we were invaded by an advance guard of seven billion salt marsh mosquitoes. They are a strange kind. They don't bite, but some ancestral memory tells them they should get in position to bite. They are large and black and fly slowly, and when you wipe a dozen off your arm, they leave black streaks like soot. They are inept at the mosquito profession, but come in such numbers they can rattle the most easygoing disposition. As you breathe them in, you find yourself asking in desperation—But what do they *want*?

Chook and Arthur had showered and changed, and it was immediately obvious they had somehow made each other totally unhappy. Arthur was leaden and remote. Chook was brisk and remote. All they would exchange were the most formal politenesses. I showered amid the fading scent of Chook's perfumed soap, in that absurd mirrored stall, big enough, almost, for a Volkswagen garage. It is a grotesque waste of space in a fifty-two-foot houseboat, even with a twenty-one foot beam, almost as much of a waste as the semi-sunken pale blue tub, seven feet long and four feet wide. I imagine that the elderly Palm Beach party who lost the vessel to me over the poker table needed such visual stimulations to do right by his Brazilian mistress.

In response to the unexplained drearies of my boat guests,

I had a vicious attack of the jollies, regaling them with anecdote, absurdity and one-sided repartee, much like a solitary game of handball. Once in a while they would pull their lips away from their teeth and go heh-heh-heh. And then politely pass each other something that was within easy reach of everyone in the small booth adjoining the galley.

I judged it a favorable development. People were choosing up new sides. Chook and I had been united in caring for the sick. Now any relationship, even a rancorous one, which shut me out, was proof that he was not entirely defeated. She had to pump some spirit into him or my chances of any salvage were frail indeed. And maybe this was a start.

FIVE

ON MONDAY we pulled the hooks and droned in stately fashion down to a new anchorage off Long Key, charging the batteries and getting beyond the range of the sooty mosquitoes which were restricting us to the belowdecks areas. During the swimming that followed, I was heartened by a small triumph. The long contest was around a distant marker and back to the boarding ladder. Halfway back she pulled even and moved a half length ahead. I knew from the pain in my side that in another hundred yards I would begin to wallow and roll and lose the stroke. Suddenly the reserves were there—missing so long it was like welcoming an old friend. It was as if a third lung had suddenly opened up. I settled into it until I was certain, then upped the tempo and went on by her in a long sprint finish, was clinging to the ladder when she arrived, and feeling less like a beached blowfish than on other days.

"Well now!" she gasped, looking startled and owlish.

"You had to let me win one of these."

"The hell I did! I was busting a gut trying to keep up." She snapped her head back and gave me the first grin I had seen since rowing back with the groceries.

"Come with me," I said, and swam slowly away from the *Flush,* rolled and floated and, looking back, saw Arthur busy at the chore I had given him, putting new lacing in a section of the nylon fabric that is lashed to the rail around the sun deck. Chook made a surface dive and came up beside me, and blew like a porpoise.

"I could put you two in the shower stall," I said. "What you do, you each take a corner of a silk handkerchief in your teeth, left hands tied behind you, six-inch knife in the right hand."

"Skip it, McGee."

"It's just that the way you two go around chuckling and laughing, it gets on my nerves. I keep wondering what could make two people so hilarious."

"Maybe you could guess. I'm a big girl. I'm a big healthy girl. And I'm leading a very healthy life. I'm sleeping with him, in that half acre bed of yours. And that's the precise word, McGee. Sleeping. Just that. So I thought maybe he was well enough, and it was going to take you a long time to get back with the groceries. I showered first, and got into a sexy little thing made of black cobwebs, and dabbed a little Tigress here and there and yonder, and spread myself out like picturesque, with my girlish heart going bump bump bump. It's not as if it had never happened with him before. And the son of a bitch acted as if I'd solicited him on a street corner. He was offended, for God's sake. He made me feel sleazy."

"Maybe you're putting the wrong interpretation on it."

"There comes a point when I stop being understanding, friend. And that was it. It's his move. And unless he makes one, there's an invisible wall right down the middle of that bed. It's made of ice cubes. All he'll get from me is some practical nursing care."

In the night I was awakened by the creak of the lines as the *Flush* was trying to go around on the tide change, swinging further each time until pushed back by the breeze. I always rig two bow hooks in such a way that she shifts her weight from hook to hook when she changes end for end. As this was the first night at the new anchorage, I wanted to check and see that she wasn't working loose with all the swinging, and that she would swing the way I had guessed. As a rule of thumb they will always swing with the bow toward the nearest shallows. But the wind can make a difference, and there can be a tide current you didn't read.

So, as the easiest way out, I went forward and up through the hatch. I pulled the line she was still on and found it firm. I have a reflector plate under my riding light, and it keeps the decks in relative shadow, but just enough gets past the plate so you can check lines when your eyes are used to the darkness. From the relation of the way she was swinging to the lights along the keys, I could tell she was going to go around the right way. I decided to wait until she was around and then check the other anchor line. I had a lot of scope, big Danforths and a good bottom, so it was a thousand to one I was fine. But there are a lot of dead sailors who took things for granted. On a boat things go bad in sets of threes. When you pull a hook and then go hustle to get the wheels turning, something will short out on you so that you go drifting, dead in the water. And that is the time when, without lights, you drift right out into the ship channel, see running lights a city block apart coming down at you, run to get your big flashlight, fumble it and drop it over the side. A boat is something that never has just one thing wrong with it.

As I sat on the corner of the bow hatch, waiting, I felt a little faraway thud. I felt it through the soles of my bare feet, wondered what the hell, then realized it was the dink tied astern, swinging in the wind, nudging mother. I padded back along the side deck, put another line on its little stern cleat and snubbed it up against the two fenders hanging over the transom. I'd gone aft on the port side, and went forward on the starboard side, and came suddenly on a pale ghost that nearly made me leap over the rail. It startled her too, and then she made a miserable snorting sound and came into my arms for comfort. She had on a skimpy white hip-length nightie. She clung, snorting again. Her body heat was high, her breath hot and humid. She had that flat-sweet unmistakable scent of female sexual effort. Her nipples were hard as little pebbles against my bare chest.

"Oh God, God!" she whispered. "He can't do it. He tried and tried and tried. I helped and helped and helped. Then he was no damn good at all, and he started crying, and I had to get out of there. Oh God, Trav, my nerves are shot, shot, shot."

"Steady, girl."

"That damn bitch might just as well have cut them off," she said, and sobbed again, and got the hiccups. She hicked and gasped and ground her face into my throat, held me in an iron grip, and, with each hick, gave me a little thud with those powerful hips. I was not unresponsive. Hell, a bronze statue three thousand years old would have made its reaction as evident to her as I did.

49

"God, darling—hic—be a dear—hic—and take me off—hic—the hook."

"And you know it wouldn't stop there, and wouldn't that do Arthur a lot of good, though? Wouldn't that brighten his hours, improve his morale?"

"But you—hic—want me, darling. Please—hic—"

"Okay, Chook."

"Bless you!" she said. "I love you so. Hic."

"I'll help you out," I said. I bent to get one arm behind her knees. She went loose, thinking, perhaps, I was going to tote her topsides to the sun pads on the upper deck. I swung her up and out and over the rail and let go.

Shriek. Ka-swash. Then some coughing, and then some strident and bitter abuse from the dark water. I strolled back to the boarding ladder, bent and gave her a hand, hauled her up onto the after deck and told her to stay right there. I brought her a towel and a terry robe.

"After all!" she said in a cold and level voice. "Really!"

"Your language is improving."

As she belted the robe, she said, "You're all bastard, aren't you?"

"Listen. Did it or did it not cure the hiccups?"

Suddenly we were laughing, and in laughing we were friends again, and went topsides to the big padded bench at the topside controls. I went and checked the anchor line, came back with cigarettes for her, a pipe for me. The running light dimmed the stars, but not entirely.

"You were absolutely right, of course," she said. "And let me believe, damn it, that it cost you something too."

"More than I care to think about."

"So maybe failure finished him off. We don't know that. But I damn well do know that I would have moved into your bed for the duration of the voyage, captain, and that certainly would finish him."

"Like that little knife they use when the matador hasn't been able to kill with the sword. Some stocky little guy, like a butcher, moves in and gives it to old bull right behind the ears. And he goes down as if he'd been dropped off a roof."

"Then those damned mules pull him all the way around the ring instead of right on off stage. Why do they have to do that?"

"A tribute, maybe."

"Trav, how in the *world* am I going to act toward

50

Arthur tomorrow? He felt so . . . wretched about everything."

"Open and obvious affection, Chook. All the little pats and smiles and kisses. Little hugs. Just as if it *had* worked."

"But why in the world should. . . . Oh, I think I get it. No penalty for failure. Encouragement to try again. No social disgrace. But if it ends up the same way, I don't think I can endure it. Oh hell, I suppose I can always run out and jump overboard, screaming."

"And hiccuping."

"Honestly, and you have to believe me, I never got in such a state before in my life. It's something about a boat, I guess. And the phase of the moon. And Frankie gone for years. And feeling . . . so *damned* sorry for Arthur. And, of course, being so bloody awful healthy. Poor lamb. He was *so* apologetic and crushed. Well, thanks for practically nothing, McGee. Night."

I made the pipe last. I sat up there, bare feet braced on the wheel spokes, and wondered why Chook should bring out the martyr in me. Twice now, with her, I had gone so noble it semi-sickened me. And such a glorious package. But was she? Maybe she was a little too much. She created a certain awe in the standard issue male. I had noted that fewer passes were made at her than she had a right to expect. All that robust, glowing, powerful vitality might actually have given me a subconscious block, a hidden suspicion that I might, in the long run, be unable to cope—an alarming prospect for male vanity, of which I was certain I had my share. When these dreary suspicions threatened to spoil a pretty night, I went forward, back down through the hatch and into my spartan bed.

Too restless to go to sleep quickly, I found another reason, perhaps just as ego-damaging, why I could resist intimate involvement with Chook. Except for her inexplicable bondage to Frank Durkin, she was uncommonly staunch and stable. Though shrewd, diligent and perceptive, she did not have any of those inner contradictions, complexities and vulnerabilities that are born of self-doubt. She was all of a piece, confident of her total survival, and—in that sense—utterly wholesome. Maybe I could be stirred only by the wounded ducklings. Maybe I could respond best to the cripples I cut out of the flock, the ones who, by contrast, could give me a sense of inner strength and unity. And a whole woman might, conversely, serve to give me a less fictional image of the inner McGee, showing the fracture

lines and the clumsy ways I had pasted myself back together, and too many tricks with mirrors. When you have
learned control over your own dear little neuroses, you can
have empathy with the ones who are shaking themselves
apart, and get your jollies out of teaching them how to
dampen the vibrations. But a sound and solid one can only
make you aware of how frequently precarious your acquired
controls can become. It could be that this wariness of the
sound ones and the true ones was one of the hidden reasons
why I had to be a roamer, a salvage expert, a gregarious
loner, a seeker of a thousand tarnished grails, finding too
many excuses for all the dragons along the way.

This kind of emotional introspection, this self-fondling, is
strange medicine. A little bit, now and again, can acrete a
small quotient of wisdom. But, like nitroglycerin for the
weakened heart, too much of it at one time can blow your
head off.

Maybe it was all a lot simpler than that. Physical attraction was strong, but without emotional attraction. Once begun, we would go the long route, and at the end of it there
would be absolutely nothing, very probably not even the
friendship. And that was good enough to warrant a knowing
abstention.

Tuesday Chook seemed to be overdoing the whole routine.
The response was perhaps as noticeable as she would have
gotten from petting a dead dog. Pats and squeezes, kind
words and quick kisses, and special little treats from the
galley. Arthur seemed too deep in humble apathy to notice
or care. But from time to time I saw him stare toward her
with a mildly baffled expression. She laid it on so thick, I
felt more comfortable at long range. I gave myself the most
rigorous day yet. There is one which can match anything
they thought up during the Inquisition.

Sit. Hook feet under something solid. Lace fingers behind
neck. Lean slowly back until shoulders are approximately
ten to twelve inches off the deck. Stop right there. And stay
there until the sweat bursts and every muscle is jumping,
and then stay there a little while longer, then come slowly,
slowly back up to the sitting position. Another: One-legged
deep knee bends, taking about two seconds to go down and
two seconds to come back up. Continue until body weight
seems to approximate seventeen tons.

Alternate ten minute rest periods with fifty minute work-
outs all day long, then soak in a tub so hot you have to get
into it by inches, then eat twenty ounces of rare beef, a peck

52

of salad, stretch out topsides and look at the stars, and blunder off to bed.

I was awake for a little while in the first gray of the false dawn, and heard the lovers. It was a sound so faint it was not actually a sound, more a rhythm sensed. It is a bed rhythm, strangely akin to a heartbeat, though softer. Whum-fa, whum-fa, whum-fa. As eternal, clinical, inevitable as the slow gallop of the heart itself. And as basic to the race, reaching from percale back to the pallet of dried grasses in the cave corner. A sound clean and true, a nastiness only to all those unfortunates who carry through their narrow days their own little hidden pools of nastiness, ready to spill it upon anything so real it frightens them.

Heard even in its most shoddy context, as through the papery walls of a convention motel, this life-beat could be diminished not to evil but to a kind of pathos, because then it was an attempt at affirmation between strangers, a way to try to stop all the clocks, a way to try to say: I live.

The billions upon billions of lives which have come and gone, and that small fraction now walking the world, came of this life-pulse, and to deny it dignity would be to diminish the blood and need and purpose of the race, make us all bawdy clowns, thrusting and bumping away in a ludicrous heat, shamed by our own instinct.

Hearing them I felt placidly avuncular. Enjoy. Find that one time that has no shred of self or loneliness. Seal it so that from now on McGee is the third wheel, all interrelationships solidly structured from now on. Celebrate the "nowness" of it, and subside into affections.

The almost inaudible pulse hastened, then slowed, and ended. I heard the faroff drone of a marine engine, fading into the distance, a commercial fisherman perhaps, heading for the grounds off East Cape. Ripples slapped the hull. What assurances, gratitudes, immediate memories were the lovers entwined whispering to each other? Did they listen to the slowing of their hearts? Were there little catches at the end of those long breaths that were deep as sighs? Was it beautiful for you too, darling?

When I awoke again it was with the sense of total well-being I had been aiming for. The pounds were gone. A few slight areas of muscle soreness were not enough to diminish that good feeling of resiliency and vitality.

The body, once you are old enough to stop taking it for

granted, becomes like a separate entity. The way it will endure neglect makes you feel guilty. Having survived trauma, and being still willing to carry you around after healing itself, it deserves better. Cherishing it and toughening it is an act of appeasement for past omissions.

In my line of work, neglect was especially asinine. Like being a front-line type with a rusty rifle, or a neurosurgeon with a hangover. One half step, or one twentieth of a second lag in reaction time can make the difference. Any violent necessity is usually the result of something having gone wrong, a probable error of judgment. But the probability is always there.

Now, with just minor versions of the total torture of the days past, it would hold its edge.

My shower serenade did not stir the drowsy lovers, nor did the banging of pots. After breakfast I broke out a small spinning rod, rigged it with a yellow jig, installed sail, rudder and centerboard on the dingy, and went off to circle the edge of distant grass flats. I released a couple of small jacks, one weakfish, and then, just as I was coming about, hooked into a stranger, a stray pompano who didn't belong in that kind of area. He ran better than three pounds, and I had him split, buttered, and on foil under the broiler as the lovers came fumbling, blinking and yawning out into the daylight. Call the pompano a sacrifice on a special altar. They claimed nothing had ever tasted as good. They finished him, every crumb, while I stood smirking like a kindly old aunt in a TV commercial.

All her actions toward him that Wednesday were precisely as on the day before. But without the Charge Nurse flavor. She had a doe-eyed glow, a lazy smugness. The gestures were returned in kind. I was the outsider. Arthur had his chin up, for a change. And he risked a few of his mild, strained jokes—rewarded with girlish howls of glee. I tried to keep out of their way. But at times *The Busted Flush* can seem small. In mid-afternoon I invented an errand at Long Key, a replacement filter, and with an identical expression of repressed anticipation on their faces, they waved to me as I went putting off toward Long Key.

Friday morning I put the essential question to him. I brought the anchors in, and he helped me spread the lines at the bow to dry before stowing them. In the early gray, so silent and eerie it gave one a tendency to whisper, the *Flush* floated dead in the water at the high tide change, with

54

the mist magnifying the sun image in the east to a gigantic ball, suitable to a science fiction movie.

Arthur was beginning to look fit. Scrawny, but fit.

"What about it?" I asked him.

Squatting, he stared at me. "About it?"

"You ready to help me go after the loot, Arthur?"

He stood up. "I . . . guess I'm ready now."

I made an appraisal. He wasn't the same fellow who'd been a part of our ever-changing group better than a year ago. He looked almost the same, though thinner. I guess it was the eyes. Before, he had been able to watch you with the same pleasant fixity of stare of a family beagle. Now the eyes came up, then fell away, came back, shifted away.

"Listen, Arthur. The attitude is not anger, nor indignation, nor hate. No heroics. No punishments. We go in cold and shrewd and savvy. And you stay out of contact. You are my intelligence officer. I bring you pieces of it and we work out how they fit. But if I need you for any contact, I want to know you'll do it exactly as I say, whether you understand or agree. I want to know you won't let it shake you up."

"Trav . . . all I can do is promise to try."

"How do you feel about it?"

He tried to smile. "Butterflies."

"You can have butterflies, but you've got to have an operational attitude too. We're going to steal meat out from under the tiger's paw. We'll divert the animal's attention. We'll keep Chook out of it. And it starts right now."

He moistened his lips and swallowed. "Where are we going?"

"On a hunch, I'm going to start at Marco."

SIX

I TOOK the *Flush* up to Flamingo, through Whitewater Bay, and out the mouth of the Shark River into the Gulf of Mexico. The Gulf was flat calm, so I took her about six miles out, figured the course to take me just outside Cape Romano, and set the reliable old Metal Marine. It began turning the wheel back and forth in fussy little movements of a few inches at a time. I checked it to see that it was holding.

Sun came hot through the slight overcast, and in the greasy calm the only breeze was from our stodgy cruising speed. At noon I got the marine forecast from the Miami Marine Operator. Fair for the next twenty-four hours, winds slight and variable. A tropical disturbance centered below the Yucatan Straits, moving north northeast at five to six knots.

Chookie brought lunch topside. They both seemed subdued. I realized uncertainty was bothering them. You have to have an instinct about how much briefing the troops should have. Too little is as unsettling as too much.

"What we're up against," I said, "is the big con. It's a quasi-legal variation of one of the little cons, the finding the wallet routine."

"What does that mean?" Chook asked.

"Once they select a mark, the operator drops a wallet, a fat one, where he'll spot it. The accomplice gets to it a fraction of a second ahead of the mark. They move into an alley. The accomplice counts the money, and the mark sees that there is, say nine hundred dollars. Then the operator moves in, a very plausible guy. An acquaintance of the accomplice, but the accomplice very respectfully calls him mister. Says he found it, alone. Operator takes the mark's side, proclaims they both found it and should share equally. Accomplice agrees, grudgingly. No name or identification in wallet. Operator says the honest thing to do is watch the want ads for one week. If nothing appears, then it is theirs to split. Gets a brown envelope, seals wallet inside with tape, accomplice and mark initial the tape as a form of seal. Okay, who is to hold it? After argument, it is decided the mark can hold it, provided he gives the accomplice three hundred dollars to hang onto as a proof of good faith. Operator holds the envelope until mark can return with the three hundred. Addresses are exchanged. Mark watches want ads for a week, gleefully tears envelope open, finds ratty old wallet stuffed with newspaper. The switch was made while they waited for him to come back with the three hundred. Or, when the mark is smarter, they make the switch right in front of him, let him carry the envelope, and go to the bank with him. These things always depend on human greed. This option con, Arthur, was a more sophisticated version of the same tired old thing, with Stebber as the operator, Wilma as the roper, Gisik, Waxwell and Watts as accomplices. When they make a hit, they go to ground. But as this one was quasi-legal, some of them had to stay out in the open—

56

Watts and Waxwell. I suspect they got small pieces. So what we have to do is put out some bait."

Chook scowled at me. "To get Stebber and Gisik out in the open? You don't look like a mark, Trav. And if you run into Wilma, she knows you."

"I have somebody all roped, and I need some competent help to pick him clean."

"Who?" Arthur asked blankly.

"We'll have to invent him. But if I have to produce him, we should have somebody in mind, somebody who could run over here at short notice and put on a good act."

"And you do have somebody in mind, don't you?" Chook said accusingly.

"You ever run into Roger Bliss?"

She didn't know him. I told them about Roger. Except for an unfortunate taint of honesty, he could have become one of the great confidence men of our times. After a fine arts education, he had gone to Italy to study and paint. There he had gotten in with the movie crowd and had been put to work doing character bits. He was a natural mimic. He'd learned he'd never make it as a painter. And, in time, the movie thing bored him. Now he owned a small expensive sales gallery in Hollywood, Florida, had nurtured a profitable list of art patrons, lived well, was often restless, particularly during the slack season, and had helped me a couple of times in the past, when I needed someone who could be, on request, a convincing psychiatrist, air force colonel, college dean or Oklahoma wildcatter. He had a wicked ability of being absolutely plausible, down to the smallest mannerism and detail of dress. I would make sure he was available, just in case. And think up a cover story which would make Stebber and company salivate freely.

So we cruised up the flank of the Everglades, past the misted shoreline of the Ten Thousand Mangrove Islands. It is dark strange country, one of the few places left which man has not been able to mess up. The great river of grass starts up near Okeechobee, the widest shallowest river on the continent, and flows south. The hammocks of oak, cabbage palm, fifty other varieties of trees, are the quaking islands in the thirty-mile width of the sawgrass river. On the broad moist banks are the silent stands of cypress. Where the tides seep up into the river, at the northernmost limits of brackishness, the dwarf mangrove starts. The Ten Thousand Islands comprise the vast steamy tidal basin where the river enters the Gulf and Florida Bay.

Man, forever stubborn, has made but a few small dents in this eternal silence. Perimeter outposts—Everglades, Marco, Flamingo, Chokoloskee. But he has never thrived. There is rich soil there, rich enough so that a hundred years ago tomatoes grown in the Everglades were bringing twenty-four dollars a case in New York during the winter season. But hurricanes thrash through, pushing salt tides that take years to leach out of the poisoned soil. The fevers, the bugs, the storms, the isolation—these things have always broken the spirits of all but the toughest, the kind of human who can describe the peak of the mosquito season as the time when you can swing a one-pint jar and catch a quart of them.

The tough Calusa Indians were there at the time Christ was born, building storm shelter islands out of the shells of the oysters and clams they ate, leaving a staggering enough tonnage of shells by the time the Spaniards totally eliminated them that miles and miles of the first rude roads into the edges of the Glades were paved with those shells.

This is the land of the great enduring myth of the Seminole. They were a ragtag ethnic jumble, driven all the way down from Georgia and the Carolinas, until finally after the forced resettlement of most of them in the southwest, there were not two hundred and fifty left—scattered, hiding, demoralized—not worth any further military effort. For fifty years their numbers remained about the same. Then slowly they reestablished a new culture composed of remembered fragments of many old ones, speaking pidgin versions of old tongues. They had even begun to acquire a kind of plaintive dignity, but then the white man pushed the Tamiami Trail across the Glades from Naples to Miami, eliminating them as a tribe, turning them into roadside merchants of such a vast gypsy cynicism that of all the artifacts they manufacture and sell to the tourists—not one bears any relation to their customs, habits, or prior way of life. They are the carnival Indians, degraded by commerce, curious heirs to the big colorful lie that they were never whipped, never made a truce. They are the comedy Indians who, never having used tomtoms in their history, never having used the tomahawks or bows and arrows like the Plains Indians, now make vast quantities of each and sell them to people from Ohio.

Now, of course, having failed in every attempt to subdue the Glades by frontal attack, we are slowly killing it off by tapping the River of Grass. In the questionable name of progress, the state in its vast wisdom lets every two-bit developer divert the flow into the draglined canals that give him "waterfront" lots to sell. As far north as Corkscrew Swamp, virgin stands of ancient bald cypress are dying. All the area north of Copeland had been logged out, and will never come back. As the Glades dry, the big fires come with increasing frequency. The ecology is changing with egret colonies dwindling, mullet getting scarce, mangrove dying of new diseases born of dryness.

But it will take a long time to kill it. And years from now foolish men will still be able to kill themselves off within miles of help, hopelessly lost among islands which all look exactly alike. It is a black land, and like every wilderness in the world, it punishes quickly when a mistake is made, quickly and with a casual, savage indifference.

I studied the chart and picked a spot. I went beyond Marco Pass to a wide pass named Hurricane Pass. The channel was easy to read from the topside controls. The *Flush* draws four feet and is heavily skegged to protect the shafts and wheels. Roy Cannon Island, deserted, lies just inside the pass. It was low tide as we came in just before sunset. The pass is so wide, Roy Cannon has a sand beach. I edged a little north to get the protection of the headland which forms the north edge of the pass. At dead slow I ran the bow into the beach sand. With Chook and Arthur helping, we put out all four anchors, the two bow ones well up on the beach, wedged into the skeletal whiteness of mangrove killed by the sand which had built up, probably after Hurricane Donna had widened the pass. I carried the stern hooks out into water neck deep, wedged them in, stomped them firm. She would rest well there, lifting free with the incoming tide, settling back at the low. I'd topped off the fuel and water at Flamingo. We swam as the sun went down, and then clouds of mosquitoes, shrill with hunger, drove us below decks to break out the bombs and drop the ones that had come in with us. It was such a hot and airless night, I started the generator and put the air-conditioning on. After dinner, over coffee, I took Arthur through the best physical descriptions of the four men that he could manage, particularly Stebber and Gisik. I wanted to be certain to know them if the names were changed.

Saturday morning early I saddled up the dinghy and, taking Chook with me, droned south inside the islands to Marco

59

Village. We achieved invisibility. There is an easy way to do it along that coast. I wore khaki pants, a white T-shirt, a baseball hat with a long bill, dark glasses. She wore white denim stretch pants, a blue halter, dark glasses, and a little pot-shaped straw hat some female had left aboard, embroidered in red yarn across the front—Drink Up. We brought along a tackle box, two rods and a red beer cooler.

Marco Village saddened me. The bulldozers and draglines had gotten to it since my last visit. The ratty picturesque old dock was gone, as was the ancient general store and a lot of the old weatherbeaten two-story houses which had looked as though they had been moved down from Indiana farmland. They had endured a half century of hurricanes, but little marks on a developer's plat had erased them so completely there was not even a trace of the old foundations.

But even the scurry of multimillion dollar development slows to a sleepy pace in the island heat of late May. Loafers identified us instantly by type as we tied up and clambered out of the dinghy, and from then on their total bemused attention was on the fruitful flexible weight encased in the white stretch denim, with Chook quite comfortably aware of admiration and speculation. I asked my question, and we got one bad lead and then a better one, and finally found a sallow, thoughtful young man who took us to where his boat sat lashed to a trailer. Sixteen foot, heavy-duty fiberglass hull, with a forty horse Evinrude bolted to the reinforced transom. Twin tanks. All required gear.

"I don't know about a week," he said. "Figured on using it some myself. I'd have to get"—he wiped his mouth, stared into the distance—"a hundred dollars, mister?"

"Seventy-five. I buy gas."

"I got fourteen hundred dollars in it, mister."

"Seventy-five right now, and if I only keep it three days, it's still seventy-five."

He made a responsible show of studying my driver's license, giving sidelong glances at Chook's scanty halter, and got very helpful and cheery when he had the seventy-five in hand, describing places where we could hook into big snook and baby tarpon. He put it in the water for us. Boldly lettered on the white fiberglass, in pink, and for some obscure reason in Old English calligraphy, was the name *Ratfink*. We took off sedately, towing the dinghy astern, dock loafers watching us out of sight. Arthur was waiting on the beach when we returned. Without the burdens of Chook and the dinghy, I took *Ratfink* out into open water and found I had made a good guess on the hull design. It was very fast and stable, and when I came smashing back through my own wake, I found it was a dry boat.

Another can of gas aboard would give it all the high speed range I'd need. It had one of the new control rigs, shift and throttle on the same handy lever. The cable control gave it a quick steering ratio. I taped a piece of white cloth over the too-memorable name, and with some black electrician's tape I made an alteration in the registration number, turning a six into an eight and a one into a seven. It would stand inspection from ten feet away.

I changed to slacks and a sports shirt, stowed a light jacket and tie in the locker under the forward deck, told them to be good kids, and took off up the inside route to Naples, an estimated twelve miles away, less than a half hour in my jazzy craft.

I found an adequate little marina just short of the highway bridge on the southeast side of Naples. I filled the tanks, bought an extra five gallon can, had it filled with the right gas and oil mix and stowed it aboard. I said I might be leaving it there off and on for a week. The man said a dollar a day. And how about leaving a car here when I'm out in the boat? I asked. Right over there next to the building, where that pickup is, it'll be okay there, no charge. I paid him a week on the dockage, and after he had shown me where to put it and wandered away, I tied it up in such a way that though the lines were firm, I could free them with one yank, shove off bow first, hit the starter button and be on my way. This was one of the elemental precautions. Never go in until you are damned well sure how you are going to get out. There are few roads in the Glades country, but more waterways than have ever been counted. With the jacket over my arm, I went up to Route 41 and walked across the highway bridge and down the other side of the bayou to the Fish House Restaurant. It was clean and quiet. The decor was seashells stuck into cement on the pillars, beams and ceiling. Tourists had pried out a lot of the ones within reach. I found they served a clam chowder with character. It would cure debility, angry the blood, and turn a girl scout troop into a baritone choir.

I didn't bother phoning Crane Watts' office. His residence was on Clematis Drive. A maid announced it as The Watts Resydense and told me, "They's at the Club." And when I asked if it was the Cutlass Yacht Club, she said, "Nome, they plays tennis at the Royal Palm Bath Club."

I looked up car rentals, phoned one and was told they couldn't deliver. Just one man on duty. I took a cab to the place the other side of town. I signed up for a dark green Chev, four door, with air-conditioning. The attendant told me to go about another mile north and then look for the Bath Club sign on a road to the left, turn and go about a half mile. I couldn't miss it. I didn't.

I found a parking place in the lot. The huge pool, behind woven fencing, was a gabbling, shrieking, belly-whomping mass of kids. They had a crescent of private beach dotted with bright umbrellas and oiled brown flesh, prone and supine. Despite the early afternoon heat, their dozen asphalt courts beyond the pool area were all full. You could see at a glance it was very proper tennis. Everyone raced about in spotless white, sweating and banging hell out of the ball, calling out Love, Add, Out and Nice Shot.

The club house was a flaking Moorish pastry onto which had been pasted a big wing in supermarket modern. I wandered in and found a bulletin board in a corridor. They are always useful. The bulletin board was folksier than the tennis. There was a mimeographed copy of the last club bulletin tacked to it. Seems that on May tenth the Taylors had given a big farewell bash for Frank and Mandy Hopson, before they left on their dream trip, three whole months in Spain. Crane and Viv Watts were listed among the guests. I found a phone booth and book, but it gave me no clue as to good old Frank's occupation, if any. I roamed until I found a door labeled OFFICE. I knocked and pushed it open. A thin girl was alone in there, typing. She had a pert look, a large toothy smile.

"May I help you, sir?"

"Sorry to bother you. I just got to town today. I called Mr. Frank Hopson at his home but I couldn't get an answer. I remember him speaking of this place, and I thought maybe Frank and Mandy might be out here."

She made a sad mouth. "Oh, dear! They went away on a long trip."

"Don't tell me they finally made it to Spain. Son of a gun."

"They were as excited about it as a pair of little kids, believe me, Mr. . . . ."

"McGee. Travis McGee. They've been after me for years

to come over and see them. Well . . . that's the way it goes. At least I got a look at the club."

She hesitated for some additional inspection. I am conspicuously large, and I have a permanent deep-water tan, and I would not look out of place on a construction crew. But the slacks and shirt and jacket were top grade and she knew it. And I smiled at her like Stoney Burke admiring a speckled calf.

"Well, I think we can do better than that for any friend of the Hopsons," she said, making her decision. "How long will you be in town?"

"Maybe a week. On business."

"Mr. and Mrs. Hopson would certainly want you to use the Club." She winked. "In fact, I *distinctly* remember Mr. Hopson saying that you should have a guest card if you ever appeared while they were gone." She pulled the sheets out of her typewriter, ran a card in and filled it out. I gave her the Bahia Mar box number. She signed the club manager's name, put her initials under it, and handed it to me with a little flourish. "These are good for two weeks, Mr. McGee. You can sign and be billed directly. The only restriction is that you can't bring guests here. Except your wife, of course."

"Unmarried. How about just one lady? One at a time."

"No one could object to that. Please don't be shy about mingling and introducing yourself. You'll find all the members very friendly, particularly toward any friend of Mr. Hopson. And please put the card number on the chits you sign. Tonight we're having an outdoor steak roast, buffet style. If you want to stay for it—it's really very good—I can take your reservation."

"Might as well. Thanks. You've been very kind, Miss . . ."

"Benedict. Francie Benedict." The smile opened her up back to the wisdom teeth. "I do wish I could show you where everything is, but I do have to finish this."

"I'll just wander around."

"You can rent swim trunks from Albie in the men's locker room."

She was typing again as I pulled the office door shut. I found a dark, cool, quiet bar in the Moorish part. The sedentary types were there and in the adjoining card room, several grim tables of male bridge. I stood at an empty expanse of mahogany bar. The bartender approached with one eyebrow shoved up in cautious, supercilious interrogation. I whipped out my card, and his smile of acceptance would have looked more plausible if he'd been outfitted with those stainless steel teeth the Russians have developed. After he served my Plymouth gin on ice, the clot of members down the bar motioned to him. He leaned across the bar. There was a whispered question and answer; they looked me over and got back into their argument.

A pudgy chap with a statesman's face and careful coiffure of white locks said in liquor-slurred tones, "But you got to face facts, Roy. The fact remains, we got the evidence right in front of us, the decay of the nashal moral fiber, mob rule in the streets, violence, punks killing decen' people. Am I right or am I right?"

I could imagine the same tired concept being stated in a thousand private clubs across the country on this May afternoon. They see the result, but they are blind to the cause of it. Forty million more Americans than we had in 1950. If one person in fifty has a tendency toward murderous violence, then we've got eight hundred thousand more of them now. And density alone affects the frequency with which mobs form. The intelligence of a mob can be determined by dividing the lowest IQ present by the number of people in the mob. Life gets cheaper. Cops, on a per capita basis, get fewer. And the imponderables of the bomb, of automation, of accelerating social change create a kind of urban despair that wants to break loose and crack heads. All the barroom sociologists were orating about national fiber while, every minute and every hour, the most incredible population explosion in history was rendering their views, their judgments, even their very lives more obsolete.

They should hark to the locust. When there is only a density of X per acre, he is a plain old grasshopper, munching circumspectly, content with his home ground. Raise it to 2X and an actual physical change begins to occur. His color changes, his jaw gets bigger, and the wing muscles begin to grow. At 3X they take off in great hungry clouds, each cloud a single herd instinct, chomping everything bare in its path. There is no decline in the moral fiber of the grasshopper. There is just a mass pressure canceling out all individual decisions.

"Am I not right, sir?" demanded the pundit, making a stately turn to include me. I had not heard the more recent statements.

"Absolutely," I said. "Right on the button."

I was roped into the group, met the mellowed and important gentlemen, heard fond words about good old Frank

64

Hopson, and discovered, fortuitously, that Frank was a realtor. "But with his holdings, he doesn't have to work at it much. It's mostly management and rental stuff on what he owns. Poor bastard, he's a land merchant, and he can't take a capital gains on anything, so he just doesn't sell it off."

One of them said, not to me, "I heard that for a while there, young Crane Watts was trying to work something out for Frank, some deal whereby he could put everything in one package, real estate business and all, give up his license and retire and sell all his holdings to an outside corporation and take his capital gains."

A man beside me lowered his voice and said, "He'd be a fool to let Watts work on anything."

"It was some time ago," another said in the same low tone, and they stared toward the card room. I spotted the one who most clearly matched Arthur's description. He was playing bridge at the furthest table, slumped, peering slack-jawed at his holding. He selected a card slowly, raised it high, whacked it down with a wolf yelp of laughter, then hunched forward, glowering, as the opposition gathered the trick in.

"I don't know how he can afford that game."

"He seems to get it somewhere when he needs it."

"She's such a *damned* fine girl."

"Sure is."

I detached myself and went wandering to the courts, looking for that damned fine girl, Vivian Watts. A kid resting between sets pointed her out to me. She was in a singles match against an agile blonde boy of about nineteen, almost ten years her junior I would guess. It was the only court with an interested gallery. She was of the same physical type as Chook, not as tall. She was dark and tanned, sturdily built but lithe. And, like Chook, she had that hawk-look of strong features, prominent nose, heavy brows. As with all natural athletes, she had an economy of motion which created its own grace. She wore a little pleated white tennis skirt, white sleeveless blouse, white band on her dark hair. Her brown and solid legs had a good spring, bringing her back into a balanced readiness after each stroke, the way a good boxer moves.

It was easy to see the shape of the match. The boy was a scrambler, going after everything, returning shots it didn't seem plausible he could reach, lobbing them high enough to give him time to get back for the smash, and preventing her from coming up to the net to put them away. She tried a cross-court volley and put it just outside.

"Broke her service again," a bald little man beside me said. He was as brown and knotty as walnuts.

"How does it stand?"

"Six-three to Viv, then seven-five to Dave. Now he's got her nine-eight."

He had a big serve and she waited well back, handled it firmly, moved to center court and drove his ground stroke right back at his ankles. He aced her, on his next serve. Then on the next serve he tried to come to the net and she made a beautiful passing shot. Her return of his next serve floated and he let it go out by six inches. He took the advantage on another service ace. At match point, she again tried the passing shot as he moved up quickly, but the ball slapped the tape and, to the accompaniment of a concerted partisan groan, fell into her court.

She went to the net and, smiling, tucked her racket under her left arm and held out her right hand to the boy in a quick, firm congratulatory handshake. The smile was the first change of expression I had seen. Her tennis was poker-face, with no girlish grimaces of despair when things went wrong.

They moved off the court as other players moved on, and I drifted along with them, over toward tables in the shade. The boy went off, apparently to get her something to drink. When I moved near enough, she looked up at me with an expression of inquiry, and I saw that her eyes were a very deep blue instead of the brown I had expected.

"Just wanted to say that was very good tennis to watch, Mrs. Watts."

"Thank you. Last year I could take Dave. Next year I won't take a set. Do I know you?"

"Frank and Mandy Hopson fixed up a guest card for me. I'm just in town for a short time. Travis McGee, Mrs. Watts. East coast."

The boy brought drinks, a Coke for himself and iced tea for Viv Watts. She introduced him. Dave Sablett. He seemed a little stiff-necked about her asking me to join them. He had a proprietary air toward her, to which she seemed quite oblivious. She was still breathing deeply, her hair damp with sweat. We chatted for a little while. They were signed up for mixed doubles beginning in a few moments. They were the club's mixed doubles champions.

I watched the match begin and it was clear after two

66

points they were going to take it readily. So I went back inside to see, perhaps, at closer range, the other half of this happy marriage.

SEVEN

IN THE SATURDAY DUSK I got a drink from the outside bar and moved out of the throng. In a few minutes Viv Watts came over to where I was standing. She had on a yellow summer cotton, a new mouth. Her manner and expression were tense.

"Maybe *you'll* tell me what happened in there, Mr. McGee."

"Nothing important. I guess your husband got a little abusive and his partner quit. So he was getting ugly about having no chance to get even. Nobody wanted to partner him. It was turning into a scene, so I . . . sat in."

"How much did you lose?"

"Not enough to matter, Mrs. Watts. When I found out what the stakes were, I said it was too rich for my blood. Three cents a point can be murder. I said I'd go for a half cent, and your husband said he'd pick up the slack."

She looked away with a slightly sick expression. "Five and a half cents a point. Dear God!"

"He wasn't in any shape to play. Oh, he wasn't leading out of turn or forgetting the bid. Nothing like that. He just got too optimistic."

"What did you lose?"

"It doesn't matter."

"I insist!"

"Twenty-one dollars. But really . . ."

She bit her lip, unsnapped her white purse and dug into it. I put my hand on her wrist, stopping her. "I really won't take it."

She gave up, saying, "I really wish you would. Did he go home?"

"No. After he settled up he didn't feel very well. He's in that small lounge off the card room . . . resting."

She frowned. "Maybe I should take him home."

"He's sacked out. So he's just as well off there, isn't he?"

She stared beyond me at nothing, her eyes bleak. "He

67

just seems to be getting wor . . ." She caught herself, gave me an awkward glance. A man going sour puts an attractive wife in a strange bind. Still tied to him by what remains of her security, and by all the weight of the sentimentalities and warmths remembered, she is aware of her own vulnerability and, more importantly, aware of how other men might well be appraising that vulnerability, hoping to use it. Feeling the weight of interest and speculation on the part of friends and neighbors, and sensing that she is moving ever closer to disaster, she feels obligated to be more circumspect. Because this, too, is a kind of loyalty. She wants, when it is over, to find no way to blame herself.

"Get you a drink?" I said.

"Please. Scotch and water, please. Tall and weak."

As I brought it to her I saw young Dave Sablett talking to her and saw her quite obviously send him away. He looked back at me, surly and indignant.

"Mr. McGee . . ."

"Trav."

"All right. Trav, do you think he might make a fuss if I tried to take him home now?"

"He well might, Vivian."

She looked startled. "That makes me feel strange. *Vivian*. Vivi when I was little, and Viv now. Vivian when my mother was really cross with me. Vivian on official papers. But it's all right. Maybe I'd like to be called that by someone. It could . . . remind me I have to be a grownup these days."

"None of my business, of course. But is something really wrong with him? Health? Business?"

"I don't know. He just . . . changed."

"Recently?"

"I couldn't say just when it started. A year ago anyway. Trav, I just can't stay here and . . . be calm and social and charming, damn it. Not knowing they're watching me and saying poor Viv. He promised it would be different this time. But if he refuses to come home . . . it could be worse."

"I could bring him along without a fuss."

She chewed her lip. "He might respond better to you. But I don't want to spoil your evening."

"I'm here only because I couldn't think of anything else to do."

"Well . . . if you wouldn't mind."

She showed me where I could bring him out the side door to the far end of the parking lot. The sun was gone, the steak grills cherry red, orange flames flickering atop the

68

Polynesian pedestals in the cookout area, music resonant over the outdoor speakers. We brought both cars around and I parked behind hers, a small white Mercedes with dented fenders. I told her to wait and start up after I put him in my car, and I would follow her home.

I shook Crane Watts up out of the murks of sleep, and he came up thrashing and whining with irritation. "Lemme lone! Chrissake!" He focused on me, the uncertain peer of the still drunk. "You, partner. Cheap half a cent bassar, and you were no damn help at all. I needed you like a head cold, partner what's-is-name. Gimme anything better than clowns and I can take that pair."

"You're going home, Crane."

"Hell you say! You being boyscout for that bitch? Screw you, samaritan. I'm staying. I'm going to have a ball."

I plucked him up off the couch and caught the fist he threw at me, opened it quickly, regrasped it in an effective come-along, a hold which leaves the index and little finger free, and presses the middle two fingers against the palm of the captive hand. Crane Watts, face convulsed, drew his other fist back, and I gave him a good taste of a pain sufficiently exquisite to bypass the alcohol. His face went blank and sweaty and the blood drained out of it. He made a small squeak and lowered the poised fist.

"Is there some trouble here?" a nervous voice asked, and I turned and saw a club employee in the doorway.

"No trouble. I was just getting ready to take Mr. Watts home."

I cued Watts with a little pressure. "Just going home," he said in a gassy whisper, and with a strange imitation of a reassuring smile. The employee hesitated, said goodnight and went away.

Crane Watts made a very cautious attempt to pull his hand free, and found that it added to the pain. He walked out very carefully beside me, quite erect, taking small dutiful steps, not wavering a bit. A Nassau police official had showed me that hold. Improperly applied, it snaps the bones or dislocates the knuckles. In correct adjustment, it pulls the nerves of the two middle fingers against the knuckle bones in a way that you can hit ten on the dolorometer. Nine is the peak for childbirth and migraine, and all but the most stoic faint at some point between nine and ten. You watch their color, their sweat and the focus of their eyes to keep it below the fainting point. And it is a quiet thing. Small pain makes people roar and bellow. The excruciating ones reduce them to an almost supersonic squeak. Also, intense pain is one way to induce a sudden sobriety. By the time I opened the car door for him, I knew he would be no further trouble. I pushed him in and went around and got behind the wheel, started up and followed the Mercedes.

"Jesus," he groaned, hugging his hand against his belly.

"It'll throb for ten minutes or so, and then it will be all right."

"It goes all the way up into the back of my neck, fella. Is it some kind of judo?"

"Something like that."

After a few minutes he slowly straightened up. "Beginning to go away, like you said."

"Sorry I had to do it, Crane. I promised your wife I'd get you home."

"Maybe I didn't give you a hell of a lot of choice. Or her." I felt him staring at me as we passed street lights. "What's your name again?"

"Travis McGee. Friend of Frank Hopson. Over here from the east coast on business."

"Look at that! She turns without any kind of signal at all."

"Maybe she's got a lot on her mind."

"Sure. Like how to get more overspin on her backhand. Don't let her sucker you, McGee. That's an ice cold bitch. She's slowing for the driveway. It's on the left there."

It was a broad driveway and one of those long low Florida block houses with a tile roof, a double carport and, beyond any doubt, a big screened cage off the rear, with or without pool. Awning windows, glass doors on aluminum tracks, a heat pump system—you could guess it all before you saw it, even to a couple of citrus trees and cocoanut palms out back. Terrazzo floors, planting areas in the screened cage and a computerized kitchen. But even at night I saw other clues, a front lawn scruffy and sunbrowned, a dead tree at the corner of the house, a driveway sign saying The Watts which was turned, bent and leaning from someone clipping it on the way in.

I parked in the drive, behind her car. He got out at once, advancing to meet her as she walked back toward my car.

"Congratulations, sweetie baby," he said. "Now you got proof I spoiled your evening. See how early it is? Now you can suffer."

She planted her feet, squared her shoulders. "There might be one member left who would trust you to write up a simple will or even search a title, dearest. So let's protect all that charming innocent faith as long as we can, shall we? Come on in the house before you fall down." She turned toward me. "I'd offer you a drink, but I guess you've had about all anyone would want of this, Trav."

"I might come in for a few minutes, if it's all right. I would like to ask Crane about something. Something maybe he could help me with."

"Him?" she said, loading the word with enough contempt for a month.

"Loyalty, loyalty," Crane mumbled.

We went into the house. She turned lights on. She kept turning lights on, even to the outside floods in and beyond the screened cage, rolling the glass doors open and, with a gaiety very close to hysteria, she said, "And this is our happy mortgaged nest, Mr. McGee. You may note a few scars and stains. Little domestic spats, Mr. McGee. And did you see that the pool is empty? Poor little pool. It's a heavy upkeep item to operate a pool, more than you'd think. And we don't care to run the air-conditioning this summer. You wouldn't believe the bills. But you know, I do have my little indulgences. My tennis, and my once a week cleaning woman for some Saturday scrubbing, in case we entertain on a Saturday night, but there aren't many people left we could invite, really. But, you see, I pay for the tennis and the cleaning woman. I have this lovely little trust fund, a whole hundred and twenty-one dollars a month. Don't you think wives should have an income of their own, Mr. McGee?"

She gave me a brilliant smile, sobbed suddenly, whirled and ran, her hands over her face. She went out of sight down a corridor and a door closed behind her.

Mumbling almost inaudibly, Crane Watts took a bottle from a bar corner and headed for the kitchen. As he passed me, I lifted it out of his hand.

"I need that!"

"Not if we're going to talk. If we're going to talk, you need a shower and you need some coffee, before and after the shower."

"Talk about what?"

"Maybe how you can help me make some money."

He wiped his face slowly with his hand, stopped and looked at me with one skeptical eye between his fingers. "Mean it?" I nodded. He sighed. "Okay. Hang around. Make coffee, if you can find the stuff."

71

I found powdered coffee. I made a strong mug of it and took it toward the sound of the shower. The bathroom door was ajar. I put it on the counter top next to the sink, yelled to him that it was there, and went back to the living room. Houses where love is dead or dying acquire a transient look. Somewhere there are people who, though they do not know it yet, are going to move in.

He came wandering in, mug in his hand, hair damp, wearing a blue bathrobe. He sat wearily, sipped the coffee, stared at me. His color was not good. There were dark stains under his eyes. He had a drinker's puffiness, not far advanced, but enough to alert the observant and the wary. But the mists had lifted.

"Why me?" he asked. "That's the best question I can ask."

"I could need a hungry lawyer."

"You found him. Maybe I'm not as hungry as I have to be. I won't know, will I, until you tell me."

"I'm doing a favor for a man. For a fee. He trusts my judgment and my knowledge of Florida land values. He just came into a very big piece of money. He wants to put half of it in securities and half in land. A broker is working up a portfolio for him. I'm . . . hunting around."

"You an agent?"

"No. If I could locate something good, a very promising investment, something in the eight or nine hundred thousand range, he'll give me ten thousand finder's fee. He's interested in raw land."

"And you need a lawyer to check out something quietly?"

"Not exactly. I found a couple of very clean deals, one near Arcadia and the other up the coast, south of Cedar Keys. Each is worth the finder's fee."

"So where does a hungry lawyer fit?"

I stood up. "Let's adjourn to the office."

Looking bewildered, he followed me to the bathroom. I turned the cold water in the shower on full, then leaned on the counter top. He understood quickly enough. "You're more careful than you have to be, McGee."

"I always am." He leaned against the countertop beside me, and we spoke over the roar of the shower. "Ten thousand seems smaller every day, Watts. If a deal could get more complex, maybe a little more would rub off. Like if something could be picked up and held and resold. You might have more ideas about that kind of thing than I would."

"Why should you think so?"

"From some bar talk today I got the idea you pulled off something pretty cute."

"Oh, it was cute all right," he said angrily. "It was even legal. But all I got was peanuts, comparatively speaking. It wasn't anything I set up. This lousy town. Other lawyers get a little tricky and everybody says how smart they are. You know what I got? A whispering campaign. I'm down to a practice that just about pays the light bill."

"Maybe you could try it again, and cut yourself a bigger piece. Legally, of course."

"Maybe your guy is too shrewd for it. The one they cleaned was truly stupid."

"My guy is no giant, and he's never held a job in his life. You said *they* cleaned. Who?"

"Some out-of-town operators."

"Would we need them?"

He frowned, tugged his lip. "It wouldn't hurt at all to bring one of them in on it. He's damned good." He straightened up. "You're acting as if we're going to try it, and you don't know a damn thing about it."

"All I want to know is that there's no ten years in Raiford afterwards."

"Nothing like that. It's all legal, believe me."

"How does it work?"

"Your guy has to go along with certain things. Like being willing to be in on a land syndicate operation. And your guy should be off balance a little. They used a woman on the last one."

"Is she still around?"

"Not that I know of. Why?"

"It could work with my man too."

"Listen. You said he trusts you. The way this thing works, it isn't halfway. It has to clean him completely, or it doesn't work. Would that bother you?"

"Not on his account. But it makes me a little nervous. We're talking about close to two million dollars, Watts."

"With family lawyers riding herd on it, maybe?"

"No. How does it work? Make it simple. I'm not a lawyer."

"You make your man believe the syndicate is going after one hell of a big piece of land. Everybody puts money into the syndicate trust account, on a share basis. The trustee is one of the syndicate. In this case it would be that man I told you about. The sucker thinks everybody is putting in cash. But, by separate letter of agreement, the trustee agrees to accept demand notes from the other partners, in

73

view of their long association and so forth. There's a clause in the syndicate agreement permitting additional assessments. Every time one comes along, the sucker comes up with cash and the others turn over promissory notes for their assessment. Another clause in the agreement says that if anyone can't meet an assessment, they are dealt out, and their share is divided pro rata among the other partners. Another clause says that if it is decided the operation is not feasible, the syndicate will be disbanded and the funds in the trust account divided among the partners pro rata. So you just assess him until he's dry, cancel him out with due notice, and a little while later close up shop and divide the pie. You have to keep him thinking that the whole thing is right on the verge of turning into a big fat gold mine."

"And you got a piece of that pie?"

"Hardly. I got a twenty-five hundred dollar fee and a five thousand bonus. I was promised ten, but after it was over there was no way I could blow the whistle on them without putting myself in a sling, and they knew it."

"What did they take the man for?"

"About two hundred and thirty thousand. When it was too late, he went to another lawyer. That's how the news got all over town."

"But you can still afford to lose five hundred dollars in a bridge game?"

He put his head in his hands. "Cut it out, will you?"

"Could you rig the same kind of operation again, for my man?"

"I don't know. It's a lot bigger. I don't know how good my nerve is. I'd have to bring that other man in on it. Maybe he wouldn't want to come in alone. Maybe he'd want to use the same people as before. They'd cut themselves big pieces."

"So how could we defend ourselves against being left the small end?"

He shook his head. "I've got a headache, McGee. There are ways. You work this thing out in the open. We could set up the trust account so it would require three signatures for any withdrawal, and with our promissory notes being as good as the others, we could get in for any percentage we could dicker for."

"He's my man. What if we go for half between us, forty percent for me and ten for you? And let them cut the rest up any way they want, just so they swing it."

74

"But wouldn't he know you can't come up with that kind of cash? I think it would have to . . ."

The bathroom door opened and Vivian stared in at us. "What the hell are you doing?"

"I'm getting rich, sweetheart. Close the door. As you leave."

I got a duplicate of the look she gave him. She yanked the door shut.

"One other thing, Watts. I suppose you have to set up a fictitious piece of property."

"Oh, no. That would classify it as fraud. We dealt with the executor of the Kippler tract, sixty-one thousand acres. We made legitimate option offers."

"So where are you if he said okay, let's deal?"

"He couldn't. It's all tied up by the terms of the will. But how could we know that if he didn't tell us?"

"And he didn't?"

"No. He wrote nice letters. Seriously considering your last offer. Must discuss it with the heirs and the tax attorneys and so on. They went in the file, in case anybody ever had to see the file. And he kept demanding a higher option offer."

"Which required assessments. So he was coached?"

"Of course. And he got a nice little gift afterward. Hell, McGee, the whole file on this thing is clean as a whistle."

"Could we use the same tract again?"

"Well . . . not on option terms. Too much money involved this time. Maybe on a purchase basis. With a good chance of resale if we could pick it up right, say at two hundred an acre. Twelve million. Then your man comes in for one twelfth . . . something along that line, where it would leave enough plausible spread to assess him out of the picture. You see, you have to know just about the absolute total the sucker can come up with. Once hooked big, then they have to keep throwing more in because they think it's the only way they can protect themselves. The beauty of it is that when it's over, they are picked so clean there's hardly any chance at all of them coming up with any civil action to recover, and it's a little too clean to make it attractive to any lawyer to tackle on a contingency basis. What's your man's name?"

"We'll have to think about this and talk about it later. What's the name of your expert?"

"He might be busy with something else. You'll get in touch?"

"Soon."

"In the meantime, just for the hell of it, and it can't do any harm, call your man and act excited and tell him you think there's a chance you can get him into something that will double his money in a year. Is he interested in doubling his money?"

"He wants to be nationally known as a wheeler and dealer."

"What line of work *are* you in?"

"Salvage and demolition."

"On your own?"

"Without overhead. Whenever the right kind of job comes along, I bid it in, rent the equipment, subcontract everything I can, come out with a low profit percentage that's big enough to live well until the next chance opens up."

He nodded. "Very smart. Very nice. So why all this sudden larceny, friend?"

"I wasn't the low bidder the last few times, and the operating capital is getting a little too puny."

"How can I contact you, McGee?"

"I'm staying with friends. I'll be in touch."

I did not see Vivian when I left. And I could well imagine how Crane Watts would feel the next morning when he remembered the conversation. The man suddenly and artificially sobered has a period of fraudulent lucidity. He thinks he is under control, but the cerebral cortex is still partially stunned, all caution compromised. Attempts at slyness are childlike and obvious. The business of the shower had reassured him. If I was that careful to drown out any listening devices, then, hell, I had to be okay.

In the sober morning it would have a dreadful flavor to him, and he would be aghast not only at all he had told me, but at the memory of even contemplating the same sort of thing with so much money involved. He'd know it was too big for that same kind of operation.

But he was hungry. His seams were splitting and the sawdust was leaking. I wondered if he was bright enough to realize that under that seedy look of failure was an old time conscience, prodding him into self-punishment. Such as playing losing bridge for high stakes.

Now I had things to go on, pieces to pry loose. The solo operator is often invulnerable. But group operations are weak as the weakest thief in the team. An equation applies. The weakest is usually the one who gets the smallest end of the take. And knows the least. But because of the

76

quasi-legality of this operation, Crane Watts had useful information. The big con often needs a plausible local front man. I could guess how Arthur's money had probably been split. A hundred thousand to Stebber, fifty to Wilma, fifty to G. Harrison Gisik, the balance to Watts, Waxwell, the Kippler executor and operating expenses. The role of Boone Waxwell troubled me a little. Beating Arthur so severely had been stupid. But maybe they felt they needed an enforcer. For whom? Watts wasn't likely to get out of line. Perhaps there'd been a germ of truth in their story to Arthur, that Waxwell was essential to negotiations on the Kippler tract. That could mean control of the executor. And where was the coldly efficient Miss Brown? And would that cheap redhead with the improbable name—Dilly Starr—know anything useful if she could be found?

I drove slowly toward the center of the very rich and pleasant little city of Naples, wondering how good old Frank was enjoying Spain.

EIGHT

WHEN I WALKED into the big drugstore on Fifth Avenue in Naples, I was slightly surprised to see that it was not yet nine o'clock. There were some rowdy teenagers at one of the counter sections, and I sat as far from them as possible. I like them fine in smaller units. But when they socialize, showing off for each other, they sadden me. The boys punch and shove, and repeat each comment in their raw uncertain baritone over and over until finally they have milked the last giggle from their soft little girls with their big, spreading, TV butts. And they keep making their quick cool appraisals of the environment to make certain they have a properly disapproving audience of squares. And have you noticed how many fat kids there are lately? And the drugstore comedians are usually the rejects. The good ones, as in any year, are taut, brown, earnest, and have many other things to do, and can even—unthinkably—endure being alone. This little fat-pack was nearing the end of their school year and, predictably, would slob around all summer, with a few of them impregnating each other. They would dutifully copy the outlook and mannerisms of their momentary idols. Some of them would check out this summer as a bloody stain on a bridge approach. The survivors, ten years hence, would wonder how come their luck was turning so bad, why life wasn't giving them any kind of break at all.

I had coffee and a sandwich, and went to a booth to check the thin Naples phonebook. Mrs. Mildred Mooney was listed. 17 Twenty-first Avenue. After the fifth ring she answered in a listless voice, said she was Mrs. Mooney.

"I wondered if I could stop by and talk to you about something. My name is McGee."

"I guess not. Not tonight. I was supposed to babysit and I got one of my sick headaches and I had to get somebody else, and I already gone to bed, mister."

"At least I can tell you what it's about, I'm trying to help a man you worked for. He needs help. Arthur Wilkinson. You might have some information I could use, Mrs. Mooney."

"He's a *real* nice man. He was *real* good to me. He had some terrible bad luck, losing all his money like that, so sudden and all. But I don't see how I could help."

"I won't take up much of your time."

After a long silence she said, "Well, I can't seem to get to sleep anyhow."

"I'll be along in a few minutes then."

She sat in a corner chair in the small living room of her efficiency apartment, sat in the dimness of a single small lamp burning in the opposite corner. Dumpy woman with a worn face and bushy gray hair, wearing a quilted wine-colored robe.

"When I'm like this," she said, "it's like bright light was needles sticking into my eyes. It comes on me about three or four times a year, and then I'm just no good for anything until it goes away. I got regular people, and I can get enough work to keep me going. Working at that big beach house last year was more than I like to take on. It was good pay, for around here, and just the two of them, but she didn't lift a finger. And I lost a lot of regular people taking steady work like that, and it took so long to get my regular people it seems like I ended up about even, except for working harder. Oh, I don't mind work, but when they come and go you have to look out for yourself so you have something coming in steady. But I want to tell you right now, I make it my rule not to talk about my people.

You start that and the first thing you know it gets around, then they don't want you. Land, the things I seen, I could fill a book, and you better believe it."

"I wouldn't want to ask you to talk about any of your regular people, Mrs. Mooney. I want you to consider something that maybe you never thought of. I want you to think back, and see if it would make any sense to you to believe that Wilma was a part of a conspiracy to defraud Arthur Wilkinson of his money."

"But wasn't she his wife like they said?"

"They went through a ceremony. Maybe she wasn't free to marry. Maybe it was just one of the ways of setting him up, to make it easier to take his money."

She made several little clicking sounds with her tongue. After a thoughtful silence she said, "I came close to quitting a lot of times out there, believe me, and stayed on account of him. She was a pretty little thing, and real lively, but I'd say older than maybe he krew. She sure did spend an awful lot of time on her face and hair. You know one thing she would do I never did hear of before? She would *sandpaper* her face, and that's God's truth, take little strokes and get it raw almost and then put on white goo and some kind of mask and lay down for an hour. She was loving to him, most of the time, nice enough to me when he was close, but with me and her alone, I was just a piece of furniture. She didn't see me, and if I said anything, she didn't hear me. She'd turn on me sometimes, just as mean as a wasp, eyes all narrowed down. Not hot angry, but cold as can be. I don't have to take that from anybody. But he was a nice nice man. I tell you, the way she used him was wicked. She had him waiting on her hand and foot, something she wanted that was closer to her than him, he had to go get it and bring it to her. He brushed her hair, that real pale thin kind of hair, a hundred strokes, putting a little bitty dab of some kind of perfume oil on the soft brush every ten strokes, with her whining if he lost count. She had him oil her head to foot for going in the sun, and another sickening thing, I tell you, she had him run her little electrical razor, shaving the fuzz off her pretty legs, then she'd feel to see if he did it good, tell him where he missed, and pat him when he finished. My husband Mr. Mooney, God rest his soul, was a *man*, and no woman ever lived could have turned him into a lady's maid like she done with Mr. Wilkinson. I felt so sorry for that poor man. I don't know, Mr. McGee. I thought it was just bad judgment, him investing in something that

79

turned out bad for him. But I guess she was the kind out for herself and no regard for anybody else."

"So let's say she was setting him up for Mr. Stebber to cheat him. Would that fit?"

"Mr. Stebber seemed like a real gentleman, the kind that thanks you nicely for any little thing. A smiley man. And you could tell he was a real big man, successful and all. She knew him from someplace. Then there was that tall sick-looking man with the funny name."

"Gisik."

"He didn't have much to say at any time. He acted as if he was busy thinking about important things happening far away. I guess if Mr. Wilkinson got cheated, then young Crane Watts must have got the same dose. They say he's going down hill something terrible, drinking and gambling and his practice going down to nothing, and probably they'll lose the house, so it's a blessing there's no children. It's children get hurt the worst in a thing like that. They don't understand. They're not regular people of mine, or ever were, so it isn't like I'm saying anything nearly everybody doesn't know already."

"I understand."

"There was one hanging around they called Boo. From out of the swamps around here from the way he talked. Low class man I'd say. And if anybody was robbing anybody, I'd say he was the one. And if she was in on it, I'd say she was in on it with that Boo fellow."

"Why do you say that?"

"I guess because he kept dropping in." I sensed reservations.

"There must have been something else."

"I'd rather not say."

"Any little thing might help."

"It . . . it isn't a decent kind of talk, and I don't want you thinking the wrong thing of me for staying on where that kind of thing was going on. It's not I'm an old maid. I was married twelve years to Mr. Mooney, God rest his soul, and had three dear babies who died, every one of them, breaking my heart every time, and breaking it for good when Mr. Mooney passed away in such terrible pain it was a blessing when it ended. What happened, it was an afternoon not long before they had to give up the house, and Mrs. Wilkinson and that Boo fellow were out by the pool, side by side in those tip back chairs, her keeping her face turned up to the sunshine. The mister had gone into town for some reason, and I just happened to look out the utility room window where I was sorting laundry. I was looking at them sideways, sort of, her in a naked little white suit, the bottom part like a little narrow band with fringe on it. And I just happened to see him reach over slow and put . . . put his hand down into her lap. It came into my mind that she was sleeping and she'd wake up fighting mad. But she didn't move. You know how you want to stop looking at something and you're kind of froze? When she did move . . . it was just to make things a little bit easier for him, her face still turned up for the sun and her eyes closed. When she did that, I stopped looking, and I worked like a crazy woman, throwing those clothes around, getting them all mixed up so I had to sort them all out again, spilling soap all over when I got them in the machine. When I heard them sploshing around I looked out and by then they were in the pool, laughing around. I knew then and there that the mister had a wicked wife, and I made my plans to give notice the end of the month, but before I could tell them, they told me they were giving up the beach house. That Boo man was around there a lot, and by then, those last weeks, Mr. Stebber and the sick one had gone away, back to Tampa I guess."

"Tampa?" I said it so loudly I startled her.

"Well, of course, it being where he lives."

"How are you sure of that?"

"Because I'm a real good cook. Mr. Mooney, God rest him, said I was the best he ever knew of. And that man loved to eat. I don't measure things. I just put things together the way they *seem* right. I did restaurant work once, but I hated it. There you have to measure everything because you have to make so much. I'm not lying when I say there've been visitors down here offered me more money than I'd care to mention to go back north with them. Mr. Stebber is one of those who lives for eating. You can tell it. Mostly it's fat happy men like him. They shut their eyes when they take the first taste, and they make a little moan and smile all over themselves. He came out there to the kitchen at that beach house and said it was just between the two of us, and when the Wilkinsons didn't need me any more, I should come to Tampa to cook for him. He said I'd have no heavy housework, and my own room and bath with color television. He said he was away a lot and when he was away it would be like a vacation for me. He said that I'd never have to cook for more than seven or eight at the most, and that wouldn't be often. He said he had a great

81

big apartment in one of those cooperative places, looking out over Tampa Bay, with a colored woman that came in by the day to do the heavy housework.

"Well, I told him that I just couldn't ever bring myself to move that far away from Mr. Mooney's grave. The three babies lived a little while, every one, long enough to have their names given to them, Mary Alice and Mary Catherine and Michael Francis, marked on the stones. There isn't a Sunday no matter how I might feel or how the weather is, I don't go out and neaten up the plot and set there and feel close to the only family I ever had.

"He said again that it was just between us, and if I changed my mind later on, then I could call him up, but the number wasn't in the book, and he gave it to me and told me not to lose it. But on that very next Sunday out there it seemed to me that Mr. Mooney somehow knew I was carrying that number in my pocketbook, so I took it out then and there and tore it up and let the wind blow it away. Are you sure it wasn't just maybe the missus and that Boo fellow cheated the mister?"

"They were all in on it, Mrs. Mooney."

"I do declare. You never can tell, can you? And they cheated that Mr. Watts too?"

"I think that's a very accurate statement."

"I can't think of anything else that would help."

"Do you know a redheaded girl named Dilly Starr?"

"I can't say as I do. I guess a person would remember a name like that."

"Or a Miss Brown, possibly Mr. Stebber's secretary?"

"Her neither," she said. "Is Mr. Wilkinson all right?"

"He's fine."

"Kindly give him my regards when you see him. He's a *nice* person. I suppose *she* ran off. Well, that's good riddance. I guess he couldn't help himself with her. When she was mad at him, she'd treat him like she treated me all the time, like a piece of furniture, wouldn't let him anywheres near her, and when he did exactly like she wanted, then she was . . . after him all the time. A woman shouldn't use *that* to break a man's spirit. That part of it is a wife's duty." She shook her head and clucked. "That little woman had him so he didn't know what end was up or what time of day it was. It makes a man a living fool."

When I thanked her for giving me the time, she said, "I'm glad you came by, Mr. McGee. It took my mind off the way I feel, and maybe I can drop off to sleep now. I hope the mister gets his money back."

At ten thirty I stopped at a gas station and picked up a road map to refresh my memory about distances in that sparsely settled area. I was wondering about taking the thirty or forty minute drive to Marco Island and seeing if I could locate Waxwell, but I didn't have any sound ideas about the approach. The radio news, announcing thunderstorms moving in from the Gulf, estimated to hit the area about midnight, made up my mind for me. I went to the marina, parked and locked the green Chev, and took a cautious fifty minutes driving the *Ratfink* home through unfamiliar waters.

The lovers had the lights out and the *Flush* buttoned up. I unlocked the after door to the lounge and went in and put some lights on. In a few minutes Chook came aft, into the lounge, black hair a-tangle, pulling and settling a flowered shift down on her hearty hips, squinting through the light at me.

"The thunder woke me up," she said. "Then I heard you."

"And didn't know it was me, and came blundering out. Without the pistol."

She sprawled into a chair, yawned, combed her hair back with her fingers. "So those things spook me, Trav. And it isn't going to get that rough anyway."

"I'm so glad to hear the reassurances of a qualified expert."

"Are you serious?"

"If somebody put neat little holes in our three heads, took the *Flush* out into that pass, headed her west, set the pilot, opened the sea cocks, dived overboard and swam back, then they could stop being nervous about a quarter of a million dollars. Some people just as alive as you, dear girl, implausible though that may seem, were probably killed today somewhere in the world for the price of a bowl of rice. If I come aboard at night again, and there's no gun in your pretty paw, I'm going to welt you pretty good, enough to keep you on your feet for a few days."

"Man enough?"

"Try me."

She made a face. "Okay. I'm sorry." She jumped at the next white flash of lightning, and the rain came with the thunder, roaring against the deck overhead, hissing into the bay waters around us.

"Have a happy day?" I asked.

83

"Nice, Trav. Nice."

"How is he?"

She gave me a wicked grin. "I think if you hung him by his heels in a barrel of ice water, he might start to wake up a little."

"Don't overdo a good thing, girl."

"And does that happen to be any of your damned business?"

"Don't flare up at me. It's a reasonable suggestion. You've got ten times his vitality. If I have to use him, I don't want some damned zombie."

"You won't have. You'll have a man. Something you wouldn't have had before. Who set you up to know everything about everything, you silly bastard? It's up to him every time. He deals every hand. So who's pushing him into more than he can handle? I want him to strut a little. To take charge. With her, you know what he got? When the cupboard was locked, nothing. Other times, she took charge. Until there just wasn't any response possible, and then she'd tell him he was a damned poor excuse for a man. That was poisonous, Trav. Poisonous. Merciless. Any woman can accept more than any one man can give. It's a question of mechanics. She can make him feel inadequate, and once she gets him really worrying about whether he can or he can't, then more often he can't.

"I tell the poor guy he's too much, that he's ruining me. Here is a great triumph. We were walking on the beach there, making dumb jokes. All of a sudden he gave me a great wallop across the fanny with the flat of his hand, laughed like a maniac, and ran like a kid with me chasing him and cursing him, just because, you see, all of a sudden he felt good. It made me want to cry. That sweet guy, he's a sexual convalescent. I don't demand. I take it as it comes and fake it when it doesn't, because right at this stage he has to feel that he's terrific. And another thing, that's the same for man or woman. When it's good, it doesn't drag you down. It refreshes. When it's a bad thing between people, bad in their heads and bad in their hearts, maybe hating a little, that's when it makes you drag around afterward, feeling sour and old. This way, you have a little nap, you wake up starved, you go around humming and whistling. So don't give me this quack about zombies, Trav. Maybe I'm being a damn fool. I don't know. I don't love him. He just isn't . . . quick enough, maybe, the way he thinks, and we don't really laugh the same way at the same things. But I am terribly terribly fond of him. He's so decent. Now it's like watching a kid grow up. Maybe it's penance for me. I've bitched up some guys, sometimes meaning to, sometimes not."

She gave me a rueful smile and shook her head. "Oh, hell. I sound as if I was making such a big fat sacrifice, huh? Yes sir, old girl, it's a terrible chore, isn't it? Such dull work. McGee, if you've earned one of those beautiful Mexican beers for yourself, I'll open one for each of us. And you can tell me your adventures. Believe me, we *did* worry about you."

"Every minute. Get the beers."

As she came back with them, the rain moved on away from us as quickly as it had come, making the night silence more intense. She listened intently, her face still, as I recounted events, facts and the resultant guesses.

She shook her head. "That club part. You've got a lot of gall, you know that?"

"People take you at the value you put on yourself. That makes it easy for them. All you do is blend in. Accept the customs of every new tribe. And you try not to say too much because then you sound as if you were selling something. And you might contradict yourself. Sweetie, everybody in this wide world is so constantly, continuously concerned with the impact he's making, he just doesn't have the time to wonder too much about the next guy."

She frowned. "You want to move fast, and find out as much as you can in a hurry. Right?"

"Right."

"Then I think this Boone Waxwell might be more up my alley."

"You have just one job, and you're doing it nicely."

"Do you want to be efficient? Or protective?"

"Both, Chook."

"But you've got no approach to Waxwell."

"I didn't until this moment."

"Like what?"

"The simplest thing in the world. Crane Watts happened to mention him. Watts won't ever be sure he didn't. Let me see. Watts said Waxwell might know where to locate the woman they'd used last time."

"But if he does, that's no good. Wilma knows you."

"I have a feeling he won't take me at face value."

"He'll get in touch with Watts, won't he?"

"And raise hell. Hell conditioned by the idea that maybe there's another pigeon to be plucked. Anyway, it never works to line it all out ahead of time. It's better to stay loose. And go in any direction that looks good."

"Tomorrow?"

"I'll run over to Goodland in the reliable *Ratfink*. Alone."

NINE

IN THE MILKY early mist of Sunday morning, the Gulf was placid, so I went out the pass. I looked back as *The Busted Flush* dwindled, looking smaller and smaller against the beach, blurring into the mist. Her lines are not lovely. She is a burly lady, and she waddles. But she has, on some intensely festive occasions, slept more than I bothered to count. In fact I have a treasured memory of one leisurely trip up the Intercoastal—destination, a big birthday binge for an old friend at his place at Fernandina Beach. On the third morning out I came across a sandy little girl up on the bow, sunning herself in a cute little suit, painting her toenails, whistling with great precision a series of riffs I recognized as a Ruby Braff improvisation. She had a great figure, and an ugly charming buggy little face, and I had never seen her before in my life. She looked up at me in pert inquiry and asked me who in the world happened to own this darling boat, because she had just decided to buy it.

There was a crowd aboard again. A crowd of two, and I had left Chook to brief Arthur when he got out of the shower.

I turned south, running a half mile off shore, watching the day brighten as the mist began to burn off. I again had the clothes and gear of the fisherman and almost became one when I saw an acre of water being slashed white ahead of me and further off shore, birds working over it. I ran at it, killed the motor at the point where momentum drifted me to the outer fringe of the activity. I peered down into the green and saw, a few feet below the surface, a combat squad of big bonita wheeling to hit back into the bait school. School bonita run all of a size, and allowing for the magnification of the water, and my momentary glimpse of them, they had to be upwards of six pounds. All they would do would be tear up my light spinning gear on the chance of boating something inedible. They are the great underrated game fish of the Gulf coast. On light gear, a six pound bonita is the equal of a twenty pound king mackerel. There is one thing they all do. Work them, with great effort, close to the boat, and they give you one goggle-eyed stare, turn and go off in a run every bit as swift and muscular as the first one. And they will keep doing that until, on light tackle, they die in the water. It seems a poor reward for that much heart in any living thing, particularly when the meat is too black, bloody, oily and strong to make edible. Bonefish quit. Barracuda dog it. Tarpon are docile once they begin to show their belly in the slow rolls of exhaustion. But the only way you can catch a live bonita is to use gear hefty enough to horse him home before he can kill himself.

I continued south, past Big Marco Pass, and put on dark glasses against the increasing glare. I have ample pigment in my hide, but a short supply in the iris. Pale eyes are a handicap in the tropics. I passed what was Collier City once upon a time, then cut inside around Caxambas. The dozers were working even on a Sunday morning, orange beetles making expensive homesites upon the dizzy heights of the tallest land south of Immokalee—bluffs all of fifty and sixty feet above sea level. I checked my chart, went around the indicated islands, and came in view of the mild and quiet clutter of Goodland, houses, trailers, cottages, shacks spread without plan along the protected inner shore, beyond a narrow beach of dark sand and rock and shell.

I cut to idle and went pooting in toward a rickety gas dock. Beyond it was an improvised boat yard with so many pieces of elderly hull scattered around the area, it looked as if they had spent years trying to build a boat by trial and error and hadn't made it yet.

I tied up. The pumps were padlocked. A gnarled old party sat mending a gill net with hands like mangrove roots. "Do any good?" he asked.

"All I saw was bonita outside. Didn't mess with them."

He looked at the sky, spat. "Won't be much now till near sundown. Big snook come in right under this here dock last night, popping loud as a man slapping his hands. Joe Bradley, he got one upwards of eighteen pound."

"That's a good snook."

"If'n you don't know how it used to be around these parts. You want gas? Stecker don't unlock till ten Sundays."

"There's a man here I was told to look up. Will my gear be okay if I leave it right there?"

"Sure. Who you looking for?"

"A man named Waxwell."

He grunted, pulled a knot tight, spat again. "There's Waxwells spread all the way from here to Forty Mile Bend. There's Waxwells in Everglades City, Copeland, Ochopee, and, far as I know, a couple way up to La Belle. When they breed it's always boy babies, and they breed frequent."

"Boone Waxwell?"

His grin was broad, showing more gum than teeth. "Now that one is a Goodland Waxwell, and he could be to his place, which isn't too likely of a Sunday morning, and if he is at his place they's a good chance he got a ladyfriend visiting, and if he's there and he don't, it's still a time of day he could get mean about anybody coming to visit. Come to think on it, there isn't anything he won't get mean about, one time or another."

"I won't let him hurt my feelings."

"You look of a size to temper him down some. But be careful on one thing, or size won't do you no good atall. What he does, he comes smiling up, nice as pie, gets close enough and kicks a man's kneecap off, then settles down to stomping him good. A few times he's done it so good, he's had to go way back into the Park until things quieted down. A couple times everybody thought we'd be rid of him for a few years, but the most it ever turned out was ninety days the county give him. He prowls four counties in that fancy car he's got now, but around here he keeps to hisself, and that suits everybody just fine."

"I'm grateful to you. How do I find his place?"

"Go out to the hardtop and go down that way to the end where it curves around to come back on itself, and on the curve two dirt roads slant off, and his is the one furthest from the shore line, and he's maybe a mile back there, little more than a mile and a half all told. Only place on that road."

I didn't see the cottage until I came around the last bend in the shell road, and then it was visible between the trees, a hundred and fifty feet away. Once it had been yellow with white trim, but now most of it was weathered gray, the boards warped and pulping loose. The shingled roof was swaybacked, the yard overgrown. But a shiny television antenna glinted high above it, outlined against the blue sky. A mockingbird sat atop it, rocking with effort as he created melodic patterns. A big Land Rover, new but caked with dried mud, was parked by a shed at the side. A large, hand-

88

some lapstrake inboard launch sat strapped on a heavy duty boat trailer. Parked at an angle, and almost against the rungs of the sagging porch, was a white Lincoln Continental four-door convertible, top up, the current model, dusty, with a rear fender bashed, taillights broken on that side. The collection of hardware was as if a very large child had been giving himself a happy Christmas. The closer I got, the more signs of neglect I saw. I went and looked into the skiff. It was loaded with extras, including one of the better brands of transistorized ship-to-shore radio units. But birds had dappled the royal blue plastic of the seats, and there was enough dirty rainwater aboard to fill the bilge and be visible above the floorboards.

I couldn't imagine Boo Waxwell having much of a credit rating. So I could estimate at least twenty-five thousand dollars' worth of toys in his yard. And guess there would be more in the house. Kids with lots of toys neglect them.

The mockingbird yelled, and insects shrilled, underlining the morning silence. I broke it up by facing the front door from thirty feet away, and yelling, "Waxwell! Yo! Boone Waxwell!"

In a few moments I heard some thumping around inside, saw a vague face through a dingy window. Then the door opened and a man came out onto the porch. He wore dirty khaki pants. He was barefoot, bare to the waist. Glossy black curly hair, dense black mat of hair on his chest. Blue eyes. Sallow face. Tattoo as Arthur had described it. But Arthur's description hadn't caught the essence of the man. Perhaps because Arthur wouldn't know what to call it. Waxwell had good wads of muscle on his shoulders. His waist had thickened and was beginning to soften. In posture, expression, impact, he had that stud look, that curiously theatrical blend of brutality and irony. Bogart, Mitchum, Gable, Flynn—the same flavor was there, a seedy, indolent brutality, a wisdom of the flesh. Women, sensing exactly what he was, and knowing how casually they would be used, would yet accept him, saying yes on a basis so primitive they could neither identify it nor resist it.

He carried a shotgun as one might carry a pistol, barrel pointing at the porch boards a few feet ahead of his bare toes.

"Who the hell are you, buster boy?"

"I want to have a little talk with you, Waxwell."

"Now int that right fine?" He lifted the muzzle slightly.

"Git on off my land or I'll blow a foot off you and tote you off."

And unless I could come up with something to attract his attention, that was just as far as I was going to get. You have to take your chances without much time to think. I knew he could check. But somehow I could not imagine Waxwell being very close to the lawyer. Or trusting him. Or trusting anyone.

"Crane Watts said maybe you could help me out, Boo."

He stared at me with a mild, faked astonishment. "Now int he some lawyer fella over to Naples?"

"Oh, come off it, for crissake! I'm trying to line something up, and maybe there's some room for you too, like the last time. The same kind of help. You understand. But this time, maybe nobody takes any of the money back to Tampa. We can use you, and we can use the same woman, I think. Watts said you'd know how to get in touch with her."

Earnest bewilderment, "Mought be some other Waxwell you want. You makin' no sense to me noways, buster boy. You stay right where you are, and I come back out and we talk on it some."

He went into the house. I heard him talking to someone, then heard a faint female response. He came back smiling, buttoning his shirt, shoes on, and a straw hat in cowboy shape stuck on the back of his curly head. He had indeed a merry smile, and he stuck his hand out when he was six feet from me. As I took it, I saw the first flick of what the old man had warned me about, and I jumped to the side. The unexpected miss swung his heavy right shoe as high as a chorus girl kick, and at its apex, I chopped down across his throat with my left forearm, driving him down to hit the ground on his shoulders with a mighty, bone rattling thud.

He stared up at me in purest astonishment, and then he began to laugh. It was an infectious laugh, full of delight. "Man, man," he gasped, "you as rough and quick as the business end of an alligator gar. Taught ol Boo a Sunday school lesson." He started to get up, and his face twisted. He groaned. "Think you bust somethin'. He'p me up." He put his hand up. I took it. He swung his heels up into my belly and kicked me back over his head, and I had enough sense, at least, not to hang on and let the leverage slam me into the ground. I hit rolling, and kept rolling, and even so his heel stomped the ground an inch from my ear before I rolled under his trailered boat. As I straightened up on the far side, he came running at me around the stern of the boat. He was a very cat-quick and deadly fellow, and he bulled me back against the lapstrake hull, screwed his heels into the ground, and began throwing big hooks with each fist, just as fast as he could swing. When they do that, it is best to try to ride it out. It is better than being bold and catching one. My defensive attitude gave him confidence. And, at best, I do not impress. I am a rawboned gangler, with a look of elbows and awkwardness. But the left shoulder is curled comfortingly around the jaw, and the right forearm stays high enough. And the best way to catch the rhythm is to keep an unfocussed stare on the other man's belly. Then you can roll and ride with it, and still be prepared to turn a thigh into the optimistic knee. He hammered away at my arms, elbows, shoulders, and my swaying crouch kept me within easy range. He got in one dandy under the short ribs, and one over the left ear that rang woodland bells. He matched each effort with a hard explosive snuff, and finally as they began to come in with less snap and at a slower pace, he seemed to realize he was doing very little damage. So he tried to change his style from alley to club fighter, moving back a little, trying the unfamiliar jab, hoping to cross with the right. But I took him down a little alley of my own. Queensberry, even when it is by way of Graziano, is bad on the knuckle bones. And that is what makes the TV gladiators so hilarious. Just one of those wild smacks in the jawbones would have the hero nestling his splintered paw between his thighs, and making little damp cries of anguish. So, half-turning, crouching, I slumped a little to make him think he'd worn me down. It suckered him into pulling in again. I came down hard on his instep and, with my hands locked, brought my right elbow up under his chops. In a continuation of the same motion, unlocking my hands, I turned toward him, whipping him across the eyes with an open backhand. Unexpected agonies in unexpected places in very rapid sequence can give a man the demoralizing feeling he has stumbled into a milling machine. I thumbed him in the throat socket, gave him a homemade thunderclap with an open slap on the ear, hooked him deeply just under the belt buckle—the only traditional blow in my brief routine, and as he bent, I clapped onto his wrist, turned it up between his shoulder blades, and ran him two steps into the side of the boat. His head boomed it like a jungle drum and he dropped loose, made an instinctive effort to come up, then went loose again and stayed down, sleepy cheek on the damp earth by a trailer wheel.

91

As I fingered tender areas, appraising damage, and feeling pleasantly loose and limber and fit, I heard high heels on the porch. I turned and saw a girl put a giant white purse and a white cardigan on the top step, then come across the scruffy dooryard, tilting along on the high heels of soiled white shoes. She wore a sheer pale yellow blouse, her bra visible through it, and a tight green skirt in a very vivid and unpleasant shade. She looked like a recruit from that drugstore group. Fifteen, I imagined. Certainly not over sixteen. Still padded with baby fat. Wide soft spread of hips, premature heft of breasts, little fat roll around the top of the waist-tight skirt. A round dumpling face, child-pretty, and a puffy little mouth, freshly reddened. She stared steadily at Waxwell as she approached, and she continued combing her flaxen hair with a bright red comb, guiding the strokes with her other hand. She stopped close to me, looking down at him. Her child-skin was so incredibly fine that even at close range in the morning light I could see no texture or grain. I could hear the whispery crackle as she pulled the comb down through that straight, healthy, blonde hair.

"Done me a favor if'n you kilt him," she said in a thin childish voice.

"There he is. Finish the job." Still combing, shifting to the other side, she looked up at me, head tilted. I had expected girl-eyes as vulnerable as the rest of her. These hazel eyes were old and cold, and with a little twist of recognition I remembered the wise old eyes of the urchins of Pusan, the eyes which remained unchanged by the appealing, begging, belly-empty smiles they gave the G.I.'s.

"Could might do jus that some time," she said. "Or somebody will. Onliest way I could get stopped from coming on over here. Hah! He jus three month from my Pa's age. But you don't kill off Waxwells. It comes out the other way around."

Boone Waxwell grunted and slowly worked himself into a sitting position, head between his knees, hands tenderly holding the top of his head. He peered up at us through lashes I had not noticed before, dense and black and girlishly long.

"Look, I'm going to be going along now, hear?" the girl said.

"So you go long, Cindy." She stared down at him, shrugged, started back toward her purse and sweater.

She stopped halfway and called back to me. "Mister, he'll be thinkin on some way to bust you up when you least expeck."

"Ain't going to work on this old boy. Get on home, girl," he said.

Waxwell pulled himself up, leaning against the boat. He shook his head, put a finger in his ear and wiggled it. "You deefed me up on this side, like a little waterfall inside. And husked up my voice box. Some kind of that judo?"

"The home study course from Monkey Ward, Boo."

Cindy creaked the shed door open and went in and wheeled out a red and white Vespa scooter. She rested it on the brace, opened the package box, put her big purse and sweater inside, took out a white scarf and carefully turbanned her hair. She did not look toward us. She took the white shoes off and put them in the compartment. She jacked down on the starter and, with it running in neutral, tucked the brace up, hitched the green skirt halfway up the heavy white meat of her thighs, pushed it off and slid aboard, shifting into forward. She wobbled a little, then straightened as it increased its snoring sound, and went off through the sunshine down the shell road, the drone hanging in the air after she was gone, then fading out.

"Little young for you, isn't she?"

"The man says they big enough, they old enough. I give her the loan of that scooter bug. Cindy, she's my nearby girl this year. A nearby girl is when it's too damn much trouble to go after anything else. She lives just over this end of Marco Village. I can swing by that shacky old place and give a long, a short and a long on the car horn, and have me time to come back home here and get settled down, and then I hear that scooter bug like a hornet coming through the night, and she says she won't never again come when I honk for her, but ever time she comes on in pantin and blowin like she run the whole way stead of ridin."

"Why don't her folks stop her?"

He gave me that warm engaging grin, and a broad wink. "Maybe ten years ago it was, Cindy's daddy, Clete Ingerfeldt, him and me had a little talk about Clete's missus, and I pure liked to whip the ass clear off him. He got such a strong memory of it, I even say hello to him, his chin gets all spitty. I tell you, fat stuff got the hang of it a lot better than her old lady ever did." He gave me a stare of amazed innocence. "You come way out here to find out about my love life?"

"I came out here to talk about making some money. Like the money you made off Arthur Wilkinson."

"Now I don't recall we made a dime. If that deal went

93

through, we were fixing to make out good. But all we ever got back was the money we put in, less the expense money that come off the top."

"All of a sudden, Boo, your diction improves."

He grinned. "Sometimes I had to go away for a spell. Got me exposed to the high and mighty. Got me some college women to learn me."

"If you give me another chance, I'll learn you too. It's a promise. If you get tricky one more time, I'm going to give you a strong memory like you gave Cindy's father. You're going to totter around like a very old man for a very long time."

He studied me carefully. "Lord God, you got a size on you. I shoulda looked more careful to start. From those wrists, you'll go twenty pound more than I guessed. First time I been whipped in four years. But I ain't Clete Inger-feldt. You could bust half the bones I got, and I'd put my mind on mending up and coming after you, and you better remember it, and knowing I couldn't take you even, I'd take you any ways seems safe, take you way up Lostman's River and stuff you under the red mangrove roots for crab food, and it wouldn't be the first time I took care of some little problem that way." There was no bluff in it. It was an absolutely cold and factual statement.

"Then I'll put it another way, Boo. If you try something, and it doesn't work, I'll make sure you never get well enough to even get in and out of a boat."

I watched him, saw the flicker of appraisal in his blue eyes, half hooded by those long lashes. He hooked his thumbs over his belt. Then, with that flashing speed which can come only from long and intensive practice, he snapped his brass belt buckle loose, yanked it free, exposing the bright limber blade holstered within the belt leather. The wrist snap came before I could hope to reach him. The blade chunked into the damp earth an inch from the outside of my left shoe, driving so deeply that only the brass buckle showed, as if balanced on end. He leaned against the boat with a lazy grin. I bent, put a finger in the buckle, pulled the blade free, wiped the earth from it between thumb and finger. The hilt was weighted to give it a midway balance point. I handed it to him. He fed it back into the scabbard, clinched the belt.

"What's the message that get through to you, friend?" he asked.

"That I can stop watching you, because you'd just as soon talk about money."

"Let's get on in the house. I'm dry as a sandy beach for sure."

He had more toys in the house. A big rack of new sporting arms, small rust spots beginning to fleck the bluing. Color television. Expensive camping and fishing gear stacked carelessly in corners. In the kitchen he had a hotel size refrigerator, its new enamel dappled with dark fingermarks, its innards stacked full of premium beer. I saw cases of very good liquor in a kitchen corner.

Everything not new was battered and squalid. I looked in the door of the tiny bedroom. The double bed was a rumpled tangle of soiled sheets marked in a leopard pattern. They looked like silk. The pattern seemed apt. The bedroom had the pungent odors of a predator's cage, a cell for the cat carnivore.

We drank beer in silence and then he said in grotesque host-like apology, "I was fixin to keep fat stuff out here to hoe this place out today, but it slipped clean right out of my mind. I guess it'll be until after exam week fore she can get to it. I don't want to mess up her schooling."

I sat on a chair with a broken arm. "Haven't they ever heard of statutory rape around here?"

"First somebody has to complain, friend. What the hell *is* your name?" I told him. He repeated it aloud. "You in some line of work?"

"Whatever happens to come along."

"That's the best kind they is, McGee. But sometimes you work with somebody who like to mess things up because they get jumpy for no reason at all. Then you don't want to work with them again. And maybe they do damn fool things like sending somebody around who could maybe be the law."

"Crane Watts," I said. "Great guy. If the law asked him for a match, he'd fink out. It makes me wonder about you, Boo baby. But maybe you went along because it was close enough to legal. Watts filled me in. I can use some of his ideas, but not him. Not to help me with *my* pigeon. A fatter one than Wilkinson. And it is not going to be split so many ways. From what Watts said, the take from Wilkinson had to be split between him, you, Stebber, Gisik, Wilma and the executor of the Kippler estate. I was hunting up a hungry lawyer, and found him. But I need a *smart* hungry one."

He wiped his mouth, and he looked very uneasy. "That dumb bassard talks awful quick, don't he?"

"You and me, Boo. We know the ways to make them talk quick. I got interested. He got pretty jumpy."

"Like to watch 'em jump," he said dreamily.

"When he got scared sober, he tried to deny the whole thing. Maybe I like that assessment bit, to keep it legal. But maybe hit and run would be easier all around. Either way I need the woman. The way I understand it, the woman works with Stebber. But do you think she'd come in on something without bringing him in?"

"How in hell should I know about that, buster boy?"

"How in hell should I know until I ask, Waxwell!"

"What did Watts say?"

"Before I got around to that he'd started to do so much lying I couldn't sort it out."

"I say it wouldn't hurt to have Cal Stebber. That fat happy little son of a bitch could sell snowflakes in hell. He makes it go smooth. But you get Watts, and you don't get Stebber or the woman. Or Boo Waxwell. He was a one-time thing. I got only one more little piece of business with lawyer boy, and that's all. You see that Viv? She look at old Boo like he's a spitty place on the sidewalk. I got it in my mind to take care of that. I had other things going then, and no time to line her up. She's got next to no man atall, and it's sure a waste. She's all solid woman, and when ol Boo gets her steadied into it one of these days, she'll come on like an ol walkin beam pump machine with no place to turn her off. I got that one marked in my mind, because any fool can see she sure ain't gettin what she come after so far." He winked. "And she was just a little *too* snotty to ol' Boo, which is always a good sign ever time. They get like that when they get little ideas in their pretty little heads, making them skitty."

I sensed it was a diversion, but could not imagine why.

"But to get back to it, Waxwell. Is the woman as good as Watts seems to think?"

He shrugged, went out after more beer, came back and, as he handed me mine, said, "She and Arthur clamped down like one of those little hairy dogs rich women tote around. She married him legal. Always does, Cal Stebber said. Gets herself Alabama divorces. Make no money claim and it goes through quick and easy. Married up with maybe eleven of them, and her and Stebber and Gisik, one way or another, picked every one clean. Averages out maybe one a year. Maybe she doesn't hit it off so good with your man. She's no kid anymore."

"Where can I find her?"

He stared blankly at me. "Why ask me?"

"Why not? Watts told me that after you cleaned Wilkinson, you and Wilma shacked up right here."

He looked around at the room as though seeing it for the first time. "Here? Why would he say a thing like that?"

"Because Wilkinson told him how it was, months later, when he showed up demanding money. Wilkinson was sent on a wild goose chase up to Sarasota. When he came back to the motel, Wilma had cleared out. Wilkinson told Watts he found you and Wilma here, and you beat him up."

Waxwell threw his head back and guffawed, slapped his knee. "Oh, that! Goddam! He sure did come around here. Drunk or sick, God knows. I had me a little friend here, waitress that come over from Miami to see me. Little bit of a woman no bigger than Wilma, silvery color hair like Wilma. About sundown and the light not too good. That fool Arthur got it in his head she was Wilma for sure. Maybe out of his head from losing the money and her taking off. Hard to say. I had to bust him up a little and run him off the place."

He shook his head, stopped smiling, looked earnestly at me. "Mind you I'm not saying I wouldn't want to a had Wilma here a while. I did give it a little try. But I struck out swinging on three pitches, man. Hurt my pride some, but it wasn't the first time I missed and won't be the last, and a man has to face it there's some you can't get to. With her, it was all business. She didn't see no point in just for the fun of it. Cold, maybe. I don't know. Or maybe no money, no kicks. Way I figure it, while Arthur was riding that bus up to Sarasota, she was long gone on her way to Miami with her end of the loot, and from there God knows where, someplace where she could live good until the money got small enough so she had to start on suckering the next one for them to squeeze dry."

I used a long drink from the bottle to make certain my face didn't show anything. The momentary diversion, and then the strange earnestness. The house and yard full of toys. Mildred Mooney could not have invented that rancid little scene by the beach house pool. Nor could Arthur have invented the telling detail of the little diamond watch he thought Wilma had peddled. Conversely, Waxwell could not have known of being seen by Mrs. Mooney, nor of Arthur's instant recognition of the diamond wristwatch. What could he have been worth in the Wilkinson swindle? Five thousand? Ten at the very top. Maybe twenty-five thousand. And it wouldn't buy many new toys. I had a sudden and vivid image of that small, delicate, pampered face, wavery under the black slow run of water, of fine silver hair strung into the current flow, of shadowy pits, half seen, where sherry eyes had been.

"So Stebber would be the one for me to ask, I guess," I said.

"Most likely to know. By now maybe they got a new one going for them."

"So if I have to work through Stebber, then he's in on it. And my end is smaller."

"McGee, what got it in your head you got to have one particular broad, just because she did good on the last one? I could pick you one right out of the air. Thinking on one right now. Little ol gal way up in Clewiston, wasting her talent. Doing waitress work. Had her teaching license, but lost it for all time. Dresses good. Acts like a lady. Pretty face but built only a little better'n fair. Sugar sweet, and a born thief. But I swear and garntee, she get any plain ordinary fella into bed just one time, from then on he can have trouble remembering his own name or how to count to ten. And that's all you need, isn't it? That's how Wilma set them up for Stebber."

"I better think the whole thing over, Boo."

"It's Rike Jefferson over to Everglades, executor on the Kippler land, writing any damn letter they tell me to tell him. He married the youngest Kippler girl, how come he got that job, and she's years dead. I yell frog one time and Rike jumps till his heart gives out. Down in Homestead is Sam Jimper, a lawyer man crooked as a ball of baby snakes, but knowing I was behind you with my eye on him, he'd sooner frenchkiss a gator than try to get cute two ways. I'm telling you the way to do is you forget Watts and Stebber and all them, and let me get Melly on down here and you look her over, and give her a trial run if you don't believe me. She won't take as big an end of it as you'd have to give Wilma. But I get a good cut because you need me to set it up, because without a genuine big piece of land, all recorded and setting there to look at, you've got no way to give a man an itch to double his money, so as to show off for his cute new little schoolteacher wife. And I tell you, Sam Jimper's got an office paneled in black cypress big enough for a ball game, nothing like that closet Watts has got. I say you give Melly five hundred dollars for front and just turn her and aim her at your man, married already or not, he's got as much chanct as a key lime pie in a school yard."

"Don't tell me how to run it, Boo. Don't tell me who I'm going to use. Maybe I don't need some nut who tries to kick my knee off before he knows who I am or what I want. I have to think this out. I don't want it messed up. It's the biggest piece of money I'll ever get hold of. Right now I'm going to let things sit for a while. Maybe you make sense. I don't know. If I decide you do, you'll hear from me."

"What if'n I think of something else that'd help?"

"Tell me when I get in touch."

"An if you don't?"

"Stop leaning on me, Boo."

He chuckled. "So you got to go talk it over with somebody. Look like you got a partner."

"What's that to you?"

He stood up. "Nothing. Not one damn old little thing, buddy boy. None of my business. Maybe you're just the errand boy, talking big. Come back. Don't come back. Ol' Boo's gettin' along sweet and fine. Leave off your car down the road?"

"Left a boat in Goodland and walked in."

"Drive you in."

"Don't bother."

"Got to go see somebody anyways. Come on."

It was going sour. I could sense it. We went in the Lincoln. The abused engine was ragged, and he took the curves of the narrow road in careless skids, spattering shell into the ditches. After coming to a noisy, smoking stop at Stecker's Boat Yard, he got out with me and strolled out to the dock, talking slurred, amiable nothings. The old man was gone. The pumps were unlocked, but I did not want to spend extra time within range of that blue-eyed stare. I gave it full throttle and at the end of the long white-water curve away from Goodland, I looked back and saw him standing motionless on the dock, watching me, thumbs hooked onto that lethal belt.

It had been all right, and then it had gone subtly wrong in a way I couldn't explain. I had the feeling it had been a near thing getting away from him at all. Something had changed him—some factor of doubt, some special alertness. A twig snapping, maybe, in the tangly backwoods of his mind, bringing the head up, ears cocked, eyes narrow. I now knew it was going to all move quickly, and I could no longer set the pace. I had done my little prying and poking. The avalanche had started its first grumblings. Then comes the time to try to outrun it.

TEN

AFTER EXPOSURE to Boone Waxwell, the look of Chook and Arthur on the early afternoon beach had the flavor of a great innocence. She was hovering around him, cheering him on with shrill yips. He was braced against an impressive bend in one of the big boat rods. When I beached the *Ratfink* near the *Flush,* she hollered to me to come tell them what Arthur was fighting.

I trotted down to where they were. I saw a slow massive boil about a hundred yards out. Arthur, grunting, was trying to horse it enough to get some line back.

"What did you use?"

She held her fingers about eight inches apart. "A shiny little fish I caught, but we think he was dead after Arthur threw him out there a couple of times."

Arthur gave me a strained grin. He and his quarry were in stasis. I waded in and felt the taut line, then felt that slow distinctive stroke, a kind of ponderous convulsion.

"Shark," I said. "Sand shark or a nurse shark, probably. Longer odds on a hammerhead."

"My God!" Chookie cried. "We've been *swimming* in there!"

"Heavens above!" I said. "And sometimes a bat will fly into a house and bite somebody. Or a raccoon will charge, snarling, into a supermarket. Sweetie, the sharks are there *all* the time. Just don't swim when the water is all roiled and dirty."

"What'll I do?" Arthur asked in a strained voice.

"Depends if you want him."

"My God, I don't want him."

"Then set the drag tight, aim the tip at him, and back away from the water."

He did. After five strenuous steps, the nine thread line

popped, out by the leader swivel. As he reeled in, there was another boil, farther out, as the shark went off to think things out.

"Sharks have no bones," I announced. "Just gristle. They have rows of hinged teeth that straighten up as they open their mouths. They shed teeth from the front row and the other rows move forward. About one third the body weight is liver. The tiny spikes on their hides are tipped with enamel of the same composition as tooth enamel. Their brains are little nubs on the front ends of their spinal cords. They have no intelligence anyone has ever been able to test. They are a roving, senseless, prehistoric appetite, as unchanged as the scorpion, cockroach and other of nature's improvisations which had good survival value. A wounded shark being eaten by his chums will continue to eat anything within reach, even hunks of himself which might happen by. End of lesson."

"Gah," said Chookie. "And thanks a lot."

"Oh, two more items. There is no effective shark repellent. And they do not have to roll to bite. They can lunge up and chomp head-on, but when they bite down, then they roll to tear the meat loose. Now, children, we go into conference, critical variety. Everybody into the main lounge."

When they were seated and expectant, I said, "I learned that it wasn't Wilma you saw with Boone Waxwell, Arthur. It was a girl who looked a little like her."

Arthur's jaw dropped. "But I was certain it. . . . Oh, come *on*! I *know* it was Wilma. Or an identical twin. And I saw her watch. She told me once it was a custom design. I couldn't mistake it. No, that was Wilma, even to the way she was asleep in there, her posture."

"I agree. It was Wilma. And ol' Boo went to great lengths to prove it wasn't. It seems it is very important to him to establish that Wilma was never there."

"But why?"

"Because that's where he killed her. And took over her share. And used it to buy himself lots of pretty toys he doesn't take very good care of."

"Killed Wilma," Arthur said in a sick voice. He swallowed. "Such a . . . such a tiny woman."

"And it's a good guess she was your legal spouse, Arthur. She'd been working with Stebber for years. Maybe he had a little stable of Wilmas. Legal marriage makes it neater, and divorce is no great problem. You might have been husband number eleven. Marriage enlarges the areas wherein the pigeon can be plucked."

"What a charmer," Chookie said softly. "Lady spiders eat their mates for dessert. I read about one real smart kind of little boy spider. He doesn't come courting until he's caught a juicy bug. Then while she's enjoying the gift, he's off and away like a flash."

"A quarter of a million dollars is a juicy bug," Arthur said.

"Made her rates pretty high," Chook said tartly. "Trav, my God, how did you figure this out?"

"I didn't. It just seems like what must have happened." And I gave them a condensed but uncensored report. His little knife trick made Chook gasp. I got paper and wrote down the names he had mentioned before they slipped out of my mind. I gave the most weight, detail and careful choice of words to the feeling I had right at the end.

"So here it is. This is his country. I'll bet he knows every boat for fifty miles around. He's not going to take me at face value. He's going to feel uneasy until he finds where I'm holed up. By now it's certain that there are people at Marco who know where we're anchored, know there's two men and a woman aboard. The more he learns, the less he's going to like the smell of it. And he's the type to make his moves and to do his thinking later. Cute as we've been, we've left a clear trail."

"So we rub it out and pick a new base," Chook said.

"Right. And then we think up some good safe way to decoy ol Boo, so I can have enough time to take that rat nest of his apart."

"What do you mean?" Chook asked.

"This is a recovery operation, isn't it? I doubt he's spent it all. He wouldn't bank it. It's in some hidey hole. And not an obvious one. He's devious, not in any reasoned way, but by instinct. He has that bluff, battered soldier-of-fortune look, and a ton of ironic charm in that grin, and he makes me think that under other circumstances he'd be the man I'd want to go ashore with in a strange port where there would be good booze and a chance of trouble. But that would be wrong. The essence of him is feline, and not house-kitty. A bigger predator. I wonder how many people he's conned with that swampy folk-talk which isn't even very consistent. It's a good cover. His way of life is a predator way of life, a cat-habit. He has his home range, most of four counties to roar around in that abused Lincoln, whipping the other

102

males so ruthlessly nobody challenges him, bringing prey back to the den, protecting the den violently and instinctively, and ready at any time to fade back into the Glades. I'm saying all this because I don't want us to make the mistake of assuming he will respond predictably to any action of ours. Something that might send another man hustling to a faraway place might make Boo Waxwell run a little way and circle back. And, when he came so damned close to stomping me, I realized it has been a long time since I have seen anyone move that fast."

"Trav?" Chookie said in a strange and subdued tone.

"What, dear?"

"Maybe . . . maybe he is *you,* gone bad. Maybe that's what he smelled. Maybe that's why you can handle him."

My immediate instinct was to get blazing mad, tell her it was a rotten analogy. It was a response the head-feelers would call significant.

"Maybe I'm being dumb or something," Arthur said. "If this man is all that dangerous, and you're pretty sure he . . . killed Wilma, well then I'd think there would be things the police could find out. I mean, maybe an identification of the gray car he had when he took her from the motel while I was gone. Maybe he went with her to the bank when she cleaned out that joint account, before I left on the bus. I could swear I saw her at Waxwell's cottage. Maybe somebody else saw her there, or when he drove her in through the village. I mean wouldn't we be better off if he was in jail?"

"Arthur, it is very nice to believe in an orderly society. By and large, all the counties of Florida have pretty good law officers. Some are excellent. But the law isn't growing even half as fast as the population. So it is selective. From their point of view, how excited could they get over the possibility of a transient woman of dubious character getting herself ki!led well over six months ago, a woman who was never reported missing. Collier County will have some deputies who know the score in the Marco Island area, and much as they might itch to put Boo away for keeps, they'd know their chances of finding a body if he was able to take it into the islands and rivers and swamps and hide it. Now after Boo beat you so badly and those nice people who found you on the highway took you in, you must have had some idea of getting the law after Boone Waxwell. Did they give you an opinion?"

"They said to forget it. They said nothing would happen, and it could make trouble for them. They said there were

103

Waxwells all over, and a lot of them were decent quiet people, but there were a lot of wild ones like Boone, and if they wanted to take it out on Sam Dunning, sheltering somebody trying to make trouble, his nets could get cut up and his charter boat could catch fire and nobody would know who did it. The best thing to do, they said, was keep your head down. Trav, I ought to see those good people. I went off and said I'd come back soon. And they haven't heard a word. . . . It isn't right."

"Another thing, Arthur," I said. "If you made the complaint about Boo, remember it would be coming from a man who recently chopped brush on a Palm County work gang. A man with no funds and no employment. When there isn't enough law to go around, it has to work on a status system. And suppose you *did* get them to take Boone Waxwell in. They'd seal his cave, and maybe they would come across whatever he has left, if anything. Then it would be out of reach for keeps." I looked at Chookie. She sat with chin on fist, scowling. "You're getting good grades so far," I said. "What else should we do?"

"I would think that if Wilma was alive, she would have been in touch with Calvin Stebber, and if she's dead, he'd be wondering about her. It would be a way to make sure. After all, this Boo Waxwell could maybe have gotten money somewhere else. And maybe Wilma told him to lie about her being there."

"And," I said, "Stebber might be the one to decoy Boo away from his cave." I stood up. "It's gone past the point where we need an imitation pigeon."

"How about the money of mine that Mr. Stebber has?" Arthur asked.

"I want to get a chance at it. So now let's unhook this beast and get out of here."

We brought the bow anchors aboard, worked the *Flush* out by hauling on the stern anchor lines. When we coasted close enough they pulled free. I hoisted the dinghy up by the stern davits and made it fast, as, under dead slow speed, Arthur took us out through the wide entrance of Hurricane Pass. We towed the *Ratfink* astern, motor tilted up and covered with a tarp. When we were clear, and headed north up the Gulf, I put it up to cruising speed and went aft and adjusted the length of the tow line until the *Ratfink* was riding steadily at the right point of our wake. The bright afternoon was turning greasy, sky hazing, big swells building from the southwest, a following sea that began to give the old lady a nasty motion, and made it impossible to use the automatic pilot. The little solenoids are stupid about a following sea. They can't anticipate. So you have to use the old-timey procedure of swinging the wheel just as they begin to lift your back corner, then swinging it back hard the other way when the bow comes up. You labor for long seconds apparently dead in the water, and then you tilt and go like a big train. Chook brought sandwiches to the topside controls, and I sent Arthur to dig out the bible on coastal accommodations.

The Palm City Marina, thirty miles north of Naples, had the sound of what I wanted. And from the way the weather was building, it was far enough. We'd begun to get enough wind to pull the tops off the long swells and the sun was gone in haze, the water changing from cobalt to gray-green. The *Flush* heaved and waddled along, setting up a lot of below-decks creaking, clinking, clanking and thumping, and about every tenth swell the port wheel would lift out and cavitate, giving us a shuddering vibration. At least I never had to slow her down. Her cruising speed was what other boats slow down to when the seas build. When the driving rain came, I sent them down to take over on the sheltered controls. As soon as I felt the wheel being taken, I pulled the lever that freed it, put a loop over a spoke, snapped the big tarp down over the topside panel and throttles and padded below, soaked through.

They had the wipers going, were peering earnestly into the rain curtain, and Arthur was misjudging the seas enough to bounce pans off their galley hooks. They let me take over with an obvious relief. Soon, as the heavy rain flattened the swells, she began to ride much easier.

"They put those little signs in boats," Chook said with a nervous laugh. "Oh Lord, thy sea is so vast and my boat is so small. Trav, you don't have any funny signs around."

"And no funny flags to hoist. I almost fell for one little brass plaque though. It said that marriages performed by the captain of this vessel are valid only for the duration of the voyage. Arthur, go see how the *Ratfink* rides. Chook, go make coffee. Busy yourselves. Stop peering over my shoulders. Then check all ports to see if rain or sea is coming in. Stow any loose gear you come across. Then, as a pagan rite I recommend—after you've brought me the mug of coffee— you people get bars of soap, go aft and strip down and try that warm hard rain out on the after deck."

After an hour, as I had anticipated, the wind direction

had shifted to the west. I made an estimate of my position along the line I had penciled on the chart, put an X at that spot, then changed to a more westerly course so I could take it as a quartering sea on the port bow rather than rocking along in the trough. She steadied, and I put it into automatic pilot, read the compass course, figured the deviation and drew a new line on my chart. According to my computations, another eighty minutes would put us at a point offshore from Palm City where we would turn and run on in. The rain was coming down harder than before, and with less wind. I prowled, looking for my companions of the storm. The clues were obvious. The closed door to the master stateroom. And, in the main lounge on the rug, a damp blue bath towel. It made me remember a line from a story of long ago, written, I think, by John Collier, about when the kid finds the foot, still wearing sock and shoe, on the landing of the staircase leading to the attic. "Like a morsel left by a hasty cat." So make this a towel left by a hasty morsel. Hard warm rain, soap, giggles and the tossing and pitching of a small boat are aphrodisiacs vastly underrated. I eeled up through the forward hatch with my soap so I could keep a watch ahead. It was a cool abundance of water, sudsing as only rainwater can. I had a few discernible bruises on my arms where Boo's fists had sledged, and a round one on the short ribs. When I took a deep breath there was a twinge there, sign that the blow had probably ripped a little of the cartilage between the ribs. Fatuously I admired the new flatness of the belly, and the absence of the small saddlebags over the hip bones. Narcissus in the rain. I dropped back below, re-dogged the hatch, toweled in a hurry, hopped into dry clothes and trotted back to the wheel house, peering through the windshield arcs for the collision course you always anticipate when a bunch of little gears are steering your boat.

Chookie, in a crisp white dress, black hair pinned high, came bearing a tray with three cocktails and a bowl of peanuts, Arthur bringing up the rear. They were elaborately conversational. Rain made a dandy shower. A little chilly but real stimulating. Then both rushed in to find a safer word than stimulating, and managed merely to underline it, giving Arthur such a steaming red face he turned away to stare out the side ports saying, my, it certainly is coming down, isn't it?

And, my, it certainly was still coming down when we got to my estimated destination. It always seems a waste when all that nice useful rain whishes down into the salty sea. I pulled it back until we barely had seaway, and turned on the little whirling red bulb of the depth finder. The Gulf has such a constant slope, the bottom is a good location guide. We had twenty-one feet under the hull, twenty-five total, and if other things were right, that would put us three and a half miles off Palm City, according to the depths on the chart. I looked up the frequency of a commercial radio station in Palm City, with a tower almost in line with the harbor. When I had picked it up on AM, a baseball play-by-play, I changed our heading to zero degrees and rotated the direction finder loop until I had a good null. I was about a sea mile short of my estimated point. I put it on the new course, again with a following sea, and we waddled and rocked on in until the sea buoy appeared out of the murk, giving me a course on the chart for the channel between the keys. Inside, we were in flat water, and it was no trick finding the private markers for the marina channel.

It was, as I had hoped, loaded with big cruisers. Two air-horn blasts brought a kid out of the dock house wearing a plastic raincoat with hood. He directed us with hand signals and ran around to the slip. I worked it around and backed it in, went forward in a hurry and got a loop on a piling and around a cleat and snubbed us down. In fifteen minutes we were all set, lines, fenders and spring lines in place, gangplank onto the dock, all identified and signed in. And the rain was slacking off.

I was damp, but not enough to change again. Chook distributed dividends from the shaker and said, "Okay. I bite. Why here?"

"Multiple reasons. If you want to hide a particular apple, the best thing you can do is wire it onto an apple tree. Lots of these big lunkers around us are in wet storage for the summer. We're one face in the crowd. We're not far from Fort Myers, where they have air service to Tampa. We're a half hour by car from Naples, a little better than an hour from Marco. If he finds out we anchored off by our lonesome once, he'd expect us to do it again. And if he does find us, and if he does have any violent ideas, it's a damned poor place for him to get away with them. Also, it would reassure Stebber if it turns out I can fix up a meeting here."

Arthur said, "I think it was across that causeway over there, over on the beach on that key where they found me stumbling around. Should . . . should I sort of stay out of sight?"

Chook said to me, black brows raised in query, "With your fishing hat and those fly-boy dark glasses?"

"See no reason why you should," I said.

Chook leaned to pat Arthur on the knee. "You have a dear face and I love you, but darling, forgive me, you aren't terribly memorable."

"I guess one of us is enough," he said, making one of his rare little jokes, waiting then with no confidence anyone would laugh.

I got the evening weather news. As I had expected, the wind was swinging around into the north, and by dawn they expected it to be out of the east at three to five knots, clear weather, occasional afternoon thunderstorms. It meant that by early morning, with the *Ratfink* bailed and fueled, I could make a good fast run close inshore down to the little marina in Naples, tie it up there at that handy and useful location, then take the rented car back to Palm City. The evening was laundered bright, the air fresh, and Chook declined a chance for a dinner ashore, saying she had a serious attack of the domestics, a rabid urge to cook. After dinner, while the two of them were policing the galley, I took the little battery operated Mirandette tape recorder into the stateroom I was using and closed the door. For some reason, I cannot perform the feat with people listening, and sometimes I cannot perform it at all. The little machine has astonishingly good fidelity, considering its size.

Try, playback, erase. Try, playback, erase. I learned that to get Waxwell's tone quality I had to pitch my voice higher, and put a harder and more resonant edge on it. The slurs and elisions were easier to manage, along with that slight sing-song cadence of the swamp lands. When I got a reasonably satisfying result, I left it on the tape.

I went up on the sun deck for the long slow evening pipe. When one is down to this mild reward for abstinence, there is only one way to cheat. I found an oversized pot in the pipe drawer, a massive Wilke Sisters product, and nearly sprained my thumb packing Black Watch into it. We all sat up there in the warm night, marina lights sparkling on the water, traffic moving across the distant causeway. They sat together, about ten feet from me, off to my right. They rustled a little now and then. And whispered. And several times she made a furry and almost inaudible chuckle, as sensuous as a slow light stroke of fingernails. It began to make me so edgy I was grateful when they said their early, husky goodnights. I think it was becoming a little more for her than she estimated. I hoped it would get big enough to pry her loose from Frankie Durkin. But any kind of future for Chook and Arthur would depend on my making a pretty solid recovery for him. If she had to support him, or share the job of supporting the two of them, it wouldn't work out so well. It would make him restive. And this was her time to have kids. And it wouldn't mix well with her strenuous brand of professional dancing. She had the body for kids, the heart for them, the need for them, and love enough for a baker's dozen.

So if you don't recover enough, do you need to clip a full fifty percent of it, McGee?

Next there will be a choir of a thousand violins playing I Love You Truly. Or, perhaps, Paddlin' Maudlin Home.

Back in my empty lonely nest, I turned the recorder on, and with the larynx memory of how I did it before, became Boo Waxwell giving a sour little talk on the joys of love and marriage. Then I played the tape from the beginning. The part I had previously approved sounded just about the same as the new addition. That meant I had it nailed well enough to risk it.

ELEVEN

IT WAS A LITTLE after nine in the morning when I tied up the *Ratfink* as before in the little marina. I went over into town in the green sedan, ordered drugstore coffee, and, as it was cooling, shut myself in the phone booth and called Crane Watts' office number.

He answered directly, sounding remarkably crisp and impressive and reliable. "Crane Watts speaking."

"Watts, this Boo Waxwell. How about you give me that number for Cal Stebber in Tampa. Caint lay my han on it."

"Now I don't know as I'm authorized to . . ."

"Lawyer boy, I git it fast, or in five minutes I'm right there, whippin yo foolish ass down to the bone."

"Well . . . hold the line a moment, Waxwell."

I had a pencil ready. I took down the number he gave me. 613-1878.

"Address?" I asked.

"All I've ever had is a box number."

"Nev mind. Lawyer boy, I plain don't like the way you give that McGee the whole story."

"Don't you think you made that plain enough last night, Waxwell? I told you then and I'm telling you now, that I didn't tell him half the things he claims I told him."

"Too dog drunk to know what you told him."

"I'm doing my level best to get a line on him, and as soon as I learn anything useful, I'll get in touch with you. But I don't know why you're upset about it. It was a perfectly legal business arrangement. Another thing, Waxwell, I don't want you ever coming to my house again, like last night. You upset my wife, the way you acted. See me here if you have to see me at all, but I'm telling you now, I'm no more anxious to have any future association with you than you are with me. Is that quite clear?"

"Think I'll come by anyways and bounce you some."

"Now *wait* a minute!"

"Talk sweet to ol' Boo."

"Well . . . maybe I did sound a little irritable. But you see, Viv knew nothing about . . . that business arrangement. You said too much in front of her. She cross-examined me half the night before I could get her quieted down. And she still isn't satisfied. I'd just rather you wouldn't come to the house again. Okay?"

"I swear, lawyer boy, I never will. Never again. Less something comes up all of a sudden."

"Please, just listen to reas . . ."

I hung up, sweating lightly, and went back to my coffee. Boone Waxwell had wasted very little time getting to the only man who might know anything about me. And had charged that man with digging up information. Watts could get my Bahia Mar box number from the club records. That wouldn't be much help. But there was a new factor. Waxwell did not seem like a patient man. Perhaps no later than this afternoon he would be phoning Watts to find out what he'd learned. And he would be very intrigued to know it was his second call of the day, and interested to know that he had asked for Stebber's unlisted number earlier. He would work that out in short order.

I aimed the Chev north up 41 through light traffic, keeping a watch front and rear for State Police, who object violently to any speed approaching three numbers. I pulled into a marina parking space at Palm City at ten o'clock. The *Flush* was locked. A note on the rug inside the rear door to the lounge said they'd gone grocery shopping. I went hunting and found them in a Food Fair two blocks away, Arthur trundling the basket, Chook mousing along, picking out things, wearing that glazed look of supermarket autohypnosis. Eleven minutes after I located them, I had a protesting Arthur locked aboard with instructions to stay put and out of sight, and I was backing out of the parking space with Chook beside me, hitching at her skirt and buttoning the top buttons of her blouse.

If the feeder flight out of Fort Myers hadn't been ten minutes late coming in from Palm Beach, we would have just missed it. And I had been too busy driving to do more than fragmentary briefing. I bought two round trip tickets to Tampa. With stops at Sarasota and St. Pete, the ETA was twenty past noon.

Once aboard, I gave it to her in more detail. "But with just a phone number?" she asked.

"And a little jump. And a prayer for luck. And the name of a yacht."

"Golly, suppose you worked all this hard at something legitimate, McGee. No telling how big you might be."

"A state senator, even."

"Wow!" She checked in her mirror and fixed her mouth. "What good am I going to be to you?"

"I'll figure that out as we go along."

At Tampa International, with Chook standing outside the booth looking serious, I tried the number. As I was just about to give up and try again, a cool, careful, precise female voice said, "Yes?"

"I would like to speak to Mr. Calvin Stebber."

"What number were you calling, sir?"

"Six one three - one eight seven eight."

"I am sorry. There is no Calvin Stebber here, sir."

"Miss, I suppose that it's one of the oldest code situations in the world. You always ask for the number to be repeated, and the party calling is supposed to change one digit. But I don't happen to have the code."

"I haven't the faintest idea what you're talking about, sir."

"No doubt. I am going to call you back at exactly quarter to one, twelve minutes from now and in the meantime you tell Mr. Stebber that somebody is going to call who knows something about Wilma Ferner, Wilma Wilkinson, take your choice."

She hesitated a half breath too long before saying, "I am

terribly sorry that all this means absolutely nothing to me, sir. You've made a mistake, really."

She was very good. So good the hesitation seemed to lose significance.

I tried it again at the promised time.

"Yes?"

"Is Mr. Stebber interested in Wilma? This is me again."

"Actually, you know, I shouldn't be so childish as to let this nonsense fascinate me, whoever you are. I suppose it's because I am having a dull and boring day. Do you think that could be it?"

"Nonsense fascinates lots of people."

"You *do* have rather a nice voice. You know, if you aren't too busy for nonsense, you could break up my afternoon with more of it. Why don't you mystify me again, say, at three fifteen?"

"It will be my pleasure. I'll be the one with the red rose in his teeth."

"And I shall be wearing a girlish smirk. Goodby, sir."

I stepped out of the booth. "What are you grinning at?" Chook demanded.

"The good ones are always a pleasure. She couldn't contact Stebber so quickly. But without giving away one damn thing, she lined me up to call back at three fifteen. Then if Stebber is interested, they open a door. If not, she gives me the girlish chitchat, and I hang up never really knowing for sure. Very nice."

She pulled herself taller. "It means you're outclassed, doesn't it, sweetie? Stebber has this terribly keen girl, and you're making do with a big dull dancer."

"Oh for God's sake, why should a little impersonal admiration raise your hackles?"

"Feed me," she said. "All women are at war all the time, and when I've got hunger pains, it shows a little more."

We went to the upper level where she ate like a timber wolf, but with more evidences of pleasure than any wolf would exhibit. There was so much of her, and it was so aesthetically assembled, so vivid, so a-churn with vitality that she faded the people for ten tables around to frail flickering monochromatic images, like a late late movie from a fringe station. She provided me, in certain measure, with a cloak of invisibility. ———Okay, fella, but describe the guy she was *with*.———Just a guy. Big, I think. I mean, hell, I don't think I really looked at him, Lieutenant.

She sipped coffee and smiled, sighed, smiled again.

"You look like a happy woman, Miss McCall." I reached across the table and touched her with a fingertip right between and a little above those thick black brows. "There were two lines here."

"Gone now? Son of a gun. Gee, Trav, I don't know. I talk. I talk my fool head off. There in the dark with him holding me, mostly. Things I've never told anyone. He listens and he remembers. I skip around, back and forth through my dumb life. I guess I'm trying to understand. I'm talking to myself at the same time, about Frankie, about how my mother made me ashamed of growing too big to fit into her dream, about running off and getting married at fifteen and annulled at sixteen, knocking around, and then buckling down and *really* working hard and making it and saving money so I could go back in style and knock their eye out. I knew just how it would be, Trav. I would wear that mink cape into that house and my mother and my grandmother would stare, and then I would let them know I hadn't gotten it the way they were thinking, and show them the scrapbook. Nineteen years old. God!

"There were strangers in the house, Trav. An impatient woman, and kids running all over the place. My grandmother had been dead over a year, and my mother was in the county home. Premature senility. She thought I was her sister, and she begged me to get her out of there. I got her into another place. A bill and a half a week for a year and a half, Trav, and then she had one big stroke instead of continuous little ones, and she died without ever *knowing*. Arthur asked me how I really know that. Maybe she had some lucid spell when she knew and was proud." Her eyes swam and she shook her head. "Okay. He's good for me. Like my head was full of little knots. I talk and talk and talk, and he says something, and a little knot loosens." She scowled. "The thing about Frankie, when he finds out something bugs you, a long time later he'll say something that'll make it bug you more. I explained that to Arthur. He says maybe that's why I need Frankie, so he can punish me and I don't have to punish myself.

"Trav, you really have to give Arthur *something* to do. I can only hoist him up so far. You treat him like a tanglefoot kid, and when I make him into a man it doesn't hold. It doesn't last. Maybe, Trav, that's a more important part than the money. He talks about those jobs at Everglades. Wistful, sort of. When he ran the store it was all kind of set. The buyers knew what to buy for that city. And he had good display and advertising people, and the merchandising was kind of all established before he got into it. But he said if you can put up rough studding and it stands true and the foreman comes around and says okay, then you think people are going to live there for years, and winds won't blow it down. I can't say it like he does. But you see, except for the store which was all set anyway, everything he ever did got bitched up. Everything except those crummy little jobs. If you trust him to do something, he'll trust himself more."

So I promised I would, and I told her we had time, before three fifteen, to get a little better set. I bought a news-stand map of Tampa and I rented a pale gray Galaxie. They are turning Tampa into the customary nothing. It used to be memorable as one of the grubbiest and most infuriating traffic mazes south of the Chelsea area of Boston. Now they are ramming the monster highways through it, and one day soon it will become merely a momentary dinginess. They've opened up the center of the city into a more spacious characterlessness, and, more and more, they are converting Ybor City into fake New Orleans. In some remote year the historians will record that Twentieth Century America attempted the astonishing blunder of changing its culture to fit automobiles instead of people, putting a skin of concrete and asphalt over millions of acres of arable land, rotting the hearts of their cities, so encouraging the proliferation of murderous, high-speed junk that when finally the invention of the Transporlon rendered the auto obsolete, it took twenty years and half a trillion dollars to obliterate the ugliness of all the years of madness, and rebuild the supercities in a manner to dignify the human instead of his toys.

I left Chook in the car and went into the reference section of the library and looked up the *Buccaneer* in Lloyd's Register of Yachts. There were a slew of them, and I found the one registered out of Tampa that was a hundred and eighteen feet long, a converted Coast Guard cutter, owned by Foam-Flex Industries. I phoned them and was shunted up through the pyramid to the Vice President in Charge of Sales and Promotion, a Mr. Fowler with a little trace of Vermont in his speech.

"On anything like that," he said, "you'd have to check with Mr. Robinelli at the Gibson Yards where we keep her. The way it works, we set up an advance schedule for executive use of the vessel, and empower Mr. Robinelli to charter her when such charters will not interfere with company plans in any way. These charters, and I wish there were more of them, help with maintenance, dockage, insurance and payroll of the permanent crew. I don't have a copy of the advance schedule handy, but I could have someone get it. I happen to know she is at the Yard right now. If you . . ."

I told him not to bother, and that I would check with Mr. Robinelli. I looked up the address of the Yard, and went back to the car and found it on the city map. There was enough time to go check it out. It was over in the big busy commercial harbor where a dozen freighters were loading and off-loading, where industrial smog hung low and heavy in the heat, where the air stank of chemicals, and where, in that manufactured haze, some huge piles of sulphur gleamed a vivid and improbable yellow. I parked by the office of the Gibson Yards, and I could see the *Buccaneer* at a dockside mooring. Two men in khakis were working topsides. She had a lot of brightwork, and I did not envy anyone the housekeeping chore of sluicing the local grime off her every day.

Robinelli was chunky and brusque, a three telephone, four clipboard, five fountain pen man, a trotting fellow with no time for small talk. I represented myself as spokesman for a group interested in chartering the *Buccaneer* for a cruise to Yucatan, say twenty days. Ten in the party. Would she be available anytime soon? At what rate?

He jumped into his desk chair and scribbled on a pad. "Call it an even three thousand. Includes food, steward service. Crew of four. Bring your own booze. Everything else laid on." He spoke more loudly, with a whip-crack in his voice, and a thin woman with a limp came at a halting half-trot to hand him a clipboard. He snapped through the top pages. "She's open as of July 10th for thirty-two days. Have to know by June 30th the latest. Certified check in full two days before departure. No charter passengers sixty-five or older. Insurance provision. Cruises at fourteen knots. Sixteen hundred mile range. Radar, salt water conversion unit, draws nine feet, seven passenger staterooms, three heads with tub and shower. Anti-roll fins. Go look at it." He scribbled a note, handed it to me. "Let me know. In writing."

I took Chook down to the dock with me. A husky kid with a blunt indifferent face, big freckled biceps, a khaki shirt tailored to fit as tightly as his young hide, looked at the note, said the Captain had gone ashore for the day and we were welcome to look around. We took a quick tour. The conversion was well done. She had become luxury transportation without losing her businesslike flavor.

Topside again, I said, "Thanks." Stuck my head in the engine room. "Solid old lunkers," I said. "With that big slow stroke, they should live forever. But in the conversion, didn't they put in a different precombustion system?" I had read the dirt under his nails accurately. Pleased alertness washed away the air of indifference, and in about four minutes he told me more than I cared to know about the brute diesels in the *Buck*.

"I heard about her from a friend of mine who had her on charter. Cal Stebber."

"Who?"

"A very important man. Short, heavy, very friendly. He was on her last summer in Naples. He was down there on a land deal."

"Oh, *him*! Yeah. Nice guy. But it wasn't a charter, exactly. We had a three week layover at that Cutlass Yacht Club on account of one job ended there, and we had to pick the next bunch up there, so Mr. Stebber made a deal with Captain Andy to stay aboard for a while. Sort of a dockside charter. Captain Andy got hell from Robinelli. Hell, if he hadn't turned in the money, Robinelli wouldn't have known a damn thing about it. I think it was fifty a day they settled for. And the deal was that Mr. Stebber had some people he wanted to look real good for, so we were briefed to say, if anybody asked us, friends had loaned it to Mr. Stebber."

"I know Cal lives right here in Tampa, and I had his unlisted number and didn't bring it. Forgot his address. One of those cooperative apartments on Tampa Bay. You wouldn't have it aboard, would you?"

"Golly, I don't think so. He got on and he got off at Naples, and we were tied up the whole time. He paid cash. There wouldn't be any reason to . . ." He stopped and tugged his ear, looking into space. "Wait a minute. There was something. Yeah. Bruno found it when he was sweeping up after Mr. Stebber left. One cuff link under something. Solid gold with some kind of gray-looking jewel in it. Captain Andy had that phone number, or got it somehow, and when we got back to Tampa he got hold of Mr. Stebber and . . ." He turned to face forward, and yelled, "Hey, Bruno. Here a minute."

Bruno, lanky and unprepossessing, came shambling aft, wiping soapy hands on his thighs, staring with great glint-eyed approval at Miss McCall.

116

"Say Bru, you remember the guy you took that gold cuff link back to last year?"

"Give me twenty bucks, man. I remember pretty good."

"Where was it you had to go?"

"West Shore Boulevard, below Gandy Bridge, like near McDill. Some number, I don't remember. Pretty nice place, man."

"Could you tell this man something so he can find it?"

"Don't lean or I come up empty. Give me room to think. It had a number, and it had a name. Pale color building, and like four buildings hooked together, him in the one closest to the water, top floor. Maybe seventh floor, eighth floor. Anyhow, the top one. Something about the name, it didn't make sense. I got it! West Harbour. Even spelled wrong. Oh-you-are instead of oh-are. And no harbor there, man, no matter how you spell it. Docks and a half-ass breakwater and more little sailboats than they had little cruisers, but nothing I'd call a harbor."

As we headed away from there, Chook said, "Half the time I don't know what's on your mind. I have to just stand there, looking relaxed. It's a weird way to come up with his address, McGee."

"There are probably other ways. Maybe not too many, if he's quiet and careful. People leave tracks. You don't know where they left them. If you range back and forth across territory where you know they've been, then you have a better chance of blundering across something. You just saw good luck. I've had a lot of bad days too. If Stebber wants to play, or if he doesn't want to play, either way I'm glad to know where he is. I think we'll call him right from there."

It was almost three thirty by the time I located West Harbour. It was rich and tasteful, the grounds spacious and landscaped, the architecture styled to avoid a cold and institutional look, without severe geometry or mathematical spacing. The main entrance drive split into three separate drives—delivery, guests and residents. I left Chook in the car, the keys in the ignition.

"I am going to be out of there by four thirty or sooner. I won't send word. If I want to take longer, I'll come down and tell you myself. So at four thirty, you drive right out of here, stop at the first pay phone you can find, tip the police, anonymously, that something very strange is going on at the Stebber apartment, West Harbour, the tower near-

117

est the waterfront, top floor. And then find your way back to the airport. Turn this car in. Here's your airplane ticket. If I don't show for the seven o'clock plane, get on it anyway. Take the other car back to the marina. Here are the other car keys. Check Arthur off the boat, lock it up, go check into a motel. Make it . . . Mr. and Mrs. Arthur McCall. Tomorrow morning, find the Chamber of Commerce. They all have visitors' books. Sign in under that name, with the motel address, including the unit number. Get it?"

"I got it."

"Need money?"

"No. I've got enough."

I used a pay booth in the West Harbour lobby to phone Stebber's unlisted number. "Yes?" the same voice said, in the same cool modulation.

"Me again, smirking girl. A little off schedule."

"The gentleman you were asking about before, sir, would be happy to meet you at the bar at the Tampa Terrace Hotel at five o'clock."

"Couldn't he see me now, as long as I'm right here?"

"Here?"

"At West Harbour, dear. In the lobby."

"Would you please hold the line a moment, sir."

It was a very long moment. She came back and said, "You may come up, sir. Do you know the apartment number?"

"I know where it is, but not the number."

"Four dash eight A. Four is the tower, eight is the floor."

I took the walk to the tower nearest the water. The path had a screen of shrubbery. There were curves, stairs up and stairs down, little public courts with benches and some curious cement statuary. The lobby of Tower Four was spacious and empty. You can equate expense with the space they are willing to waste. Two small self-service elevators. At eight the door hissed open and I walked into a small foyer, indirectly lighted. B on the right; A on the left. I pressed a stainless steel button. There was a three inch circle of mirror set into the door. I winked at it.

The girl behind the voice opened the door and said, "Do come in, sir."

I did not get a really good look at her until she had led me through a short entrance hallway and down two carpeted steps into a large living room, where she turned and smiled her greeting again. She was medium height, and very slender. She wore pants carefully tailored to her slenderness, of a white fabric worked with gold thread in ornate and delicate design. With it she wore a sort of short coolie coat of the same fabric, with three quarter sleeves and a wide stiffened collar which stood up in back and swooped down around her shoulders, making a theatrical frame for a slender, pale, classic, beautiful face. Her hair, a very dark and rich chestnut brown, was combed smooth and straight, falling to frame her face, soft parentheses, to chin level, with copper glints where daylight touched it. But the eyes were the best of her. Crystal mint, that clear perfect green of childhood Christmas, the green you see after the first few licks have melted the sugar frost. In walk and smile and gesture she had all the mannered elegance of a high fashion model. In most women who have that trick, it is an irritating artifice. Look, look, look at gorgeous incomparable me! But she managed, somehow, to mock herself at the same time, so the effect was of elegance shared. It said: Having it, I might as well use it.

"I'll tell him you're here. It would be nice to tell him a name, wouldn't it?"

"Travis McGee. You have a name too."

"Debra."

"And never never Debbie."

"Never indeed. Excuse me." She swayed off, closed a heavy door softly behind her. And for the first time the room came into focus. Probably thirty by fifty. Twelve foot ceiling. Window wall with a spectacular view of the bay, terrace beyond it with a low wall, chunky redwood furniture. An almost transparent drapery had been pulled across to reduce the afternoon glare, and there was a heavier drapery racked at the side of it. Giant fireplace faced with coquina rock. Deep blue carpeting. Low furniture, in leather and pale wood. Bookcases. Wall shelves, built in, with a collection of blue Danish glassware, and another, glassed in, with a collection of the little clay figures of Pre-Columbian Latin America. The cooled air was in slight movement, scented very faintly with pine.

It was a very still room, a place where you could listen to the beating of your heart. And it seemed to lack identity, as though it might be a room where executives waited to be called into the board meeting beyond the dark and heavy door.

After long minutes the door opened and Calvin Stebber came smiling into the room, Debra two paces behind him and, in her flat white sandals with gold thongs, maybe an inch taller. He marched up to me and stared up at me, smiling, and I could feel the impact of his superb projection of

119

warmth, interest, kindliness, importance. You could be this man's life-long friend after ten minutes, and marvel that he found you interesting enough to spend a piece of his busy life on you. It was the basic working tool of the top grade confidence man.

"Well now, Mr. McGee, I do respect Debra's instinct, and I must say that she was correct. You have not the faintest odor of the law. You do not look irrational, and you do not look a fool. So do sit down, young man, and we will have our little chat. Sit there, please, where you won't get the glare in your eyes."

He wore a dark green blazer, grey flannel trousers, a yellow ascot. He looked ruddy and fit, chubby and wholesome as he smiled across at me.

"And," he said, "our little telltale in the foyer has advised us you are not carrying some lethal hunk of metal. Cigar, Mr. McGee?"

"No thank you, Mr. Stebber."

"Please, Debra," he said. She went to a table, took a fat foil-wrapped cigar from a humidor, peeled it, and, frowning in pretty concentration, clipped the ends carefully with a little gold gadget. She lit a kitchen match, waited until the flame was right, then lit the cigar, revolving it slowly, getting a perfect light. She took it to him, her every move theatrically elegant, and this time all elegance was directed at him, and without irony, more as if it was her obligation to herself and to him to be as consciously lovely as she could manage to be. A gift for Calvin.

"Thank you, dear. Before we begin, Harris phoned up here about your companion, Mr. McGee, and I suggested he bring her up."

"It might be a pretty good trick."

"Harris can be very persuasive." A buzzer sounded. "There they are. Do let her in, dear. And tell Harris to bring the car around at five."

I did not get a look at Harris, but Chook told me later that he was so much beef in a grey chauffeur's uniform, he would make me look shrunken and puny. She said he had plucked her out of the car the way she would lift a kitten out of a shoebox. I realized later that the long wait when I had phoned upstairs was to give Debra time to alert Harris on another phone, possibly a house line to the service area.

Chook came into the room, thin-lipped with fury, rubbing her upper arm. "Trav, what the hell is going on!" she demanded. "That big clown lamed me. And *you*, fat little man, I suppose you're the chief thief."

Stebber scurried over to her, great concern on his face. He took her hand in both of his and said, "My dear child, the last thing I wanted was to have Harris hurt you or anger you or frighten you, really. I merely thought it rude to have you waiting down there in the car in the hot sun. But seeing what a striking creature you are, my dear, it's doubly a pleasure to have you here. Come over and sit with me here on the couch. There! Now what is your name?"

"But I . . . Look, I only . . . Well . . . Barbara Jean McCall." It was a measure of his charm that I had never known her name until that moment. She made no attempt to pull her hand away. She looked bedazzled. I glanced at Debra and she gave me a wise, measured wink. "Chookie, people call me. Chook sometimes. I . . . I'm a professional dancer."

"Chookie, my dear, with all that grace and vitality and presence, I can't imagine you being anything else. I bet you're *very* good!" He released her hand, gave her an approving little pat on the arm, turned and looked up over his shoulder at Debra, leaning against the back of the couch and said, "Debra, dear, say hello to Chookie McCall, and then you might fix us all a drink."

"Hello, dear. I'm tremendous with daiquiris if anyone cares."

"Well . . . sure. Thanks," Chook said. I nodded agreement.

"Four coming up swiftly," Debra said, and Chook did not take her eyes off the willowy grace of Debra until a door swung shut behind her.

"Spectacular creature, isn't she," Stebber said. "And, in her own way, quite natural and unspoiled. Now let's get to it, Mr. McGee. You used a name over the phone. A password. And you show a certain amount of resource and ingenuity. But, of course, we have a problem. We don't know each other. Or trust each other. What is your occupation?"

"Semi-retired. Sometimes I help a friend solve a little problem. It isn't anything you need an office for. Or a license."

"And this handsome young woman is helping you help a friend?"

"Something like that. But when a friend gets caught in a big con, it isn't easy. Old grifters like you keep the action safe and almost on the level. Maybe you even pay taxes on the take. And you train your ropers and shills and let them take the risks. I suppose you're so used to living nice, Stebber, you don't want to risk taking any kind of a fall. How badly do you want to avoid a fuss? When I know that I know how much pressure I've got." I kept it very casual.

He stared at me for long alert seconds. "Certainly not bunko," he said. "Wrong type, completely. Could you have been with it?"

"Not with it. Close to it a few times. Helping friends."

Chook said irritably, "What's going *on*?"

Debra reappeared, bringing four golden-pale daiquiris on a teak and pewter tray. I said, "Cal Stebber's in the bait business, honey. He gets the hungry ones, and they get hauled aboard and gutted."

Debra made a face at me as I took my drink from the tray. "What a dreadful way to say it. Really! You must have made some very bad investments, Mr. McGee."

"Debra, dear," Stebber said. "Have we given up waiting for our cues?" It was said with loving patience, and with an almost genuine warmth. But the girl's color changed, the tray dipped, the glasses slid an inch before she regained control. She made an almost inaudible murmur of apology. Discipline was rigid on this team.

After one imitation sip, I put my drink aside. Debra sat graceful and subdued on the arm of the couch. Stalemate. I decided I'd better gamble on my knowledge of the type. Perhaps, twenty years ago, he could have taken chances. Now his life would seem shorter to him. If I had no information he wanted, I wouldn't have gotten into the apartment. Now he was regretting even that. And I could say with almost total certainty that my chance of prying any of Arthur's money out of this one was zero. I had to give him some confidence. And I thought I might have the name that would do it.

"Know The Moaner, Cal?" I asked him.

He looked startled. "My God, I haven't thought of Benny in years. Is he still alive?"

"Yes. Retired. Lives with his son-in-law in Nashville. Phone is under the name of T. D. Notta. You could say hello."

"He knows you?"

"It isn't a real warm friendship."

He excused himself and left the room. Chook said, "*Somebody* could give me a scorecard."

"When the Moaner was young and spry, back, they say, in

122

Stanley Steamer days, he got his start in Philadelphia, diving into the front end of slow-moving cars. He'd bounce off and roll away and moan like to break your heart. His partner wore a cop suit and came running up and spilled the fake blood on the Moaner when he bent over him to take a look at him. He worked up from there. Fake masterpieces, they say. And he worked the ships. Ran bucket shops, telephone swindles. All the long-time grifters know each other." Debra made a sound of amusement. Her morale was returning. But when I tried to pump her, she was both silent and amused.

When Stebber returned he had shed large hunks of his public personality. "The old bastard sounds pretty shaky, McGee. He doesn't like you. One of the last scores he made, a little one, you got it back before he could get out of range."

"For a friend."

"He says you don't holler cop. He says . . . Debra, dear, why don't you take Miss McCall to your room and make girl-talk?"

When Chook looked at me in query I nodded approval. They left.

As the door closed, Stebber said, "Benny says you can get cute. And he says it isn't a good idea to send anybody after you. He said you made two good boys as sorry as could be. He said don't try to figure you for a mark in any direction. And you're pretty much a loner. But if you say you'll deal, you'll deal."

"So you want to know what I've got and what I want."

"I know Wilma didn't send you. She's not damn fool enough to think of making a deal to come back in. And she would have given you the phone code. It's a simple number switch, based on what day of the week it is. Seven digits in the phone number. Seven days in the week. When she asks the caller to repeat the number, you just add one to whatever digit represents that day. You would have said seven one three - one eight seven eight."

"And having told me, to show how much you trust me, you'll change the code as soon as you can."

"You hurt me, my boy."

"The secretarial type who fed Arthur the knockout at the Piccadilly Pub. Could have been Debra, I suppose."

"You have a good eye. Few men could see how severe and plain she can make herself look. And how is poor Arthur?"

"Insolvent."

"It had to be him, of course. Wilma's most recent venture.

123

Your Miss McCall. She has a special interest in Arthur?"

"You could put it that way."

He awarded me a sad, sweet, knowing man-of-the-world smile. "Odd, isn't it, how those very vital and alive ones are attracted to such shadowy, indistinct men. Poor Arthur. Not much sport there. Like shooting a bird in a cage."

"You must have felt sorry for him, Stebber. Or you would have taken his last dime."

"Wilma had her way. No pity, no mercy. He was just another symbol of what she has to keep killing, over and over."

"That's one of the shticks of the half-educated, this bite-sized psychiatry, Stebber. You do it pretty well."

Ruddiness deepened and then faded. It was nice to mark him a little in an area where he least expected it. "But we aren't progressing, McGee. We want information from each other. And the magic word is Wilma."

"For a top operator in the big con, which you seem to pretend to be, Stebber, you put together a damned shaky team. Crane Watts and Boone Waxwell are weak links."

"I know. Also Rike Jefferson, the executor. Weakness and unpredictability. But it was a . . . sentimental flaw. I couldn't take the time to set it up more soundly. Harry couldn't spare the time. Mr. Gisik. An old associate. A valued friend. He died six weeks ago in New Orleans after heart surgery, God rest his soul. As this venture was . . . reasonably legal, I took the risk of operating with weak people. But they were paid what they were worth. Your being here is, I suppose, one of the penalties of a clumsy operation. But let me assure you, Travis McGee, clumsiness stops out there beyond the main gate."

"I think there's another penalty too."

"Yes?"

"I think Wilma is dead."

It hit him very solidly. He reverted to that mask face which can be acquired only in prison or in the military. It shows nothing, asks nothing. He stood up slowly, paced to the window and back. "I've thought so too," he said. "Without quite admitting it. Let me put it this way. She was with me for fifteen years. And it is not an emotional loss. It's the end of . . . an effective professional relationship."

"Fifteen *years!*"

"She was nineteen when we found her. I had a steady partner at the time. Muscle. I went in for more active gaffs at that time. Southern California. She was in a place that catered to movie money. In little frocks and jumpers and

124

pinafores, Alice in Wonderland haircut, face scrubbed, talking in a thin little lisp, doll in the crook of her arm, bubblegum in her little jaw, she could pass for eleven or twelve. There's a steady demand at good rates for that sort of thing. But they couldn't control her. She kept going on the gouge on her own. Greedy and reckless and merciless. We took her off their hands. She responded to discipline when she found we weren't at all squeamish about it. We improved her diction and cleaned up her vocabulary. We put her in full make-up, high fashion clothes, and worked the class lounges and hotels. She had a good natural eye for a mark. After the fun and games, the gaff was to hit the mark in broad daylight on his grounds—home or office—the three of us, Wilma as a scared, bawling fourteen-year-old saying she truly loved the scared clown, my muscle as her murderously inclined father, me as an officer of the juvenile court, with her faked birth certificate in hand. The way out we'd finally give him was for him to spring for two or more years in a private institution for her, with the fee adjusted to how we had checked him out before the visit. You want to see real horror, you should have seen their faces when we laid the gaff on them. When we were home free, my God how she would laugh! A laugh to chill the blood. She learned fast. She was a quick study. She read a lot, remembered a lot. And lied a lot about herself. I think she even believed most of it."

He sat in silence on the couch, almost unaware of me. He was a dumpy, tired little thief dressed for a costume party.

"I gave up the rough lines. She became a partner. She'd cruise on her own, rope them, bring them back within range, set them up, clean them out, divorce them. Had she been more merciful I think she would have been a poisoner. Mercilessness can be a flaw. And believing your own lies. And she had another flaw too. She could never get any sexual satisfaction from the marks. After the scores she'd almost invariably find some brute stud, usually ignorant, rough, dirty and potentially dangerous. But she always kept the whip hand, drove them hard, walked out when she was ready." He sighed, stirred, pumped himself back up to full con-artist scale, aimed personality at me like a two-mile flashlight.

"McGee, do I do all the talking?"

"I think she must have been carrying her share in cash. And was killed a few days after she left the motel in Naples while Arthur was off on his bus trip. I'd guess the playmate

125

who killed her has spent at least twenty-five thousand. Cars, a boat, guns, toys. I'm helping my friend Arthur. If I could come up with a good way of making a recovery from you, I'd give it a try. I take expenses off the top and keep half the net salvage. So moving in on her playmate could be full of ugly surprises, and if I knew how much she was carrying on her, I'd know if there was a balance worth the risk."

"And if I give you the figure?"

"Then I'd have to figure out whether to tell you who and where. And if you're lying. Suppose she was carrying just twenty-five. So you tell me a hundred so I will go prodding and maybe get jammed up in a way that will keep me from ever coming back with some cute idea for you. Or maybe I eliminate the playmate, which would satisfy you up for the way he cooked your future plans for Wilma. Or suppose she was carrying a hundred and you tell me it was twenty-five. I say who and where and you send muscle after it."

He pondered it. "Stalemate again. I see your point. There's no way I can get you to take my word that the very last thing I would do these days is go after a hijacked take, or send anyone. Risks alarm me, Travis McGee. I have too much to lose. You could check something out. I own twenty percent of the West Harbour Development Corporation. And some other things here and there. Muscle is seldom combined with wits. You seem to be a striking exception. Someone gets killed and the muscle gets tricked into a state's evidence revelation, and the middleman I would use implicates me. No thanks. Besides, Debra and I are negotiating a score as big as the one Arthur contributed. By falsifying records, bribing minor officials, making some careful changes in old group pictures—school and church—and with the help of some brown contact lenses, some minor changes in hair and skin texture, we have given Debra an iron-clad identity as a mulatto, as a pale-skinned girl who actually did disappear at fourteen. This curious revelation has come as a horrid shock to her young husband of four months, and an even worse shock to her wealthy father-in-law, the ex-governor of a southern state, a fevered segregationist, a man with political ambitions. The positive rabbit test—also faked—is bringing things to a climax. The fat settlement is for divorce, abortion and total silence. There was a real chance they might solve it by having her killed. But Debra is not squeamish. Actually, she takes too many chances. Very good family. She was risk-hunting when I found her. Jumping out of air-

126

planes, racing overpowered little boats and automobiles, skin-diving alone and too deep, potting at cape buffalo with a hand gun. She's incredibly quick and strong. Now she has found something, finally, which satisfies her. The hunt. Along with the constant and very real danger of displeasing me.

"McGee, all I can ask you to do is accept my story of what happened. There was a hundred and thirty-five thousand left in that trustee account for the syndicate in the Naples bank. I arranged in advance for them to have cash available. It is not difficult in Florida where cash is used so often in real estate closings. The day Arthur came up to meet me, my man Harris drove me to Naples. I closed out the account at noon, kept five thousand for incidental expenses and took the balance to that grisly motel room and gave it to Wilma. She was almost packed. We had arranged she would return to Tampa in the car with me in time to catch a Nassau flight. I had her ticket. The money represented the final take for both of us. I gave her the prepared deposit slip for my share. Bahamian banks have a pleasant policy of never divulging information on an account unless the depositor appears in person and signs a specific authorization. She said she'd made other arrangements, that someone was going to drive her to Miami and she would fly over from there. I made mild objections."

"And you let her fly off with all that money?"

"She liked money. Without me, she'd have a lot less to spend. We were together fifteen years. Taking cash into the islands is easy. She was shrewd and tough. And far from retirement."

"So, as I said at first, maybe you're fattening the figure."

He called Debra in. I gave them no chance for signals, made her face me with her slender back toward him. She verified the details and the amount, asked no questions, left without a word when he told her to go.

I could have gathered up Chookie and left. I doubted he'd have tried anything. But there was an implied obligation. And if he did indeed come after what Boo might have left, it could turn into a diversion I might be able to use.

"Boo Waxwell picked her up at the motel. Arthur went to Waxwell's place at Goodland and found her there. Boo beat him badly. I jounced Crane Watts around first. I used his name to open Waxwell up. I invented the yarn that Arthur had gone to Watts and told him he'd seen Wilma at Waxwell's. I said I was trying to set up a similar kind of operation to the way you cleaned Arthur out, and needed the

127

woman. He claimed, wide-eyed, it was a little ol' waitress friend from Miami. But Arthur remembers Wilma wearing the watch he thought she'd sold in Miami. He wouldn't invent that. And, of course, he has all his new toys."

Stebber nodded slowly. "Her usual type. A little more complex, probably. Whenever she tamed them, that finished it for her. I tried to keep him away from Arthur's beach house while we were still building the con. Hard man to control. Yes. Of course. It fits. She wouldn't have waved the money at him. He smelled it somehow."

Debra knocked and appeared with a blue extension phone. "Crane Watts," she said. "Do you want to take it in here, darling?"

"Or take it at all? Please." She stooped lithely, plugged it into a baseboard jack receptacle, brought it to him and drifted out.

In full heat and radiance he said, "How *nice* to hear from you, Crane, my boy! . . . Start from the beginning. Slow down, boy. . . . Yes . . . I see. . . . Please, no assumptions. Confine yourself to the facts."

Watts talked for a long time without interruption. Stebber made a sad face at me. Finally he said, "That's enough. *Do* pull yourself together. No person named McGee or named anything else has tried to contact me on that matter. Why should you think in terms of an official investigation? As a lawyer you must know it was a legal business matter. This McGee is probably some sharpshooter who found out Arthur had lost some money in an unwise investment and is trying to shake some of it loose. Tell Waxwell too that neither of you should be so agitated. Please don't phone me again. I retained you for legal work. It's finished. So is our association."

He listened for a short time and said, "The status of your career could not mean less to me, Watts. Please don't bother me again."

As he returned the phone to the cradle I could hear the frantic tiny buzzing of Crane's agitated voice. Frowning, Stebber said, "Strange that Waxwell should be so eager to bully my phone number out of Watts. He says he gave him the number but not the code—as if he expected congratulations. I would think, if your guess is right, I'd be the last person he'd . . ."

Changing the pitch and resonance of my voice, I said, "Ol' Boo make that lawyer boy itchy."

It astounded and delighted him out of all proportion to

128

the accomplishment. Patience and a good tape recorder can make a respectable mimic out of anyone.

"Maybe some day we could find a project to our mutual advantage," he said.

"I can think of one right now. Decoy Waxwell up here and keep him here for one full day and I send you ten percent of all we recover."

"No thanks. I don't think the man is entirely sane. And he goes by hunch. I wouldn't risk it. Decoy him with a woman, McGee. The McCall girl could keep him occupied long enough."

"Let's say she's squeamish, Stebber. Loan me Debra for the same cut. Ten percent."

"I wouldn't consider it for one . . ." He stopped suddenly. His shy glance was more obscene than any wink or leer could have been. "If you could have her back in three days. And . . . if you could leave Miss McCall here with me. As a guarantee of good faith."

"How bulky would the money be?"

"New hundreds in Federal Reserve wrappers. Thirteen packets, one hundred bills thick. Perhaps not quite enough to fill a fair-sized shoebox. You didn't answer my question about Miss . . . Chookie."

"Given a choice, given time to think, I imagine she'd pick Boo Waxwell."

"Why give her a choice, dear boy? You'd find Debra charming company. And I can assure you few men make the impact on her you've already made. And when you get Miss Chookie McCall back, you'd find her quite anxious to be agreeable, and not at all contentious. Truly effective disciplines, McGee, leave the loveliness untouched and the soul just an interestingly bit queasy and apprehensive. It's a superimposed useful anxiety."

"Speaking for Miss McCall, no thanks."

"Some day, perhaps," he said and went and called the girls. They came walking slowly back into the big room, and I saw Chook wearing an odd expression, Debra looking secretively amused.

They both walked us out to the elevator, all charm and assurance, convincing us we were lovely people who had stopped in for a lovely drink. As the elevator door closed, my final look at them showed their gracious smiles, the smiles of an elegant couple, tastefully appointed, mannerly. And virulent as coral snakes.

Chook stayed lost in her silence and did not explode until

129

we were a half mile away. "Girl talk! *Girl* talk! Do you know what that skinny bitch was doing? She was trying to . . . to *recruit* me. Like a gawdam Marine poster. See the world. Learn a trade. Retire in your prime."

"Recruit you as what?"

"She didn't say right out. She inspected me like a side of meat and said I was prime. Too bad I was wasting myself in such hard work for so little money. Damn it, I make *good* money. Men, she said, the right kind of men, could get so expensively intrigued with a big, dark, fierce-looking girl like me. And that man, Trav. He made me feel weak and silly and young, and he made me feel anxious to make him like me. At first. But at the end there, I was thinking how nice it would be to squash him like a bug. They scare me, Trav. In a way I don't think I've been scared since I was a kid, when my grandmother got me so worked up about white slavers, if I saw two men standing on a street corner, I'd cross the street so they couldn't jab me with a needle and sell me to the Arabs. Trav, if we have to have anything to do with those people, something really awful might happen. My God, Trav, you should see the clothes she's got. Furs and originals and nine drawers of undies and a shoe rack, I swear to God, with a hundred pair of shoes at least. And all the time she was kind of laughing at me inside, as if I was a dumb oaf of a girl, a nudnik. What *happened*, Travis?"

"In short form, he confirms the hunch Waxwell killed her. She was carrying her share and his of Arthur's money. She was to put his end in a Nassau bank account. A hundred and thirty thousand dollars. I think he already had taken a fat slice of the rest of it. Everybody else had been paid off. But he writes her off and the money off. He wants no part of it. He says. Maybe I believe him. I don't know. He might send somebody down. We have to play it that way."

"A hundred and thirty thousand!" she exclaimed.

"Less what old Boo has blown. Rough guess, eighty-five or ninety left."

"But that's good, isn't it? Isn't that better than anything you expected?"

"Putting my hands on any part of it, Chook, is going to be better than I expected. And I haven't done that yet."

TWELVE

IT WAS AFTER nine at night when I parked at the marina and we went aboard *The Busted Flush*. No light showed. I had the irrational hunch that something had gone wrong. Maybe I had been exposed to too much calculated deviousness for one day. But as I flicked the lounge lights on, there was Arthur slouched on the big yellow couch. He had a tall glass in his hand, dark enough for iced coffee. He gave us a big crooked glassy grin, hoisted the glass in such an enthusiastic salute of welcome that a dollop of it leapt out and splashed his shirt.

"Warra sharra numun!" he said.

Chook stood over him, fists on her hips. "Oh boy! You've done it real good, huh?"

"Shawara dummen huzzer," he said, in pleased explanation.

She took the glass out of his hand, sniffed it, set it aside. She turned to me. "As you remember, it doesn't take much. The poor silly. It was such a strain to be shut up here all this time." She took his wrist, braced herself. "Upsy-daisy, darling."

She got him up but with a wide loving grin, he enfolded her in big arms and, utterly slack, bore her over and down with a mighty thud of their combined weights. Chook worked free and stood up, rubbing a bruised haunch. Arthur, still smiling, cheek resting on his forearm, emitted a low buzzing snore.

"At least," she said. "It's not what I'm used to. A happy drunk."

Between us we stood him up, draped him soddenly over my shoulder. I dumped him into the big bed. "Thanks, Trav. I'll manage from here," she said, and began to unbutton his shirt, looking up from the task to give me a slightly rueful smile. "Rich warm memories of Frankie Durkin," she said. "But there the trick was to keep from getting a split mouth or a fat eye before he folded."

Up on the sundeck I heard the sound of the shower, and a

131

little while later she came climbing up into the night warmth in her robe, bringing two beers.

"Rockaby baby," she said. "Tomorrow he'll be a disaster area." She sat beside me. "And what now, Captain?"

"Confusion. I was thinking that, at the right distance, in the right garments, you might pass as Vivian Watts, tennis player. And if Viv left a message for old Boo to join her in assignation at some far place, it might intrigue him. But it won't fit together. The odds are she despises Waxwell and he knows it. Then it struck me that she could properly blame Waxwell for her husband's downhill slide. And she might leap at the chance to give him a bruise if there was a chance of a piece of money to square all overdue accounts and have enough left over to move along to a place where Crane Watts could start all over again. That means sounding her out. Quietly and soon. But with something specific. That's as far as I've gotten."

"Hmm. And Waxwell would think it fishy if she made a play. But he does have . . . a certain interest in her?"

"Avid."

"What if he found out somehow that she had left her husband and gone off someplace alone to think things out, all alone in some hideaway place, away from people. A place hard to get to. She wouldn't be there, of course, but it would take him a long time to get there and find out and get back."

"And when he got back and found out he'd been cleaned out, who would he go after first, Chook? That isn't a happy thought."

"See what you mean. But what if she and her husband got all set to take off, so then you could give them some of the money and they'd be gone before he got back?"

"And if I can't find the money?"

"Then he wouldn't have much to be sore about, would he?"

"And she could say that she started off and changed her mind and came back to her husband. If he asks. You have a talent for this, Miss Chookie."

"Thanks a lot. Trav, I don't see how you *can* expect to find it, even if you had a whole day."

"I have an idea about that. Remember the story of Bluebeard?"

"What's that supposed to mean?"

"I'll tell you if it works."

"And you have to think of a place she might be likely to

132

go. And some way of getting the word to Boone Waxwell. And you have to talk her into it in the first place."

"I think she's desperate. I think she's ready to try anything. And she would be the logical one to ask about a place she might go. Meanwhile, playing it by ear, we've got ourselves located on the wrong square on this board maybe. Maybe not. Hell, I guess not. With the car, and with the little boat at Naples, maybe right on the edge of the board is the best square to occupy."

"And you'll use Arthur somehow, dear? Some safe way?"

"I promise."

She patted my arm. "Thank you very much. Do men's work. Leave the lady home to give tearful thanks at the safe return."

"I can't take him with me tomorrow. Or you. Not for the morning mission."

"What is it?"

"I want to see if the Bluebeard idea is any good before I take the Viv idea any further."

Tuesday morning at nine thirty, from a gas station a quarter mile from the junior high school, I phoned the administration office and asked to speak to Cindy Ingerfeldt. A woman with a tart, skeptical voice said, "This is the next to the last day of exams. I can check to see if she is taking an examination or if she is in a study period, but I shall have to know who you are and the purpose of the call."

"The name is Hooper, ma'm. Field investigator for State Beverage Control. I'll have to ask you to keep that confidential. The girl could have some useful information. Could you give me a rundown on her, what kind of a kid she is?"

"I . . . I don't imagine you'll find her cooperative. Cindy is quite mature for her age. A very indifferent student. She's just marking time here, as so many of them are. I take it her home life is not too pleasant. She's not a popular child. She keeps to herself. She's tidy about her person, and would be really quite pretty if she lost some weight. Mr. Hooper, if you want to interrogate the child, you could come here and I could turn over a private office to you."

"I'd rather not do it that way, ma'm. Word could get back to some pretty rough people. I wouldn't want to cause her that kind of trouble. That's why I ask you kindly to keep this to yourself."

"Oh dear. Is the child . . . involved in anything?"

"Nothing like that, ma'm. You know, if you really want to

cooperate, rather than me trying to get anything out of her over the phone, I'd appreciate it if you could just make some reason to send her down the road to the Texaco Station. I won't take much of her time, and send her right back."

"Well . . . let me check her schedule." About a full minute later, as I stared through the booth glass at the distant building and the ranks of yellow buses behind it, she came back on the line and said in a conspiratorial way, "She'll finish her History test at ten. I think the most inconspicuous way would be for me to go and see her in person as she comes out, and I will send her along then. Will that be all right?"

"Just fine, and I certainly do appreciate your cooperation."

At a few minutes before ten, I moved the car, parked it fifty yards closer to the school, aimed in the direction of the gas station. At a few minutes after ten I saw her in the rear vision mirror, trudging along toward me, both arms hugging a stack of books to her bosom. She wore a green striped cotton blouse, salmon-colored pants that ended halfway between knee and ankle, white sneakers. When she was near enough, I reached over and swung the door open, saying, "Good morning, Cindy."

She stared at me, came slowly toward the car, stopped a few feet away. "Oh. You, huh." She appraised me with those wise old eyes. "What's on your mind?"

"Get in."

"Lissen, if Sunday give you any ideas, forget it. I don't know you, I'm not in the mood, and I got enough problems, mister."

"I want to fix ol Boo's wagon, Cindy. And he'll never know you were involved in any way. I just want to ask some questions. Get in and we'll drive around and I'll drop you off right here in fifteen minutes."

"What makes you think I should want to mess Boo up someways?"

"Let's just say you could be doing your father a favor."

She pursed her small mouth, gave a half shrug and climbed in. She plunked her books on the seat between us and said, "No driving around. Go like I tell you."

Her directions were terse and lucid. They took us three blocks over, two blocks to the left, and into a sheltered grove with picnic tables and fireplaces, willows thick around a pond. When I turned the engine off she sighed, undid a button of her blouse, poked two fingers into her bra,

134

squirmed slightly, and pulled out a wilted cigarette and a kitchen match. She popped the match a-flame with a deft thumbnail, drew deeply, exhaled a long gray plume that bounced off the inside of the windshield.

"How'd you get old Mossbutt to leave me loose?"

"I said it was official. Beverage Control investigation. When you go back she'll want to know. Tell her Mr. Hooper said not to talk about it to anybody."

"That your name?"

"No."

"Is it official?"

"What do you think, Cindy?"

"Prolly not."

"You're right. Sunday you gave me the impression you wish Waxwell was out of your life. Was that an act?"

"I don't know. Guess not. If he wasn't so damn mean. And not so old. Don't take me no place. Miami he keeps saying. Sure. I should live so long. The way it goes, shit, I've gotta make some kind of move myself, because I hang around, it's going to be the same, no matter what. A bunch of the kids, they got a chance to bus up and work tobacco in Connecticut this summer. Working hard and being far away, I could get over being so hooked, maybe. Goddam mean old man, he is."

The last drag drew the fire line down close to her thumb. She snapped the butt out the window, holding her breath, then exhaled, openmouthed. She turned toward me and rested her plump cheek on the seat back. "What d'ya wanna know?"

"Do you know Boo murdered a woman out there at his place last year?"

She hooded her eyes, examined a thumb nail, nibbled the corner of it. "Friend a yours?"

"No. Just the opposite. It didn't seem to surprise you."

"I guess I had the feeling something happened. She a midget or something?"

"That's a funny question."

"There was some black lace panties I tried to get on. I'm fat but not that fat. I busted them trying. When I asked too many times he popped me on top of the head with his fist so hard I got sick an heaved up."

"She was a very small woman. I understand he makes you work around the place."

"Oh Christ, I don't mind that. He lives like a hog. It's just he won't let me keep ahead of it. He lets it go, then it's twice as much work."

135

"Is he always there when you're cleaning up?"

"When I'm there, he's there. What he says, I ever come around when he's gone, or come without him calling me he's got something special he's saving for a big surprise. I'm not fixing to get any surprise from him for sure."

"All right, when you are cleaning the place, is there any particular part of the house he won't let you touch?"

"Huh? I don't get it."

"As if something could be hidden in the house?"

"Huh? No. Nothing like that. But I sure God stay clear of the grove there back of the shed. One time, back in March I think, it got hot unexpected like. He'd come by and give me a blast on the horn pretty late. At like three in the morning, him asleep and snoring by then, I was there smelling some stinking fish he'd forgot about and left on the porch maybe since that noon. Redfish. They turn fast when it's hot. It got my stomach rolling over finally, so I up and pull my dress on and go out and pick them up by the stringer, get a shovel from the shed and go off back into the grove to bury them, holding my breath mostly. I hardly dug half a hole and he come at me, running flat out, grunting, that belt knife of his winking in the moonlight, charging bareass crazy right at me. Me, I take off through the grove and hear him hit a root or something and go down hard. Then he's coming on again, yelling he's going to kill me, and I'm yelling I was burying his stinking fish before the stink made me snap my lunch.

"Then he was quiet, so I snuck in a circle and see him back in the open part of the grove, finishing digging the hole. He dabbed the fish in and covered them over, then he hollers for me to come on in, saying it was okay, he was just having a funny dream and he woke me up. Hell he did. A long time after he went back in the house I get the nerve fin'ly to sneak back in, and the way I got grabbed sudden in the dark from behind, it like to kill me. But what he wanted to do was just horse around. You know. Laughing and tickling. And he got me all turned on prakly before I got over being scared. And I tell you one thing. I never seen any shovel anywhere around his place since. But he isn't so dumb he'd bury that dwarf woman onto his own place. Not with a couple million acres of 'glades close by, where he could put a little dead woman back in there so far and so deep, the whole army and navy couldn't find her in a hundred years. Why, he could just float her into a gator pool and them gators would wedge her down into the mud

136

bottom for ripenin' and have her et'n to nothing in a couple weeks. Maybe they can catch him *killin'* somebody, but they'll never get him for it afterwards. I'll tell you one more thing for sure. If'n you mess him up good, and he knows who done it, you're best off leaving him dead your own self. That's the thing about that tobacco work. I get maybe up past Georgia someplace and the bus stops and there he is, leanin on that white Lincoln grinnin, and I pick up my suitcase off'n the rack and get off that bus, because that's all there'd be to do. And he knows it."

On one of her notebook sheets I drew a crude sketch of the cottage and shed and road, and she made an X where she had started digging, and drew in some lopsided circles to indicate where the trees were standing.

As I let her off, she looked at me for a moment, eyes squinty and her lips sucked in. "I'd hate for you to say I told you this stuff."

"Cindy, you're fifteen years old, and you're going to get out of this mess and in another couple of years you won't remember much about it."

There was a bleak amusement in her woman's eyes. "I'm three weeks from sixteen, and it'll keep right on going on until Boo gets tired of it, and there won't be a day in my life I don't remember some part of it or other."

I drove into Naples, on the alert for Land Rovers and white Lincoln convertibles. I found a hardware store several blocks along Fifth Avenue, parked in their side lot, bought two spades and a pick and put them in the trunk. Then I thought of another device that might be useful, a variation of the way plumbers search for buried pipes. I bought a four foot length of quarter inch steel reinforcing rod, and one of those rubber-headed mallets they use for body and fender work. Naples was drowsy in the heat of the off-season, pre-noon sun. I phoned Crane Watts' office number, and hung up when he said hello. Next I phoned his home number. It did not answer. I tried the club and asked if Mrs. Watts was on the courts. In a few moments they said she was, and should they call her to the phone. I said never mind.

When I arrived at the club the parking lot was nearly empty. There were a few people down on the beach, one couple in the pool. As I walked toward the courts I saw only two were in use, one where two scrawny elderly gentlemen were playing vicious pat-ball, and, several courts away,

137

the brown, lithe, sturdy Mrs. Watts in a practice session. The man was apparently the club pro, very brown, balding, thickening. He moved well, but she had him pretty well lathered up. There were a couple dozen balls near the court. He was feeding her backhand, ignoring the returns, bouncing each ball, then stroking it to her left with good speed and overspin. She moved, gauged, planted herself, pivoted, the ball ponging solidly off the gut, moved to await the next one. The waistband of her tennis skirt was visibly damp with sweat.

It seemed, for her, a strange and intense ritual, a curious sublimation of tension and combat. Her face was stern and expressionless. She glanced at me twice and then ignored me. Gave no greeting.

Finally as he turned to pick up three more balls she said, "That'll do it for now, Timmy."

He took a handkerchief from his pocket and mopped his face. "Righto, Miz Watts. I make it three hours. Okay?"

"Anything you say."

As Timmy was collecting the balls in a mesh sack, she walked to the sidecourt bench, mopped her face and throat with a towel, stared at me with cold speculation as I approached.

"Pretty warm for it, Vivian."

"Mr. McGee, you made an excellent first impression on me the other night. But the second one was more lasting."

"And things might not have been what they seemed."

She took her time unsnapping the golf glove on her right hand, peeling it off. She prodded and examined the pads at the base of her fingers. "I do not think I am interested in any nuances of legality, Mr. McGee, any justification of any cute tricky little things you want to involve my husband in." As she spoke, she was slipping her rackets into their braces, tightening down the thumb screws. "He is not . . . the kind of man for that kind of thing. I don't know why he's trying to be something he isn't. It's tearing him apart. Why don't you just leave us alone?"

As she gathered up her gear, I picked the words that would, I hoped, pry open a closed mind. "Vivian, I wouldn't ask your husband's advice on a parking ticket, believe me."

She straightened up, those very dark blue eyes becoming round with surprise and indignation. "Crane is a *very* good attorney!"

"Maybe he was. Once upon a time. Not now."

"Who *are* you? What do you *want*?"

"I want to form a little mutual aid society with you, Vivian. You need help and I need help."

"Is this . . . help I'm supposed to get, is it just for me or for Crane too?"

"Both of you."

"Of course. I get him to do some nasty little piece of crooked work for you, and it will make us gloriously rich and happy."

"No. He did his nasty little piece of crooked work last year, and it didn't do either of you any good."

She began to walk slowly, thoughtfully, off toward the distant entrance to the women's locker room, and I walked beside her. She had been laboring in the sun for three hours. Under the faded cosmetic and deodorant scents of a fastidious woman was an animal pungency of work-sweat, a sharpness not unpleasant, the effluvium of ballet schools and practice halls.

"What I can offer, if things can be worked out, is a long odds chance and a suggestion. I think he's whipped himself here. I think you're both whipped. If you had some cash, right now, you should settle up what you owe around here and get out. Try it again in a new place. What is he? Thirty-one? There's time. But maybe he's lost you along the way, and you're not interested."

Under the shade of big pines the path narrowed and I dropped behind her. Her back was straight and strong, and the round of her sturdy hips, in tempo with the smooth brown muscular flex of her calves, gave the tennis skirt a limber sway. She stopped suddenly and turned around to face me. Her mouth, free of the tautness of disapproval, was softened and younger. "He hasn't lost me. But don't play games. Don't play cruel games, Travis. I don't know what's been going on. He says he got into something and he didn't know it was a bad thing until too late."

Sometimes you have to aim right between the eyes. "He knew from the start. He knew it was fraud, with a nice little sugar coating of legality. They paid him well, and he helped them screw a man named Arthur Wilkinson out of a quarter of a million dollars. It got around, Vivian. Who'd trust him now? He's terrified that somebody is going to wipe off the pretty icing and expose the fraud. He consorted with con artists and trash like Boone Waxwell, went into it with his eyes open for the sake of what he thought was going to be twelve thousand five. But he doesn't have the nerve to be a good thief. He began to shake apart. They kissed him off with seven thousand five, knowing he didn't have the nerve to get hard-nosed about it. And if he keeps dithering around, spilling his guts to strangers like me, maybe they'll get so tired of him they'll send somebody around to put a gun in his hand when he's passed out, and stick the barrel in his ear."

She wobbled on those good legs, and her color went sick under the tan. She moved off the path and sat, quite heavily, on a cement and cypress bench, staring blindly through the shade toward the bright sea. Her mouth trembled. I sat beside her, watching that unhappy profile.

"I . . . I guess I knew that he knew. Sunday night, after Waxwell left, he swore on his word of honor Waxwell had been lying, trying to needle us by all those little hints that Crane had been in on something all along."

She turned and looked at me in a pleading way, her color getting better, and said, "What makes him so *weak?*"

"Maybe what's left of your good opinion of him is the only thing he has left, Vivian. Would you still want to try to save it?"

"His best friend at Stetson, his roommate, wanted Crane to quit here and go in with him in practice in Orlando. He might still . . . I don't know. And I don't know about me even. I think if I could get him straightened out again, then it would be time to decide about me."

"If what I want to ask you to do works out, I want you and your husband to be ready to leave any moment, to get ready so you can leave. Arrange the big things later, like getting rid of the house and so on."

"Right now our equity in that might buy one day's groceries," she said bitterly. "One way or another, I can make him do it."

"How much would it take to clean up your bills here and give the two of you say a month or six weeks a good long way from here, in some hideout. Don't look so skeptical. You wouldn't be hiding from the law. It would be a chance to get him dried out. And then he might begin to make more sense to himself, and you."

"My father left me a cabin on a couple of acres of ridge land near Brevard, North Carolina. On Slick Rock Mountain. It's so lovely up there. You can look out across ridge after ridge, all gray-blue in the distance. Wood fires on summer nights." Her mouth twisted. "We honeymooned there, several thousand lifetimes ago. How much to settle up here? I don't know. He's been so secretive. Maybe we owe more

140

than I know. I'd think three or four thousand dollars. But there might be other debts."

"And getting started in Orlando later on. Call it ten."

"Ten thousand dollars! What could I do that would be worth ten thousand dollars to anyone? Who do I have to kill?"

"You have to be bait, Vivian. To lure Boone Waxwell out of his cave and keep him out for as long as you can, a full day minimum, more if we can manage it."

Those good shoulders moved slowly up. She locked her hands, closed her eyes and shuddered. "That man. God, he makes my flesh crawl. The few times I've ever seen him, he's never taken his eyes off me. And he acts as if he and I have some special secret we share. All those little smirks and chuckles and winks, and the way he struts around me, puffing his chest and rolling his shoulders, laughing with a little snorting sound, like a stallion. And he puts double meanings in everything he says to me. Honestly, I freeze completely. He makes me feel naked and sick. That pelt of hair sticking out of the top of those ghastly shirts, and all that black hair on the backs of his hands and fingers, and that sort of . . . oily intimacy in his voice, it all makes my stomach turn over. Travis, if what you have in mind involves his . . . even touching me in any way, no. Not for ten thousand dollars, not for ten thousand dollars a minute." She tilted her head, looking at me in a puzzled way. "It isn't because I'm . . . prissy or anything. No other man has affected me that way. I am certainly not . . . unresponsive." And again, the wryness around her mouth. "Of course I haven't been able to check that in some time. When one becomes a very infrequent convenience for a drunk, an accommodation, the opportunity for any kind of response is very goddam rare."

A dime of sunlight came through the pine branches overhead, glowed against the firm and graceful forearm, showing the pattern of fine golden hair against the dark skin. She shook her head. "It's like nightmares when you're a kid. I think that if Boone Waxwell ever . . . got me, I might walk around afterwards and look just the same, but my heart would be dead as a stone forever. Oh, I guess I'd make nifty bait all right. He did everything but paw the ground Sunday night."

"The point is to make him think you have gone to a place where he can get at you. A far place, that'll take him a long time to get to. And a long time to get back when he finds it was a trick, and when he gets back, both of you will be gone. But you can't let your husband in on it. Because in his present condition, Waxwell can spread him open like a road map. We have to make Crane believe you *have* gone to a specific place, and somehow give Waxwell the idea of prying it out of him."

"Then you can get the money, while he's gone off after me."

"I had the idea you'd be just this quick and bright, Vivian."

"The money . . . Crane helped steal?"

"A good part of it."

"But then it's still stolen money, isn't it?"

"Not when, this time, you get it with the blessing of the man they took it from."

"The man you're working for?"

"In a sense. Arthur Wilkinson. And I think he should tell you in person that he approves the arrangement. You think of how we can best set it up, this decoy operation. Maybe Arthur and I can meet you tonight?"

"I could have some specific plan by then, I think, Travis. You could come to the house at eleven."

"What about your husband?"

"The big suspense in my life every evening is whether he'll pass out in his big leather chair or totter to bed first. I try to cut down the intake. I make his drinks, on demand. It is a delicate problem. If I make them too weak, he comes blundering out into the kitchen and snarls at me and puts another big slug in the glass. He stares at television and doesn't see a thing or remember a thing. It's no problem, really. Tonight I'll make them strong, and frequent. And by eleven you could march a fife and drum corps through without him missing a snore. When he passes out, I'll put the light on over the front door." She took a very deep breath, let it out in a sigh. "Maybe it *can* work. Maybe people can go back and start the race a second time."

Back aboard the *Flush* I was in time for lunch only because Chook had delayed it until there was an improved chance of Arthur keeping it down. He was wan and humble, reeking of guilt, his eyes sliding away from any direct glance.

"All these empty boats around us," he said. "I don't know. I kept hearing things. A little creak or a thump, after it got dark. Each time I *knew* he was sneaking aboard. And I knew what he has to do, Trav. He has to get rid of every-

body who can link him with Wilma. And I *saw* her there.
I went back and forth in the lounge in the dark, with the
loaded gun, and I'd peer out the windows and see things,
see some shadow duck across an open space over there,
coming closer. I felt I could empty the gun right into him
and he'd come right on at me, laughing. He certainly found
out the name and description of this boat, and I just *knew*
he'd hunted until he'd found it. Then I thought a drink
would give me some confidence. And one didn't. But the
second one worked so good, I thought three would be even
better. Hell, I can't even remember what I *did* with the gun.
We hunted all over. Chook found it. In a corner up against
a locker. I must have dropped it and kicked it. I'm a lot of
help to everybody."

Chook stepped from the galley to the dining booth and
glowered down at him. She wore pale blue stretch pants
that rode low on her hips, and a red bikini top so narrow
that only a perfect adjustment, which she attained but seldom, kept the umber nipple areas entirely covered. Half-
leaning over the booth in that cramped area, in the glow
of sun off the water shining through the ports, it seemed
an almost overpowering amount of bare girl.

"Why don't you go sit in the garden and eat worms,
lover?" she demanded. "Your self-pity rends my girlish heart.
You got drunk, a condition so rare you can find it only in
medical books. God's *sake*, Arthur!"

"I got terrified."

"That man beat you within an inch of your life, with
Wilma watching it and enjoying it, and if that railing hadn't
broken, maybe he would have killed you. Do you think a
thing like that shouldn't leave a mark?" She hissed with
exasperation. "Since when is it a sin to be scared? Am I
going to move out of your bed because you can get fright-
ened? Are people going to spit on you on the street? Drop
this *boy scout* bit. Every day in every way, nine out of
ten people in this big fat world are scared pissless. You
have some obligation to be different? Even the mighty Mc-
Gee isn't immune, believe me. God's *sake*, Arthur!"

She strode back into the galley area, made a vicious banging of copper pots.

"Wow," Arthur said in a low tone of awe.

"She's right," I said. "And tonight you get another chance
to get a little jumpy, Arthur. You and I are going calling."

His throat slid up and down in a large dry swallow. He

put his shoulders back. "Fine!" he said heartily. "Just fine! Looking forward to it."

Chook appeared with a big scarred pewter plate for each of us, banged them down. "Huevos rancheros," she said. "There's enough chili in those eggs, lover, and enough heat in that sausage to give your stomach something brand new to think about." She brought her own plate and slid in beside him. "Ours are merely hot, my lamb. Yours is volcanic. And choke it down or you'll wear it like a hat. It's an old home remedy for the squeams."

Arthur made it. It was a noble effort. It gave him tears, the snuffles and the sweats, and frequent glares of astonished agony before snatching at the soothing blandness of buttered bread.

"You briefed him?" I asked her when we'd finished.

"On the whole thing, at least when he wasn't clattering off to go whoops."

"Cut it out, Chookie!" Arthur said firmly. "Enough is enough. Let's drop it for good." He stared her in the eye.

Suddenly she grinned, nodded, patted his arm. "Welcome back to the human race."

"Glad to be aboard," he said politely.

"Wilma's background too?" I asked.

"It's so strange," Arthur said. "I never knew her at all, did I? I realized something odd today. I can see her very vividly, the way she stood and sat and walked. But in every memory, she's turned away from me. I can't bring her face back at all. I can remember the color of her eyes, but I can't see them. So now somebody I never knew is dead. And . . . she was married to somebody I didn't know very well. I see two strangers living in that beach house. Does that make any sense?"

"It does to me," Chook said. "Trav, please, what happens tonight? Until you're both back safe, I'll be half out of my mind. Please tell me."

THIRTEEN

IT WAS VERY CLOSE to eleven when I turned the dark green sedan onto Clematis Drive. The other houses were dark. There were more vacant lots than houses. As I approached the Watts home I saw that the light over the front door was not on. And so I touched the gas pedal again and started by, saying to Arthur, "I guess lawyer boy is still semi-conscious."

Quite a few lights were on in the house. And just as I passed it, I saw, in the darkness of the side lawn beyond the carport, something that made me give a little sound of surprise.

"What's the matter?" Arthur said in a strained voice.

"Good ol Boo's white Lincoln tucked nearly out of sight at the side there. Top down. See it?"

"Yes, I see it. My God. We better go back, don't you think?"

I did not answer him. I turned left onto the next street, and after the first few houses, there was nothing but the emptiness of development land, where asphalt turned into damp dirt with deep ruts. I backed and filled and got the car turned around, and on the last swing I turned the lights off, proceeded slowly by faint watery moonlight. I bumped it up over curbing and tucked it into the shadows of a clump of cabbage palm. In the silence a slight wind rattled the fronds, making a rain sound.

"What are you going to do?" he asked. There was a tremor in his voice.

"Take a look. Both the Watts' cars are there. I'll cut across and come out behind the house. That's it, over there. The lighted one. You wait for me right here."

"And what if you g-get into trouble, Trav?"

"I'll either come back on the double, or I won't. Then, if I don't, if you think you can handle it, get as close as you can and see what you can see. Don't take any chances. Use your judgment. Here." I took the pistol out of my jacket pocket and shoved it into his hands. Morale builder. I had to turn my frail reed into something stauncher, just in case. Even at the expense of making me feel naked.

"I don't like this," he said. He was not alone in that appraisal.

"If it turns very very sour, go and get Chook and get out of the area fast. Use this car and drive all night, right up to Tallahassee. In the morning get hold of a man in the State Attorney General's office. Remember this name. Vokeler. Truman Vokeler." He repeated it after me. "Don't talk to anyone else. If he's away, demand he be sent for. And you and Chook level with him. Everything. He'll take it from there. Trust him."

"Why don't we just . . ."

I got out of the car and closed the door. I walked fifty feet into the field, stopped and waited until I had enough night vision to pick up the contour of the ground, and keep from falling over palmetto and small bushes. I kept the vision by not looking directly at the house lights. Brush was thick beyond their rear property line and I moved toward a gap and came upon a woven cedar fence, low enough to step over. Once in the back yard, I stopped in the shadows, examining the house, refreshing my memory of the layout. Kitchen windows were lighted. Light from the living room shone out into the cage, on plantings and shadowy terrace furniture. I could hear no sound. There was an odd flickering light which puzzled me. After moving a little way to the side, I could see through the cage and into the living room. Crane Watts was slumped in a big green leather wing chair, legs sprawled on a hassock, head toppled to the side. I could detect no sound or movement in any part of the house, nor see any other person.

I moved around toward the carport side, crouched and ran to the side of the convertible, waited there, resting on one knee, listening. I came up cautiously and looked into the empty car, then leaned and felt cautiously. The keys weren't in it. I went to the rear, crouched and felt the nearest tail pipe. There was just a slight residual heat. Recalling how he drove it, I could guess it had been there some time. I moved close to the house and around the corner and along the front of it, ready to flatten myself among the unkempt plantings should a car come down the street. The awning windows across the front of the living room were almost wide open. I crouched below them, raised cautiously. I saw Crane Watts from another angle. All I could see of him was the sprawl of legs on the hassock, one hand dangling. The chair faced the television set. It accounted for the flickering light. The sound was completely off. A handsome Negro girl was singing. The camera had moved in for a closeup, the white teeth, tremolo of tongue, effortful throat, vast enunciations of the lips. All in a total silence, total until I heard a faint buzzing snore from the man in the green chair, and another.

I ducked down and continued across the front to the far corner. As I went around the corner I saw the long shadow I cast, and knew that I was outlined against the single streetlight on the other side of Clematis Drive, and knew it would be a Very Good Thing to get back where I had been. Out of darkness ahead came a sound. THOP. And with it a whisper of air movement touching the right side of my throat, and immediately thereafter the workmanlike chud of lead into a palm trunk a hundred yards behind me.

They would say, when Whitey Ford made that incredible motion to nip the base runner off first, that the man was caught leaning. The man was leaning one way, and realized what was happening, and yearned to go the other way, but he had to overcome the inertia of himself before he could move back. I was off balance. I yearned for the safety I had left. Either it was a cheap silencer he was using, or a home-made one, or a good one used too many times. Good ones go THUFF. Not THOP. I did not review all my past life in a micro-second. I was too busy changing balance and direction, and thinking, How stupid, how idiotic, how . . . Arthur-like. I did not hear the next THOP. I heard only the monstrous tearing blast as the slug tore the whole top left side of my head off with such finality, the world ended in whiteness without even any residual sense of falling.

. . . my head was in a fish bag, in a fetid closure of stink, laced with engine oil. My hand was way off, around a corner, down another street, utterly indifferent to the master's demands. So if you won't come, I told it, wiggle a finger. It wiggled a finger. No problem, boss. Try the other hand. The right hand. The good one. But that is im-possible, en-tirely. Cleaved I am, from crown to crotch, the right half discarded, wound fitted with plexiglass so they can see all the moving parts in there, all the little visceral pumps and pulses.

The rebel hand floated up and came drifting, unseen, all the way back, caught upon something, pushed, and the fish bag was gone and I lay in a black fresh wash of air, made one little hitch, another, looked at two moons riding, two half moons absolutely identical. Well now. That *is* unusual. Each star had a twin, both in the same relationship as were the twin moons. I struggled with some massive concept of duality, something which, could I but grasp it and put it into coherency would alter the whole future of mankind. But some nagging little temporal worry kept trying to intrude. A graveyard slab was over me, tilting. Actually two of them, one merging into the other. I stared and the slab became two white leathery backs of a front seat, merged in the same way, and by painful deduction I established that I was on the rear floor of a car. And suddenly it was Boone Waxwell's car, and I was dead. Caught leaning. I got my hand up there to find out how I died. It felt very bad up there, and very tall. All caked and torn meat. Stickiness and miscellany which could not be me. I tried to find the other half of myself. The hand, more docile and obedient, went a searching. It found dull dead meat, and I thought someone was tucked in there with me. But when I prodded it and squeezed it, there was some deep and muffled tenderness announcing itself as my right arm. My efforts brought the edge of the stinking tarp flapping down over my face once more, and I pushed it down and away. Dead was one thing. Becoming crab food was a further unpleasantness. The fellow was certainly casual about it. Kill me, dump me in his car, throw a tarp over me, take care of the body when he found the time. But if the body happened to be gone. . . .

Reaching up, I found the release on the rear door. It clicked and I shoved with my good leg. I slid over the sill a little, forcing the door open. I pushed again and again until my shoulders were over the sill, but my head hung down. I got the good hand under the back of my head, pulled it up, shoved again, and I slid out until my shoulders were on turf, hips still up on the sill. Two more shoves and my hips fell onto the ground. Then I could push against the outside of the car with the good leg. The dead leg followed me out. Rolling over was a major feat, requiring careful planning, proper shifting of dead parts into positions where leverage would work. Twice I got up to the balance point and the third time I flopped over.

Rested, then with the help of my hand, got my head up to take a look. Two of everything. Far things were doubled. Close things were two things merged, blurred into each other. Blinking did no good. I was between his convertible and the side of the carport. I had begun to wonder if I might not be entirely dead. The raw scrubby land out back would be . . . *that* way. Worry about the fence when I got to it. If I got to it. Go that way. Get to back corner of carport, turn left. Go along back wall of carport and house. Come to cage. Turn right. Go along edge of cage and then straight out across yard.

In a little while I found the only possible method of locomotion. Roll onto the dead side, stay propped up by pressure of left hand against ground. Bring left knee up as far as I could get it. Use leg as brace and reach as far ahead as possible with left hand. Dig fingers into soil. Then pull with hand, and push with edge of left shoe, and slide on the dead side. Not quite as dead. It had begun to tingle in a

148

very unpleasant way. Pins and needles. But it wouldn't respond to command. I estimated that five or six good efforts took me my own length. I awarded myself a brief rest at the end of each McGee-length. Four rests brought me to the carport corner. Four more rests and I seemed to be halfway to the cage. It seemed to me that a long time had passed since he had shot me in the head. There seemed to be only one light in the house. I felt I was rustling the half-dead leaves of the plantings too loudly. At least I was in moon-shade on the back side of the house.

I stopped for an earned rest, face down in moist grass. I was ordering a dead-hand finger to wiggle when, directly over me, in a voice that was half a hard resonance and half a husky whisper, with a dreadful, intimate jocularity, Boone Waxwell said, "Gone play dead now, hey?"

I waited to feel the cool fat end of that silencer against the nape of my neck.

"You answer ol Boo now, hear?" he said in that same wheedling, jolly imitation of affection. "Gone play dead? Little ol country club pussycat gone try that little game that didn work the other times neither?"

And suddenly it was all clarified by the thin, faint, weary sound of Vivian's voice. I could not hear the words. It was utter hopelessness. I turned my head slowly and looked up at the side of the house. Even with the irritating double vision I could see what the situation was. Sliding glass bedroom doors were open. The screening was not eighteen inches from my face, and the terrazzo floor level perhaps eight inches above ground level. In a faint illumination through a half-open door to the hallway, I could see the bottom corner of a bed, possibly twelve inches from the other side of the screen.

My impulse was to scramble away like a crippled bug before he looked out and saw me. Realization of the situation was like smelling salts, pushing the mists out of my mind, bringing me from stubborn dreamy labor of escape up to a vividness of alarm, awareness of life. At the edge of panic I heard, distinctly, a rustle, slow shift of weight, sigh, whispery sound of flesh stroked. And if I could hear them so distinctly, it was only wild luck he had not heard my labored squirming.

"Now why'd I want to go away, pretty pussycat?" he asked in mock astonishment. "What for I'd do that when we ain't even half finished off?"

Again her begging, toneless plaint, her tired whining.

"Pore little dead pussycat, thinks she's all wore down. Ol Boo, he knows better. Such a sweet piece you are now. And you do so fine, so real fine."

I heard an aimless shifting, rustling, small thud of elbow against wall or headboard, a sudden huff of exhalation, a silence. Then he said, in the voice people use to play games with small children. "What's this! And this here? How in the worl' can this be a-happenin to a pore dead pussycat? It beats all!"

There was a small thrashing, a silence, a whine, another silence.

In a voice suddenly tightened and gritty with effort, he said, "Now how this for you?"

There was a scampering rustle, a loud whimper, a restraining clap of hand onto flesh. And a silence longer than before.

"AAAAAAA," she said. And again. "AAAAAAA." It was not a sound of pain or of pleasure, of fright, of want, or of denial. It was simply the sound of sensation, purified, dehumanized, so vivid that I could visualize her head thrown back, eyes wide blind staring, mouth wide and crooked.

And the random and meaningless sounds of motion began a cyclic repetition, steadying into a slow heavy beat.

Across that beat, in a rhythmic counterpoint, she cried "OGodOGodOGod!" in a voice of that same clarity and formality and impersonality I had heard her use to call Love and Ad and Game and Let.

"Stay with it," he gasped.

And, released from my unwilling voyeurism by the sounds of them, I went hunching and scrabbling along, turning away from the house, heading out across the open yard, aching to get out of earshot of what they had built to, away from that furnace-gasping, whumpety-rumpety, plunging, wall-banging, flesh-clapping prolonged crescendo of the pre-wearied flesh, crawling and hitching, weeping inwardly sick weak tears for the plundered wife, wondering how in God's name I'd ever had the benign stupidity to formulate the jackass theory that the sounds of love could never be sickening. This was as pretty as the raw sound of a throat being cut. Or the sound of the great caged carnivore at feeding time.

The hurt on the dead side was beyond pins and needles. Though the surface felt numbed, each pressure brought a dead aching pain, as though I had been burned. I felt as if each grunt of effort was tearing the inner lining of my throat. Finally, reaching, I stubbed my outstretched fingers against the fence. I hitched closer to it, reached up and got my

150

hand around the top edge of it. I rested there, breathing hard. Distance had faded the sounds of them, losing those sounds in bug shrilling, frond clatter, mockingbirds, a dog barking two streets away. The little fence was improbably high. I had an arm ten feet long, thin as a pencil reaching up and up to take a weak grasp on the roof-edge of a building, and any idea I could hoist myself up and over was absurdly optimistic. From the mortgaged house came the finishing cry of the tennis player, a tearing hypersonic howl like a gut-shot coyote. Her eyes were a very dark blue, and with sun-coin on the tawny forearm, she had closed her eyes and shuddered at the thought of any Waxwell touch. I borrowed from her cry the energy of desperation, pulled myself up and up, hooked my chin over the bruising wood, and got just enough response from the dead arm to swing it up and over, fence edge biting into armpit. I writhed and pushed and worked, hung there with the edge across my belly, reached and found a tough curl of root, pulled, tumbled, rolled onto my back on the slight slope beyond the fence.

So die right here, McGee. Cheat the bastard out of that much. But maybe, with a light, he can follow you. Torn and flattened grass. Wetness that could mean you leave blood. Maybe it's as obvious as the sheen a snail leaves on a sidewalk. And Boo would act with the same jolly and intensely personal manner, giving death the same intimacy as assault. Now what's ol' Boo found hisself here? My, my, my.

I tried the dead arm and it came up slowly, as remote from me as those coin games where you look through glass and work the claw to pick prizes out of the bin of candy. It steadied, outlined against the double images of the stars. I put the good hand up and took hold of it. No feeling in the skin, like taking a stranger's hand. But when I squeezed it a bone ached announcing identity.

So scrabble on, this time getting a partial use of it, a slight helpful leverage of elbow. Then, when next I rested, I heard a clumsy thrashing and stumbling coming toward me. I felt more irritation than alarm. A damn fool way to go busting and blundering through the night. It came on and was going to pass me, ten feet away, and I saw it, the shape and posture of the doubled silhouette familiar.

"Arrar," I said in a voice I'd never heard before. It stopped him. There was something loose and sloppy and wrong about the right side of my mouth. I firmed it up with effort. "Arthur."

"Trav?" he said in a nervous whisper. "Is that you?"

"No. It's just one of us gophers."

He felt his way to me. "I . . . I thought you were dead."

"You . . . could be right. Gemme *outa* here!"

He couldn't carry me. It was not the kind of terrain to drag people across. We got me up, with fumbling clumsiness, dead arm across his shoulders, his left arm around my waist, dead leg dangling and thumping along between us like a sack of putty. It was damned high up there. Like standing on the edge of a roof. And he kept coming close to losing me when we'd get off balance. He would brace and heave and I would manage a little hop on the good leg. Several weeks later, we came upon the car. During the final fifty feet I had been able to swing the dead leg forward, sense the ground under it, lock the knee and lurch forward on it. He fumbled me into the passenger side of the front seat. I slumped, resting my head on the seat back. He went around and opened the door and got halfway in and stopped. The courtesy light shone down on me. I rolled my head and looked at him. The double image slowly merged into one and then separated again. Double or single, he wore a look of horror.

"My God!" he said in a thin high voice. "My God!"

"Get in and close the door. He shot me in the head." I had to speak slowly to make the right half of my mouth behave. "It isn't supposed to make it pretty."

He piled in, anxiety making him breathe hard, fumbling with the ignition, saying, "I got to get you to a doctor . . . a doctor . . ."

"Hold it. Got to think."

"But . . ."

"Hold it! How much time's gone by?"

"Since you. . . . It's quarter of two."

"Took you long enough."

"Trav, please try to understand. I . . . I went after you a long time ago, when you didn't come back. I sneaked over there, like you said. I got into the side yard, behind a tree, looking at the house. I couldn't hear anything. I didn't know what to do. And all of a sudden he came around the side of the house, in sort of a springy little trot, grunting with effort and he . . . he had you over his shoulder. He passed the light from a window. Your . . . arms and head were dangling and bouncing all loose and dead. And . . . he trotted right to the car and stopped short and gave a heave and you . . . you fell into the car, in back. He didn't open a door or anything. You made such . . . such a thud, such a dead thud. He stood there for a little while and I heard him humming to himself. He opened the trunk and got a blanket or something out of there and leaned into the car, apparently covering you up. Then he went back into the house. Lights started going out. I heard a woman sobbing like her heart was breaking. And I . . . couldn't make myself look at you. I crept away. Please understand. I got far enough to run, and ran back to the car, and started up to Palm City to get Chookie like you said. I went very fast, and then I went slower and slower. I pulled off the road. I wanted to come back. I tried. I couldn't. Then I went all the way to the marina, but I stopped outside the gates. I'd have to tell her what happened. I'd say it was the only thing I could have done. But it wasn't. She'd know that. I couldn't face her. I couldn't come back. I wanted to just run away. I turned around and came back, and it took me a long time to make myself get out of the car and . . . come looking for you. The only way I could do it was telling myself he was gone, he'd driven away with you. Trav . . . is he gone?"

"He's still there."

"How did you . . . get to where I found you?"

"I crawled. Arthur, you came back. Hang onto that. It can be worth something to you. You came back."

"Why is he still there?"

"I . . . I guess it's the hospitality. Shut up. I'm trying to think."

"But maybe . . . we're waiting too long," he said. "I should put you in the hospital and call the police."

"You have a very conventional approach. But shut up."

When I had it worked out, I had him drive east on the Trail into the empty night land of cypress, billboards and roadside drainage ditches. With no traffic from either direction, I got the automatic pistol. I had to keep my right hand folded around it with my left hand, and give the trigger finger a little help. I emptied it into the wilderness. On the way back to the hospital, I coached him carefully.

He parked near the emergency entrance. He helped me walk in. Double vision had become infrequent. The life in the dead arm and leg felt closer to the surface. Now they felt as if I had a thick leather glove on the arm, fitting firmly to the armpit, and a similar stocking on the leg. It was a trim little hospital, and they were doing a big business. The staff was trotting around. Fresh blood dappled white nylon. Doctors and relatives were arriving. Somebody in the treatment room kept screaming until suddenly it stopped, too suddenly. A woman sat weeping in a chair in the corridor next to the check-in desk, a red-eyed man clumsily patting her shoulder. Arthur made ineffectual attempts to attract attention. I got a few absent glances from staff people until finally a harried burly nurse hastened by me, skidded to a stop, came back and stared at me, lips compressed with concern. She got me over to a chair, down to a level where she could look at my head.

"Gunshot," she said.

"Yes indeed," I said.

"It's all we need," she said. She grabbed an orderly, told him to get me bedded down in Trauma Room C right away. I was there five minutes with Arthur standing by before a young, squat, redheaded doctor came swiftly in, followed by a tall, narrow, pock-marked nurse. He pulled the light down, hunched himself over my head. His fingers felt like busy mice, wearing cleats.

"How long ago?" he asked Arthur.

"Three hours, approximately," I said. He seemed a little startled to get the answer from me.

"How do you feel right now?" he asked me.

"Shot."

"We're not in the mood for smartass remarks around here tonight. Seven local young people were in a car that didn't make a curve north of here about three quarters of an hour ago. We lost one on the way in, another here, and we're trying like hell to keep from losing two more. We'll appreciate cooperation."

"Sorry. I feel mentally alert, doctor. I'm not in pain. When I first regained consciousness, I had double vision, and no feeling or control in the whole right side of my body. The symptoms have been diminishing steadily, but my right side feels . . . leaden, as if every muscle had been strained."

"Why has it been so long, and how did you get so messed up?"

"I was alone. I had to crawl to where I'd be noticed."

"Who shot you?"

"I did. It was an accident. A very stupid accident. That gentleman has the gun."

"Outside the city?"

"Yes."

"We'll get a deputy over to make out a report. It's required."

He turned the overhead light out, shone a pencil beam into each eye, taking his time. The nurse took pulse and blood pressure, and I gave my name and address. Redhead went

154

out and came back with an older doctor. He looked me over, and they went over into the corner and I heard some of the words they feed Ben Casey. One is practically a television cliche. Subdural hematoma.

The older doctor left. Redhead came back and said, "You seem to have your luck with you, Mr. McGee. The slug hit right at the hairline at such an angle it grooved the skull but didn't penetrate, traveled about a full inch under the scalp, and then, probably tumbling after impact, tore free. A sharp blow on the so-called funnybone can numb the hand. The left hemisphere of the brain controls the motor nerves and sensory nerves of the right half of the body. We feel that a shock of that severity could well have stunned and deadened the synapses on that side, the nerve functions, the ability to originate and transmit orders to the right side of your body. Sensation and control are returning so rapidly, we feel you should be back to normal feeling and use in a day or so. I see no clinical evidence of concussion, but there could be a rupture of small blood vessels in the impact area, and slow bleeding. So we'll keep you here a few days for observation. Now the nurse will clean the wound and prep you for a little stitching." He got a hypo, held it up to the light. "This is just to deaden the area to save you discomfort."

He pricked me twice in the scalp and once in the left temple area and went away. The nurse tested, and when I could not feel her touch, she cleaned and shaved the area. She went and summoned the redhead. I could hear, inside my head, the sound as he pulled the stitches through. When he drew them tight, I could feel the pull in my left cheek and temple. When the cleaning had started, Arthur had gone into the hall. Not until the antiseptic dressing was in place did he come back in, looking queasy.

Then they rolled me down the corridor to what seemed to be a combination treatment room and storage room. Bright lights were on. The deputy got up when I was wheeled in. He was elderly, florid, heavy and asthmatic, and he licked his indelible pencil after every few words he wrote on the form in his clipboard. I swung my legs over the side of the wheeled stretcher and sat up. There was a mild wave of dizziness, a momentary recurrence of double vision, and that was all. He put the clipboard on the foot of the stretcher and hunched over it.

"Got the name off the records. Let's see identification, McGee." He took my driver's license and copied the number on his form. For local address, I gave him the name and registration number of my houseboat and told him where it was docked.

"Scalp wound, self inflicted," he said.

"Accidentally self inflicted, Deputy."

"Weapon?"

Arthur handed it over. He took it with the familiarity of the expert, pulled the slide back and locked it back, checked chamber and clip, sniffed the muzzle, then pushed the clip ejector. It doesn't work. I've been meaning to have a gunsmith fix it. You have to pry it before it comes loose.

He fiddled with it and said, "Jammed in there."

"That's how come I got shot, Deputy."

"You carry this around on your person?"

"No sir. I'd have to have a permit to do that. I keep it in the car or on the boat. What happened, I had it in the car, and I wanted to get that clip out. I thought it would be safer to empty it first. So I drove off the Trail down a little road, away from any houses, and fired it until it seemed empty. I didn't count the shots. Then, let me take it a minute, I sat down on the door sill of the car where I could see by the dome light what I was doing. Like a damn fool I held it this way to get the slide back. My hand was sweaty, and I guess there was a misfire on the last one in the chamber. But it fired when it got a second chance. Next thing I knew, I woke up on the ground beside the car. When I felt able, I decided the best thing to do was try to crawl back to the main highway. It numbed my whole right side. But that's going away now. You see, Deputy, my friend here was making a long distance call from a roadside phone booth. He was having trouble getting it through. I got bored. I thought I'd just get off the highway, empty the pistol and get the clip out of it. It had been on my mind. I told him I'd be back in a few minutes. When I didn't come back, he thought I'd gone down a side road and got stuck in the mud. He looked and looked, after he got through phoning. I guess it was the third road where he found me, almost all the way back out to the highway."

"Third road," Arthur said. "So I walked in and got the car and brought him right here. I thought he was dying."

"He don't look dead. But them kids out there do." He bounced the pistol on his broad tough hand, handed it to Arthur and said, "See he gets it fixed, mister." He left.

I slid off the stretcher. Arthur started toward me to help me and I waved him back. In cautious balance I plodded slowly around the little room. I had to pivot and swing my

156

hip to get that leaden leg forward, but with the knee locked it took my weight.

My light-weight jacket was a ruin, dirt, rips and grass stain, slacks not quite as bad, but bad enough. I balanced and took the jacket off, checked the pockets, tossed it to Arthur and pointed to a porcelain can with a lid worked by a foot pedal. He balled it up and stuffed it in. A blank doorway led, as I hoped, into a little wash room. With the dull clumsy help of the reluctant right hand and arm, I got the mud off my face and hands, the dark scabs of dried blood on the left side and the back of my neck. I used a damp towel to scrub down the right side of the slacks, the side I had dragged. I studied myself in the mirror. I didn't look like a disaster case. I looked as if I had been rolled in a waterfront alley. The dressing was too conspicuous.

"They'll clean you up when they put you to bed."

"Hat," I said. "Go right when you go out this door and find another way out of here. I tossed the hat on the shelf behind the back seat of the car. And get back to me with it the same way you get out. And fast."

"Listen, I won't do it! You *can't* leave. It's dangerous!"

"So are home-canned vegetables. Get the hat."

I sat on a white stool and waited. Merry McGee, the valiant quipster, with a hole in his head and the horrid conviction it *was* bleeding in there. My precious, valuable, irreplaceable head. Under the bullet groove would be some little white needles of splintered bone, sticking down into the gray jelly where everything was stored, all those memories unique to me.

A fat nurse opened the door and said, "Mr. McGee? Come along."

"I was told to wait here until they check something out."

"Tests can be taken in the ward, sir."

"Something about radiology."

She frowned. "Seems odd. I better go find out what's up."

She bustled away. When I saw Arthur in the doorway, I heaved myself up and got out of there in my curious hitching gait, putting the baseball cap on as I went down the hall. I did my very best walking as we passed a woman at a desk near the main entrance. I waited in shadow by the curb, leaning against a tree. Arthur brought the car around, something he should have thought to do when he got the hat. I didn't remark on it. He was managing better than I could have hoped.

"Clematis Drive," I said as he got behind the wheel.

"But how can you . . ."

"Arthur, my friend, you will be orderly and agreeable and stop twitching. I want you near me. I want you to stay near me. Because I am highly nervous. And if I stop making sense, or my speech goes bad, or my leg and arm get worse again, you hurry me back there so they can saw a little round hole in my head. Otherwise, just take on trust the strange idea I might know what I'm doing, because I'm too pooped to argue. Just drive. And pray my hunch is wrong. What time is it?"

"Five something. Chook will be . . ."

"She'll sweat it out."

As we turned onto Clematis, I looked over and saw the first paleness in the east. The dark trees and houses had begun to acquire third dimensions as the first candlepower of Wednesday touched them. The Watts' house was lighted up again, almost completely. The big white convertible was gone.

"Turn into the drive . . . No, keep going, and put it in the driveway of the next house. Hurricane shutters are on. It's empty for the summer. Turn out the lights before you turn in."

As we started back down the sidewalk, I said, "If anything comes, car or bike or pedestrian, either way, help me hustle into the brush and flatten out."

"Okay, Trav. Sure."

Nothing came. We went around the side of the house. Waxwell had taken off with typical flair, wheels digging deep gouges in the soft lawn.

I tried the outside screen door of the cage. It was latched on the inside. As I wondered whether it was worth trying to call her I smelled, adrift in the predawn stillness, a faint stench of fecal matter. I turned to Arthur and said, "When we're in the house, don't touch a thing unless I tell you. Stay away from the windows in the front of the house. Squat low if you hear a car."

Bracing myself against the frame, I put a knee through the screen, ripping it. I reached through, unlatched it, and, when we were inside, smeared the metal handle where I had touched it, with the palm of my hand. The odor was stronger in the living room. The television set emitted a constant cold light, the random snow pattern after broadcasting is over. The odor was much stronger. Crane Watts had slid down between chair and hassock, half sitting, head canted back on the chair seat. His face was unnaturally fat, his eyes bugging wide, pushed out by pressure behind them.

It was a moment or two before I found the point of entry, the charred ear hole. And I knew. I knew exactly what else I would find in the silence of that house. The husband had slept through too much. Too many empty evenings slack in the chair, while the wife's heart grew more hopeless. But when Boo came in, came at her, she would have cried out to the husband. Many times, perhaps, before she knew it was too late, and he was too far gone and would sleep through every endless lift and stroke, every new and demanding invasion, every cuff and slap, every jolly instruction, every rough boosting and shifting of her into new postures for his pleasure. So, having slept, husband, sleep longer yet. Forever. I wondered if she remembered who had said a nonsense thing about a pistol barrel in the ear. And, accustomed only to the antiseptic violence of television and the movies, I imagined that the sudden ugliness had shocked her. After such a small tug at the trigger. The huge terminal spasm had flounced him off the chair, opened his bowels. And hydrostatic pressure had bloated his face to an unrecognizable idiocy. I even knew what she would instinctively cry at such ghastliness. "I'm sorry! I'm sorry!" It would end her auto-hypnosis, the trance state of the amateur murderer, and leave her no choice at all but to do what I knew I would find.

I heard the dry gagging behind me and saw Arthur with his back to the body, hunched over, hands to his mouth. I bumped him away, saying, "Stop it! Not in here, you damn fool!"

With a struggle he gained control. I sent him to wait out in the screened cage. I hobbled into the kitchen and, with my thumb nail, turned the lights off. It's what they so often do in the night. Maybe some forlorn fading desire to keep the darkness back. But if they could turn on all the lights in the world, it wouldn't help them. I knew where I'd most probably find her. She was in the empty tub, and had slid almost flat, head over on her shoulder. She wore a floor-length orange housecoat, with white collar and cuffs, buttoned neatly and completely from throat to hem. It had been a good vibrant color for her swarthy handsomeness. She had fixed her hair, made up her mouth. The dark stain between her breasts, and slightly to the left was teacup size, irregular, with one small area of wet sheen remaining. I bent and put the back of my hand against her calm forehead, but there was no warmth. The weapon, a 22 caliber Colt Woodsman with a long target barrel lay against her belly, the butt under her right wrist. She was barefoot. Though she had fixed herself up for dying, there were marks she could not conceal, swollen lips, blue bruise on the cheek, long scratch on the throat—marks of that long hard use.

I sat on the edge of the tub. Dishonor before death. And more effective with that popgun than she would ever know. Two shots, even with the barrel against the target, seldom kill two people. Her death was not as messy as her husband's. Heart wounds give a tidier result. To prove a guess, I went to the shower stall. The soap was moist. There were water droplets on the shower walls. A big damp yellow towel had been put neatly on a rack. So, after she had heard Boone Waxwell drive off, she had dragged herself out of bed and plodded in and taken a shower, probably just as hot as she could endure it, scrubbing herself mercilessly. Dry off. Go take the pretty housecoat from the closet and put it on. Sit at your dressing table, and fix your hair and your bruised mouth. The mind is numb. Get up and walk through the house, room to room, turning on the lights. Stop and look at the snoring husband. Breadwinner, mate, protector. Pace some more. Reach deep for the rationalizations. Women have been raped before. It hasn't killed them. There is a legal answer. Let the police handle it. Turn him in.

"Now let me get this straight, Mrs. Watts. Waxwell was there from ten something last night until two or three this morning? And you claim that during that time you were repeatedly raped, during that whole time your husband was sound asleep in front of the television set? And Waxwell was a client of your husband? And you had met him before? And he left his car parked at your house, a very conspicuous car, all that time?"

So she paces and tries to think clearly, and she knows that if she does nothing, Waxwell will be back. Next week or next month, he will be back, again and again, as he promised he would.

And that brings her to the thing she has been trying so desperately to force out of her mind. Had he taken her quickly, she could have merely endured him, been a helpless vessel for him. But he was so damned sly and knowing, so crafty and so patient that each time, even the last time, he had awakened the traitor body so that while the soul watched, the body gasped and strained to hungry climax, to dirty joy, grasping powerfully.

So she would pace and stop to look at the husband who

160

had let that hunger in her grow so big she could betray herself. And then . . .

I found the note on her dressing table. Her personal stationery, monogrammed. A downhill scrawl with an eye-shadow pencil. "God forgive me. There is no other choice left. My darling was asleep and felt nothing. Sincerely, Vivian Harney Watts."

On the other side of the room, beyond the plundered bed, the lowest drawer of his chest of drawers was open. Cartridges a-spill from a red and green cardboard box. Extra clip. Little kit with gun oil and collapsible cleaning rod. The shells were medium longs, hollow-point. So, with luck, the one she used on herself might not have gone through her to chip or stain the tub. I went back in and cupped the nape of her neck and pulled her up far enough to see. The back of the orange housecoat was unmarked. I made my gimpy hitching way out to the screened cage.

"She's dead too. I have some things to do. I'll try to make it fast."

"D-Do you need help?"

I told him no. I went back and looked for signs of Waxwell. He would not go without leaving some trace. Like a dog, he would mark the boundaries of the new area he had claimed. But I found nothing, decided I needed nothing. First, on a table by the bedroom door, I made a little pile of things to take away. The note, the gun, the other things from the drawer that belonged with the gun. By the time I had gotten her half out of the tub, I wished I could depend on Arthur to help me with this sort of grisly problem. She was a very solid woman. She had not begun to stiffen. Death gave her a more ponderous weight. Finally I was on my feet with her in my arms. Her dead forehead lolled over to rest against the side of my chin. Carefully bracing the bad leg, and willing the bad arm to carry its share, I hobbled into the bedroom with her. I put her on the bed. Out across the back yard the morning was a pearl pale shade of gray. I closed the draperies. She was on her back on the bed. I grasped the hem of the housecoat and with one hard wrench tore it open to the waist. Fabric ripped, and the small white buttons rattled off the walls and ceiling. I tucked the bottom of the housecoat up under her, pulled it up around her waist. She lay in dead abandon. On the white of her hips and upper thighs were the myriad blue bruises left by Waxwell's strong fingers. Begging silent forgiveness, I thoroughly tousled the black hair and, with my thumb, smeared the fresh lipstick on her dead mouth. She had gotten all prettied up to die. In the bedroom lights I could see little segments of dark blue iris where the lids were not quite closed. Sorry I ruined the housecoat. Sorry they'll see you like this, Vivian. But you'll like the way it works out. I promise you, honey. They'll pretty you up again for burying. But not in orange. That's a color to be alive in. To be in love in. To smile in. They won't bury you in it.

I tipped the dressing table bench over. Using a tissue, I picked up a jar of face cream and cracked the dressing table mirror. I turned the other lights out, left just one of the twin lamps on the dressing table on, and shoved the shade crooked so that it shone toward her, making highlights and deep shadows on the tumble of dead woman.

I crammed the stuff from the table into my pockets. I left one light on in the living room, a corner lamp with an opaque shade. Day was beginning to weaken the lights. With my thumbnail I turned the sound control on the television until the hiss of non-broadcast was loud. We left. I saw no one on the way to the car, or when Arthur drove us back up Clematis Drive.

"What did you do?" he asked.

"She didn't live long enough to have her chance to decoy him off his place. I've given her a chance to do it dead."

On the north edge of town, up the trail, I had him pull over and park near a phone booth near the curbing, at a gas station showing only a night light. I had one dime in change. Just enough.

The sergeant answered by giving his name.

I pitched my voice lower than usual. "Look, you want to do me a favor, you write down a license number, okay?"

"Give me your name, please."

"I shoulda phoned you hours ago. Look, I can't sleep. Maybe it's nothing. But the thing is, I don't want to get mixed up in anything. I don't want to get involved, see?"

"If you'd tell me where you're calling from."

"Knock it off, Sergeant. Write down the number, hey?"

"All right. License number what?"

I gave it to him and said, "A white Lincoln convertible with the top down, this year's maybe. The other two cars, I figure they *belong* there, see?"

"Belong where?"

"At this house I'm telling you about. The Lincoln was on the lawn over to the side. Listen, I'm just passing through and I don't want to get involved in anything. When I get a little buzz on, I got to walk to clear my head, okay? So I went over and found some damn back street. I looked at the street sign later. Clematis Street, or Drive, I think. Yeah, it was Drive. I parked and started walking. You know, you walk around a couple of blocks, you feel better in the morning. Right?"

"Mister, will you get to it?"

"What do you think I'm doing? It was hours ago. Maybe around three sometime. I didn't check close. Okay from this house comes this sound of a broad screaming. Honest to God, my blood runs cold. I'm right in front of the house. Then I hear a kind of sharp crack, not like a shot but sort of like a shot, and the scream stopped like her throat got cut. Maybe the crack was her old man giving it to her across the chops. What I did, I turned around and headed back to my car, and I made a mental note of the license number. You can tell the house because of the other two cars, one is a little light color Mercedes and the other is a tan Plymouth. Tan or gray. So maybe you should check it, I don't know. I just got a feeling about it somehow."

"And can you give me your name?"

"John Doe, Joe Citizen. Jesus, Sergeant, I just don't want to get mixed up in anything. I don't know the house number. I couldn't see it. But it's not what you'd call a mile long, that street."

I hung up and got back into the sedan.

"Now can we go back?"

"Yes. Keep the speed down."

FOURTEEN

CHOOK WOKE ME at twenty minutes before noon, as I had asked. She sat on the side of the bed. I hitched myself up, flexed my right hand. Arthur appeared in the doorway, stood there watching me.

"How is it now?" Arthur asked.

"Better. It just feels asleep. The leg too. The hand feels weak."

"She's been coming in every half hour at least to see if you looked all right," Arthur said.

"And you don't look so great," she said.

"I feel as if I'd been hung up by the heels and beaten with ball bats."

"Head ache?" she asked.

I fingered the dressing, lightly. "It's not an ache. It's a one inch drill bit. It makes a quarter turn every time my heart beats. How about the gun?"

"It was too rough to go outside in the dinghy," Arthur said earnestly. "I got as far as the middle of the pass and dropped it there. Okay?"

"That's just fine, Arthur."

Chook said, "I guess . . . you didn't know you were going to walk into anything so rough." I interpreted the appeal in her eyes.

"Damned glad I took you with me, Arthur. Chook, between us we managed."

"I was nearly out of my mind! Trav, I'm still scared. I mean now there's no way to prove she did it, is there?"

"Waxwell killed them both. He didn't pull the trigger. He killed them. And if his slug had hit a sixteenth of an inch lower. . . . Wish I could have seen the bastard when he looked into the back end of that car. Nothing will go wrong, Chook. They'll find enough to prove he was in the house. There's a busted screen to show how he got in. And he isn't a pillar of any community. How has the news been?"

"Like you thought, so far."

I shooed them out, got into my robe and joined them in the lounge. I found I could manage an inconspicuous gait, if I kept it slow and stately. I put the big set on AM and cut the volume when a noontime used-car commercial over the Palm City station blasted us.

Their local news announcer had the usual airedale yap and the usual difficulty with long words. "This morning state, county and other law enforcement officials are cooperating in a massive manhunt for Boone Waxwell of Goodland on Marco Island, wanted for questioning in connection with the rape murder of housewife Vivian Watts of Naples and the murder of Crane Watts, her husband, a young Naples attorney. Based on an anonymous tip from a passerby who heard screams and what could have been a shot emanating from the thirty thousand dollar home on a quiet residential street in Naples in the small hours of the morning, city police investigated at dawn and found Mr. Watts in the living room, dead of a small caliber bullet wound in the head, and Mrs. Watts in the bedroom, the scene of a violent struggle, shot

164

through the heart. The anonymous tipster gave police the tag number and description of a car he saw parked in the side yard at the time of the shot he heard, and the car has been identified as belonging to Boone Waxwell, Everglades fishing guide, who for some years has been living alone in a cottage over a mile west of the village of Goodland.

"When County police arrived at the Waxwell cottage this morning, they found the car reported as having been at the scene of the crime. Goodland residents state that Waxwell had another vehicle, an English Land Rover, as well as an inboard launch on a trailer. The truck and boat trailer are missing, and a thorough search of all waterfront areas is now under way. Goodland residents say Waxwell kept to himself and did not welcome visitors. They said he seemed to have ample funds, but could not account for how he had acquired them. Waxwell is about thirty-seven or thirty-eight years old, five foot eleven, about a hundred and ninety pounds, blue eyes, black curly hair, very powerful, and believed to be armed and dangerous. On forcing entrance to his cottage, police found quantities of arms and ammunition. He has been in difficulty before for minor acts of violence, and has successfully fled on two other occasions to avoid prosecution, returning after those who filed the charges had dropped them.

"The preliminary medical opinion, pending a more detailed examination, is that Mrs. Watts, an attractive twenty-eight year old brunette, was criminally assaulted prior to her death. Waxwell apparently gained entry by forcing a screened door which opened onto the patio in the rear of the house. Time of death is estimated for both husband and wife as occurring between two and four A.M. today. Mrs. Watts will be remembered as one of the finer amateur tennis players on the lower west coast. A close friend of the family, not identified by police as yet, hearing of the double murder, reported that on Monday Mrs. Watts had complained about her husband being annoyed by Boone Waxwell over some business matter. It is reported that Crane Watts was the attorney for a land syndicate operation in which Waxwell had a minor interest.

"Authorities, fearing that Waxwell may have gone back into the wilderness areas of the Ten Thousand Islands, plan to organize an air search using the facilities of the Coast Guard, the National Park Service and the Civil Air Patrol. It is believed that. . . . Here is a flash which has just come in. The English truck and the boat trailer have just been found pulled off into deep brush near Caxambas, adjacent to a shelving beach often used by local fisherman for the launching of trailered boats. The effort to hide the vehicle and trailer seems to indicate that Waxwell sought to conceal his avenue of escape. This station will issue further bulletins as received.

"And now to other local news. The Fort Myers Chamber of Commerce today issued a statement regarding . . ."

I snapped it off. "I wish they'd got him," Chook said.

"They will," I said. "And he won't have the money with him. He's not that much of a damn fool."

They both looked puzzled. "But it would take him only five minutes to dig it up and take it along," Arthur said.

"Think of the timing. He thought I was dead. He risked stashing me in the car while he spent three hours with the woman. My guess is he tricked or scared her into saying I was coming by at eleven. Then he tied her up or locked her up while he played games with me. If she heard those sounds, she wouldn't have recognized them as shots. He wouldn't have told her he killed me. His style would have been to tell her he'd scared me off, probably. Okay, so he found the body gone. Either I woke up and got the hell out of there, or somebody took the body away. Whoever took it away hadn't called the police. Or at least hadn't had time. I think he would want to clear out until he could figure out what was going on. If I was dead, who could prove he did it? I think he was too sure of himself with the woman to think for a moment she'd charge him with assault. In fact, she'd be more likely to swear he was never there at all. If he got back to his cottage by three o'clock, which I think is a good guess —good enough for our purposes—he would be feeling easier in his mind every minute. After all, the woman had obviously enjoyed it. The husband had slept through it. He would have checked the three o'clock radio news. All quiet. So why would he complicate his life by carting all that money around with him? If he was picked up, how would he explain it? He thought then he would be coming back to his shack. It was better off in the ground. He'd take some with him, not enough to be awkward. By first light he could be way back in Big Lostman's Bend country, setting up camp on some hammock back there. I saw the radio rig on that boat. It's a big one, including an AM band. So what does he find out when it's too late to go back for the money? Boone Waxwell is wanted for rape and murder. So we get to the money first. They'll have the area sealed and staked out. So we run a bluff. If

166

we find fresh holes in the ground I will be one very astonished McGee."

"Bluff?" Chookie said uncertainly.

"Arthur looks very reliable and respectable. And I know
he's got the nerve for it." Arthur flushed with pleasure. "So
we do a little shopping first. I mean you two do. I'll make out
the list."

There seemed to be an unusual number of cars and people
in Goodland when we drove slowly through at two thirty,
and we were stared at with open curiosity. There was an
official car parked at the entrance to the shell road that led
to Waxwell's place. Two men squatted on their heels in the
shade. One sauntered out and held up his hand to stop us.
He was a dusty little lizard-like man in bleached khakis. He
strolled back and stared in curiously. Chookie, secretarially
severe in white blouse, black skirt, horn-rimmed glasses, hair
pulled back into a bun, was driving. She rolled the window
down and said, "This is the way to the Waxwell place, is
it not?"

"But you can't go in there, lady."

Arthur rolled the rear window down. I was in the back
seat beside him. "What seems to be the trouble, officer?"

He took his time looking us over. "No trouble. You can't
go in."

"Officer, we're working on a very tight timetable. We're
advance technical staff for network television. The generator
truck and the mobile unit will be along within the hour. I'm
sure they've cleared everything. We have to mark locations,
block out camera angles and placement. I'd like to get it
done before they get here."

"The shack is sealed, mister."

"I don't have to get into the shack. That's up to the lighting
people. That's their problem. We're setting up the outdoor
shots and interviews, officer. And we'll lay some cable so
it'll be all ready for them to hook on."

Arthur was very earnest and patient. He wore my bright
blue linen jacket, white shirt, black knit tie. I yawned and
turned a little more to make doubly certain the man would
see the CBS over the breast pocket of my work shirt. Mail-
box letters from the five and ten, backed with stickum. Gold.
I hoped he had noticed the same letters on the big tool box
off the boat, resting on the floor beside my feet.

I said, "Hell, Mr. Murphy, let em sweat it when they get
here."

"I don't like your attitude, Robinson. They depend on us to do a job."

"I was told no kind of reporters at all," the dusty deputy said.

"We are *not* reporters, sir!" Arthur said indignantly. "We're technicians."

"And you don't want to git into the shack?"

"We wouldn't have time if we wanted to," Arthur said, and looked at his watch. My watch. A gift I never wear. It tells the day, month, phase of the moon, and what time it is in Tokyo and Berlin. It makes me restless to look at it.

"Well, go on ahead then, and you tell Bernie down there that Charlie says it's okay."

Bernie was on the front steps, and he came out with a shotgun in the crook of his arm. He had one of those moon faces which cannot look authoritative. And when he found out Charlie said we were okay, he was delighted to be so close to the mysterious functioning of something he watched every day of his life. Too delighted. The gold letters and the reel of cable were symbols of godhead, and his smile was pendulous and permanent. We could not sustain the myth of locating proper areas to ground the equipment with Bernie hovering over every move. Chookie took him away from the play, notebook in hand, easing him back to the porch to get his expert opinion on who would be the best people to interview, and who had known Waxwell the longest, and what other interesting places were there in the area where the mobile unit could be set up.

I'd had them pick up another length of rod, and Arthur had sharpened both of them with a file from the ship's tool supply. I picked two likely spots, and with Bernie out of sight, we each began an orderly search pattern, working out from the initial probe, an expanding checkerboard pattern, six inches between the deep slow stabs into the moist earth of the open area in the grove.

"Trav!" Arthur said after about twelve minutes. I took him a spade. It was eighteen inches down, a super kingsize special bargain glass jar that had once held Yuban powdered coffee and now held three packets of curled new bills. The jar went into the car trunk, tucked back behind the spare. I moved to the border of his area. Six feet from the first find I struck something that felt metallic at about the same depth. Prince Albert tobacco can that had once held a pound and now held three more curled packets. Put it with

168

the jar. Fill the holes. I checked my watch. We worked as fast as we could. I could not move well yet. Arthur was faster. We covered a continuously expanding area. When the total elapsed time was forty minutes, I said, "Knock it off."

"But there could be . . ."

"And there might not be. And we want to get out with what we've got. Move!"

As planned, he sank a rod deep, and I taped a cable to the exposed stub. We put the other rod down ten feet away, ran cable from it back toward the cottage, and I wired the two ends into the impressive heavy duty receptacle they had picked up in a hardware store.

We drove out. Chook, eyes on the narrow road, said, "I knew the time was running out. You didn't get anything, did you?"

"Not what we expected. Just a token. Sixty thousand."

She hauled the car back from the brink of a damp ditch. She stopped at the entrance. Arthur rolled the window down. "We're all set, thanks," he called. "We're going to go out now and check with Project Control, officer. These things change very rapidly, depending on the news breaks. At least, if they do decide to use that location, it's all set for them. I personally appreciate your cooperation."

"Glad to help out, mister."

"If there's a change of plan, don't worry about the gear we left there. It shouldn't be in anyone's way, and somebody will be through later on to pick it up."

Out on the main road off the island, heading toward the Trail, Arthur began to giggle. And it became infectious. And soon we were all roaring and howling, with, for Chook and Arthur, a potential edge of hysteria in it. Gasping, we told Arthur Wilkinson he was superb. He was big media, through and through.

"Next let's try a bank job," Chook said. And we were off again.

In the interest of avoiding any unfortunate coincidence, we turned north on 951 before we reached Naples, then west on 846 to come out at Naples Park Beach eight miles north of the city.

Once aboard the *Flush,* and with the amount verified, and the cash locked into the safe up forward, I felt the nervous tension easing in my neck and shoulders. A good man with the right tools could probably peel that box open in an hour. But once upon a time I invited a qualified expert to see if he could locate the safe without ripping out any interior trim.

After four hours of delving, rapping, tapping, measuring, he said there was no safe aboard and he damn well didn't appreciate that kind of practical joke.

At quarter after five, the three of us sat, drink in hand, in the lounge. We were trying to sustain the mood of celebration, but it was dying fast, the jokes forced, the grins too transient.

"I suppose," Arthur said, "that if you look at it one way, if what they did was legal enough, then we've stolen the money."

"Hijacked is a better word," I told him. "And if your marriage was legal, and if she's dead, then the money is her estate."

"And some of it is Stebber's."

"Which he has no interest in claiming."

"For goodness sake, Arthur," Chook said. "Don't split hairs. Trav, how does it work out for Arthur? What will he have left?"

I got pencil and paper from the desk drawer. As I wrote, I explained the figures. "Sixty thousand less about nine hundred expenses is fifty-nine, one. From that we will deduct that fifty-one hundred and fifty you borrowed from friends."

"But that isn't fair to you!" he said.

"Shut up. Half the balance of fifty-three thousand nine fifty is . . . twenty-six thousand nine seventy-five to you Arthur. Or a little bit better than a ten percent recovery on what they took you for."

"You are certainly in a lovely line of work," Chookie said with a small dash of malice.

"What's *wrong* with you, woman?" Arthur demanded with unexpected heat. "Without Travis I wouldn't have gotten dime one back. What's he supposed to do? Take a chance of getting killed for . . . for a per diem arangement?"

"I'm sorry, darling. I didn't mean it," she said, looking startled.

"And if we recovered nothing, then he'd get nothing. He'd be out what he's spent."

"I told you I'm sorry."

"That's what trips up thieves every time," I said. "They start quarreling over the split. Arthur, why don't you take your end of it, your lousy little recovery and buy a lot and build a house."

"Huh?"

"Get a construction loan. Get Chook to help on layout and decoration. Do every possible part of it you can manage

170

by yourself. Put it up and sell it and build another."

He looked at me in a startled way, and then with a growing enthusiasm. "Hey!" he said. "Hey now! You know, that might be just . . ."

"Gentlemen," Chook said, "Don't let me interrupt anyone's career, but I think I would be a very much happier girl if we got the hell out of here. The weather report was good. We can run at night, can't we? I don't want to seem frail and foolish, but I would just feel better to be . . . out of touch."

"Let's humor the lady," I said.

"To make me really happy, gentlemen, let's make it a non-stop flight all the way home."

"One stop at Marco," I said. "To tell that kid where to pick up his *Ratfink,* and give him transportation money to go get it."

"And another stop," Arthur said, "if nobody minds too much. I mean Sam and Leafy Dunning were very good to me. Too good for me to just write a letter and say everything is fine. And . . . they saw me when I was so whipped by everything . . . I'd like to have them see me . . . the way I should be. I want to see if Christine is getting along all right. And maybe see some of those men I worked with. I don't know if they'd take it, but I'd like to give the Dunnings some of that money. They need a lot of things. Maybe just a thousand dollars. And . . ."

"And what, dear?" Chook asked.

"My carpenter tools are there. I had to buy them out of my pay. I guess it isn't even forty dollars worth, but I'd like to have them. I *used* them. And they might be good luck if I . . . try to build a house."

FIFTEEN

ON THURSDAY at high noon, on the last and most beautiful day of May, we turned into the marked channel leading through the islands to Everglades City. Pavilion Key was south of us. I had checked the charts and decided we would do best staying with the official channel, entering the Barron River where it flows into Chokoloskee Bay, going a little way up the river to tie up at the big long Rod and Gun Club dock. I could have wiggled my way down Chokoloskee Bay to Chokoloskee Island, but it would have to have been high tide going and coming. And it was just as simple for Arthur to find some way to get across the causeway to Chokoloskee.

I stood at the topside controls, chugging the *Flush* along the channel between the Park islands. Down on the bow deck, Chook sat on the hatch wearing little red shorts and a sleeveless knit candy-stripe top. Arthur stood in an old threadbare pair of my khaki shorts, pointing out places to her, probably telling her of things that had happened when he had crewed for Sam Dunning on his charter boat. The slow diesel grind of the *Flush* obscured their words. I saw the animation on their faces, the shapes of laughter.

Arthur, though still too thin, was looking better. The months of labor in this area had built muscle tissue which malnourishment had reduced to stringiness. Now muscle was building smoothly again, rippling under the pink-tan hide of his back when he pointed. Chook had put him on isometrics, and I had come across him a few times, braced in a doorway like Samson trying to bring the temple down, trembling from head to foot, face contorted. It embarrassed him to be caught at it, but the results were showing—the results of that, and the limbering exercises she gave him, and the huge calorie intake she was forcing on him.

And then, after the straight shot across the bay, we came into the Barron River, into the smooth green-brown flow of it, with the old frame houses of the mainland shore off to port, clumps of cocoanut palm standing tall, skiffs tied handy. On the right, with its thousand feet of concrete dock, running along the river bank, was the Rod and Gun Club, first the long two-storied, citified, motel wing, then the high screened pool area that connected it to the old frame part, then the cottages beyond. Four presidents of the United States have hidden out here, finding a rustic privacy and some of the best fishing in the hemisphere. Giant poinciana trees were in bloom, many of them reaching heavy branches low over the water, breezes dropping the flaming petals into the smooth flow of tide and current, and a gigantic mahogany tree shaded the main entrance to the old part, the steps and the porch.

A stubby, sturdy, white charterboat was tied up there, a man hosing her down, probably after a half-day charter. A boy knelt nearby on the cement dock, cleaning three impres-

172

sive snook. I saw a tarpon that would go about ninety pounds hanging on the club rack.

I decided to put it ahead of the old white cruiser. Arthur, in the bow, readied a line. At dead slow the engine noise was reduced so I could hear voices forward. As we passed the fishing boat, the man with the hose looked over and said, "Well now, hydee Arthur!"

"How you, Jimbo?"

"Fine, fine. You crewin on that there?"

"Seen Sam?"

"Busted his foot up some. Hoist slipped and the engine out of his skiff fell on it. He's over home mendin."

"Sorry to hear it."

When I balanced forward motion and downstream current, Arthur jumped to the dock with a line and I waved him on to the piling I wanted. With it fast, I cut off the engines and the flow swung the stern in. I put on a stern line and spring line. Chook asked about fenders, and I saw that the rub rail would rest well against the pilings and told her not to bother.

We had lunch in the old paneled dining room, under the glassy stare of wall-mounted fish. Just a few tables were occupied. The season was dwindling with the club a month from closing until fall. We had hot monster stonecrab claws with melted butter. Arthur introduced us to the waitresses, and as they served us efficiently, they filled Arthur in on all local news and gossip, including the latest rumors on the manhunt for Boone Waxwell.

A coastguard chopper had made a tentative report about seeing a glimpse of a boat answering the description, about thirty miles south of us a little way up the Clark River from Ponce de Leon Bay, just as it disappeared under overhanging trees. A fast patrol launch had been sent to investigate.

The opinion was that years ago a man could hide out from the law almost indefinitely in all that cruel silent maze of swamp and hammock, creek, river and island, but not now. Not if they really wanted him. The choppers and the patrol boats and the radio net would inevitably narrow the search area and they would go in and get Waxwell. Probably not alive, considering what he was like and what he had done. They were saying that his best bet would be to get as far in as his boat would take him, sink the boat in the black water, and try to make it sixty miles across that incredible morass, heading northwest, keeping to cover, and come out maybe way over in the Westwood Lakes area. A Boone Waxwell might manage that, but three miles a day might be all even he could manage, so it could be three weeks before he came out the other side, if he didn't founder in bottomless black gunk between hammocks, if he could keep the mosquitoes and stinging flies from swelling his eyes shut, if he didn't get fever, if he kept out of the jaws of gators, moccasins and other venomous species of water snake, if he could tote or trap the food he'd need to see him through, if he could avoid the swamp buggies and air boats they'd be sending in on search patterns.

There was one detail I had overlooked, and from the lobby I phoned the hospital in Naples and got the cashier. She said with considerable severity that I had left AMA, Against Medical Advice, and it had been so noted on my record. She gave me the total amount of the fee, including use of emergency room space, tests, the four X-rays and the repair job. I said I would put a check in the mail, and she softened enough to tell me that I would be foolish to avoid seeing a doctor. The wound should be examined, dressing changed, stitches removed in due course.

After making the call, I found Chook out on the porch, and she said that Arthur had borrowed a car and had gone off to see the Dunnings. We went to the boat and she changed to white slacks. We anointed ourselves on all exposed areas with Off, and walked around the town. The original Collier, having made his fortune in advertising placards in streetcars in the north, had come down and created Everglades City by keeping a huge dredge working around the clock for over a year, building it up out of the swamplands. It served as a survey base and construction base for the building of the Tamiami Trail across the Glades to Miami. It had been a company town until finally, not long ago, the Collier interests had moved out. So there was an empty bank, an abandoned hospital, an abandoned headquarters, an unused railroad station, the rails long since torn up, the ties rotted away. But it was coming back now with the big boom going on at Marco, with the Miami population pressure moving ever westward, keyed by the land speculators.

My leg could take only so much of it. At four o'clock we were back aboard. I took a shower. Showers created an eerie effect on the desensitized skin of my arm and leg, as if they were wrapped in cellophane which dulled the needles of the hard spray. I wore Chook's shower cap to keep the dressing dry. After the shower I took a nap. Chook woke me a little after six to say Arthur wasn't back and she was getting concerned about him.

174

"Maybe it's taking him a long time to get them to take that crisp new thousand."

"I wanted to get out of here, Trav."

"We'll get out. The weather is still holding. The days are long. I'd like a little light to get through the channel, and then it doesn't matter. A south southeast course after we're clear, and when we pick up the lights of Key West off the starboard bow, we'll pick us an anchorage, or, maybe better, I'll lug it way down so that by dawn we'll be about right to pick up the channel markers to go up Florida Bay. Stand watches."

"I just feel as if we ought to get going."

Arthur came trotting along the dock at seven, carrying his wooden box of carpenter tools, grinning and cheerful, apologetic about taking so long. He said he had a terrible time about the money, particularly with Sam, but when he had finally put it on the basis of the kids, Leafy had argued his way. It was finally decided they'd put it in the bank and consider it Arthur's money and touch it only in case of emergency, and then consider it a loan. He said that Christine was placidly, healthily, happily and obviously pregnant, and she'd found a nice boy from Copeland who was going to marry her, much to Leafy's satisfaction.

As we chugged across the bay toward the channel through the islands, toward the last burnt orange sunset line, the first stars were visible. Chook, with a holiday gayety, had changed to what she called her clown pants, stretch pants that fitted tight as her healthy hide, patterned in huge diamonds of black, white and orange, very high waisted, and with it a white silk blouse with long full sleeves. She moved in dance steps, brought the helmsman a lusty drink, lucked onto a Key West station doing the best efforts of the big bands of yesteryear, and turned it loud. Between her dancing, her happy jokes, her bawdy parodies of the lyrics she happened to know, she would hustle below and take a few pokes at what she promised would be a gourmet adventure. She turned us into a party boat.

We were in the winding and sometimes narrow channel between the mangrove islands when I heard a curious sound which I thought came from one of my engines, as if something had caused it to rev up. I checked the panel and saw that the rpm's were normal. Chook and Arthur were below. The loud music had masked the sound I had heard.

But I heard Chook's scream. And just as I did, I saw something out of the tail of my right eye and turned and saw, in the deceptive dusk light, the empty white boat moving astern of us, turning slowly as we passed it. The boat I had seen on the trailer in Boone Waxwell's yard.

There is damned little you can do in a narrow channel. I yanked the twin levers into reverse, gave the engines one hard burst to pull the *Flush* dead in the water, and put the shift levers in neutral. The only thing that immediately came to hand was the fishkiller, a billy club near the wheel. I forgot the damned leg. When I hit the lower deck it crumpled and spilled me. I scrabbled up and went in the after door to the lounge, into the full blast of the music. Lights were on in the lounge. Mr. Goodman was doing Sing, Sing, Sing, the long one with all that drum. Arthur stood in the posture of a man with severe belly cramps, staring at Chookie McCall standing in the corridor just beyond the other doorway, Boone grinning over her white silk shoulder. One arm was pulled behind her. She looked scared and angry. She tried to twist away. Boone's arm went up, metal in the hand picking up a gleam from the galley brightness beyond him. It came down with wicked force on the crown of her dark head, and I saw her face go blank as she fell forward, falling heavily face down, with no attempt to break the fall, landing half in and half out of the lounge. With one bare foot he tentatively prodded her buttocks. The flesh under her circus pants moved with an absolute looseness, a primitive and effective test of total unconsciousness. When faking or semi-conscious, those muscles will inevitably tighten.

Arthur, with a groan audible over the drum solo, charged right toward the muzzle of the revolver Boone had clubbed her with. Boone merely squatted and put the muzzle against the back of Chook's head and grinned up at him. Arthur skidded to a clumsy, flailing halt and backed away. Waxwell shifted the revolver to his left hand, put his right hand to his belt, deftly unsheathed the narrow limber blade. He moved forward a little, picked her head up by the hair, put his right hand with the blade under her throat and let the head fall, forehead thumping the rug. Arthur backed further. Waxwell aimed the gun at my belly and made an unmistakable gesture of command. I tossed the fish club onto the yellow couch.

"Cut the music off!" Waxwell yelled.

I turned it off. The only sound in the silence was the idling rumble of the diesels.

"McGee, you want your bilges to pump pink for the next three month, nobody gets cute. Right now we got things to

176

do. McGee, you get on up topside and keep this barge off'n the stubs, and ease on back to my boat, very gentle. If you can transmit from topside, I'll hear your power generator whine, and I'll slice this gullet here wide open. Arthur, boy, you get you a boat hook and fish up the bow line and make it fast when we come up on it, hear? Now *move!*"

It did not do me a bit of good to realize how he had managed it. He'd been tucked back into some little bayou under overhanging mangrove, had let us move by in the narrow channel, all lights and music, and then had come out and come up on us in a fast curve from astern, up to the starboard side, amidships, making the roaring sound I had heard, had cut his engine, jumped and grabbed the rail, come in though the doorway onto the side deck to take Chook unawares in the galley, gun in his hand.

We were in a turning drift toward a channel island, and I eased it away from trouble, put one engine in forward and the other in reverse to bring it cautiously around within its own length. I needed no special warning to watch for stubs. Tide currents undercut the old islands. Mangrove and water oak settle deep and die, and the above water parts weather away. But the underwater segment hardens, usually one blunt-tipped portion of the main trunk, curving down to where the hard dead roots still anchor it. It will give when you run into one, spring back and maybe slide along the hull. But if the angle is right they will punch a hole through one inch of mahogany.

I brought the *Flush* around, then scanned my spotlight across the water and picked up the white boat.

"Get it at the port stern," I called to Arthur. When we were on it, I heard it bump the hull once, and looked back and saw him get the line, stoop and bend it around a transom cleat.

"Now you go on just like before," Waxwell bawled to me from below. "Only dead slow. You see any traffic, you sing out. Keep it in your mind, ol buddy, ol buster boy, I can as well ditch the three of you and run it myself, so be real good. Arthur, hike your tired ass in here and bring me a bucketa cold water for fancypants."

Arthur went below. I kept to the channel, barely maintaining steerage way. I thought of fifty splendid ideas, and maybe half of them would work and all of them would leave Chook shrunken, bleached and dead. In my great cleverness, I had left him with nothing to lose.

As we came out of the channel, moving out toward the sea

buoy, and as the first swells began to lift us, I heard voices aft, turned and saw the three of them back there. Chook stood in a listless slump, hands lashed behind her, head bowed, dark hair spilling forward. Waxwell held her with a companionable hand on her shoulder, upright knife clamped under his thumb. I watched Arthur, at Waxwell's instruction, bring the white boat close, refasten it, clamber over and drop into it and hand up a bulky duffle bag, a rifle, a wooden box, apparently heavy. We were past the sea buoy and out into deep water. At Waxwell's orders, Arthur freed the smaller stern anchor, lifted it high overhead and smashed it down into the bottom of the towed boat. He retrieved it by the anchor line, smashed it down twice more. By then Waxwell's boat was visibly settling, and putting enough drag on that stern corner so that I had to turn the wheel to compensate. When the gunnels were almost awash, he had Arthur free the line. He yelled up to me to put the spotlight on it. When it was fifty feet astern, it showed a final gleam of white and went down.

"Give it a south southwest heading, McGee," he yelled. "Put it up to cruising, put it on pilot, and get on down here."

He sat on the couch beside Chook. He lounged. She had to sit erect, hands behind her, and she kept her head down, chin on her chest. He put us in front of him, a dozen feet away, on straight chairs, with the request to keep our hands on our knees.

He looked at us and shook his head. "Couldn b'lieve my ol eyes. *Had* to figure to take me a boat. Holed up where I figure the best chance to get me a good one, rough up some of them power squadron types, get em on the way out from Everglades with the best chance of full tanks, teach em to do exactly like ol Boo wants. And by God here comes this *Busted Flush* I heard about in Marco from when you were anchored over off Roy Cannon Island, folks that rented Arlie Mission's outboard, the one you come to Goodland in with the name covered over. One teeny little son of a bitch of a world. My, my."

He beamed. "Now would you look at ol Arthur there. I plain give him the cold sweats. You know, I heard them Dunnings tooken you in, and you were working around that part. No need to come look you up, I figured. I needed just one time to put ol Boo's mark on you. Never did think you'd get sassy again."

"Did you kill Wilma?" Arthur asked.

But Waxwell was studying me. "You're more surprise than

178

this broadass barge, friend McGee. I'd a swore you were drippin loose brains when I toted you to the car." He chuckled. "Give me a real turn findin you gone. But I figured it out."

"Congratulations."

"It had to be that fat little son of a gun, Cal Stebber. A smart one. He would have had somebody along on account of Arthur here wouldn't be any use to anybody. Come took you outen the car to take you to get patched up. It was you got him worked up about me, McGee, lettin him know whereat Wilma was seen last. So I figure after I drove off, he went on in and shot them two dead, phoned in my license, knowing he could lay it onto me and it would be safer the law takes care of me than him trying it. With me on the run, maybe he even figures to get aholt of the cash money Wilma was toten, but I have the idea it'll stay where it is till I'm ready to go back for it. That fat little fella messed me up for sure. And kilt off one of the best ol pieces a man could hope to find, afore I even got her broke in real good. But there come ol Boo's luck like always, bringin him one on the same style, oney bigger and younger, hey, pussycat?"

Lazily he touched the blade point to her upper arm near the shoulder. She gave a little jump, but made no sound. The fabric was pulled tight where he had touched. A bright red dot appeared where he had touched.

"You did kill Wilma," Arthur said.

Waxwell gave him a pained look. "Now Boo isn't one to waste something that fine. Little tiny bit of a gal, but I tell you, she was just about as much as ol Boo could handle. What happened, Arthur boy, she liked things real rough, and I guess it was the second night after you were there, we boozed up pretty good and it went wrong somehow, caught her wrong some way, and wrenched up her back, real bad. She couldn't even get up onto her feet come morning. And my, how she talked mean, like she was the queen and I was some bum. I was supposed to lift her gentle into the car and tear-ass off to a hospital. But I felt right sickly, said I'd get around to it sooner or later. Never did hear such a dirty mouth on a woman, the things she called me. And she wouldn't be still, even when I asked her nice. So I went over there and, just to give her the idea, with my thumb and finger I give her one little quick pinch in her little throat. She looked up at me and her eyes begin to bug out and her face gets dark red. Her little chest was pumpin, tryin to suck air in. I must have bust something. She waved her arms, flapped

179

around a little, shoved her tongue out and next thing you know, she's dead as a mullet, her face all purpled out. Arthur, I sure didn't mean to do it like it happened, but after I been through her stuff, I found enough cash money, had I knowed it was there to start, I'd have done it more on purpose. She's up the Chatham River, boy, down in the deep end of Chevelier Bay, her and her pretties sunk down with cement block, wired real good, even that little diamond watch down there with her, because enough money can make a man afford to be smart."

"Half smart," I said.

He looked at me with mild disapproval. "I tried to like you, boy, and I just couldn't work it out."

"You bought a lot of fancy gear with that money, Boo. It makes people wonder where you got it. And bought a scooter for poor fat little Cindy. That attracts attention. You tried to make me swallow a clumsy lie about a girl who looked like Wilma. You got nervous about me and went flailing around, getting Crane Watts all rattled. Hell, man, you didn't even get rid of all Wilma's stuff. How about the black lace pants Cindy tried to get into and couldn't?"

"I din find them until . . . you're all mouth, McGee. Cindy told you that, hah? What else she talk about?"

"Everything she could think of."

"I'm going to get back to her some day. And real good. Enough talking. I got to look this boat over. Arthur, you go find me some pliers and some wahr. Move, boy!"

When Arthur came back with them and went slowly toward Boone, even I could tell he was going to make a play. I gathered myself to do what I could, feeling no optimism. There was a clumsy rush, a fleshy smack, and before I was halfway up, Arthur was tottering back to turn and fall heavily. I sat down again. Arthur sat up, his eyes dazed and his mouth bloody.

Boone lifted Chook's heavy dark hair out of the way, took the top of her ear between thumb and finger and laid the knife blade against her temple. Without any trace of anger he said, "Just one more time, one more little bitty thing, and I slice off this pretty little piece of meat and make her hand it to you, lover boy."

Arthur got slowly to his feet. "Now you pick up that wahr and pliers and wahr McGee's ankles together, and when he lies down and puts his arms around that table leg that's bolted fast to the deck there, and you wahr his wrists good."

In a little while we were neighbors, Arthur and me, tightly and efficiently wired to the adjoining legs of the heavy wall table, and Waxwell had gone off to make a tour of inspection of the *Flush*, pushing Chook ahead of him, speaking to her with that same heavy, insinuating jocularity I had heard him use on Vivian Watts, saying, "That's right, that's fine. You just go along there, pussycat, and ol Boo'll stay right with you. My, my, you a big sweet piece of girl for sure." His voice faded as they went past the galley and staterooms toward the bow.

"My *God*, my *God*!" Arthur moaned.

"Steady down. Aside from one damn fool play, you're doing fine."

"But she acts half alive."

"She's still dazed. That was a hell of a rap. He did it very neatly, Arthur, getting aboard. We have to just hope he's smart enough to know he needs us."

"What for?" he demanded bitterly.

"If he doesn't know, I'll tell him. They'll check all boats leaving the Everglades area. He'll have to have us handy to get us a clearance, while he keeps us in line by staying out of sight with a knife at her throat. So we wait for a chance, one that we can make work."

"He'll never give us one. Never."

"Let me take the lead. Try to be ready all the time. Your job is Chook. She's his leverage. The minute I make a move, your job is get her away from him. A flying tackle, anything."

They came back to the lounge, Boone chuckling to himself. "You got this thang as prettied up as a Tallahassee whore house, McGee. This big old gal says her name is Chookie. Now ain't that one hell of a name? Come on, darlin. We're going to see what she's like topsides."

After they went out, I said to Arthur, "Act as if that last punch broke you down completely. You're whipped. It will make him less wary thinking he only has me to watch."

"But, my God, Trav, if he . . . if he leaves us right here like this and takes Chook back there and . . ."

"There won't be one damned thing you can do about it, I can do about it or she can do about it. It will happen, and be over and done, and we'll still have exactly the same problem."

"I couldn't stand that."

I did not answer him. I felt a change in movement of the boat and knew he was at the topside controls. He added rpm to both engines. They were out of sync at the new throttle setting. In a few moments he smoothed them out. I identified the clunk as he put it back into automatic pilot.

He brought Chookie back into the lounge. "Sure can't turn much knots in this tub. But she's fueled up and got a good range. I figured the heading to the Marquesas Keys, McGee."

"Congratulations."

"How it's going to work, we're going to cut between Key West and the Marquesas, then make like we were heading along the keys to come on up to Miami. But what we're going to do, we're going to cut it real real wide outside the keys, and come dark tomorrow night, we douse all running lights and run for Cuba as fast as this here bucket will go. Time them Cuban patrol boats intercept us, the only folks aboard will be a poor simple ol backwoodsy guide, and his real quiet lovin girlfriend, both runnin from the capitalists. If you both behave nice, I'm going to set you loose in that little dinghy halfway to Cuba. If you make me one piece of trouble, you get to go swimming with an anchor. Clear?"

"Yes sir, Mr. Waxwell sir."

"Now if I was half smart, like you claim, McGee, I'd just run this sweet thing back into that big bed and settle my nerves down a little. But she feels poorly and it would play pure hell if somebody run up to check us over. So once we pass a check, there's time to wahr you on up again, hoe this beard down, rench off the swamp water in that fancy shower and bed this pretty thang down."

I could turn my head and look up at them. Boone turned her, snipped the scrap of nylon line from her wrists with a flick of the knife blade, scabbarded the blade and snapped the false buckle into place. He turned her around and she stood staring dully down at her wrists, rubbing them. He took the revolver from the waistband of his pants where it had been snugged against a softness of belly.

"Now you gone be a sweet pussycat. You see this here? You gone go hot up some food for ol Boo. He's gone loose these boys for a time, and you play any games, he goes eeny meeney miney and whichever one it comes out, ol Boo blows his kneebones to pebbles."

She gave no sign of hearing or understanding. His right hand flickered, cracked her cheek so hard it took her a quarter turn around, making her take a long step to catch her balance. He pulled her back by the arm and said, "I getten through to you, gal?"

182

"Please, please," she said in a wan little voice.

"Sure hope you got more life in you on your back, pussycat, than you got on your feet." He fondled her roughly and casually, breast and belly, flank and hip while she stood flatfooted, enduring it like a mare at an auction. He pushed her toward the galley. She took two jolting steps to catch her balance, and then walked on slowly, not looking back. She could have been, I thought, in a sleep-walking concussive state, or it could be her own game of possum. If the former, it might deaden things for her. If she was being clever, I had to be alert for the opening she wanted to give me.

When Boone bent over Arthur with the cutting pliers, I tried a little idea of my own. "Better do me first, Boo."

"Why?"

"I've got the reserve batteries on charge, and there's no regulator on that bank. It's past time to change back. I go by an estimate of time. It could burn them out. So if you set me loose first, then you can take me forward so I can switch them over."

"Now why you fret about batteries that ain't hardly yours any more?"

"It's rigged so the lights feed off the bank being charged, Boo, and if the lights went out all of a sudden, you might get nervous with that gun."

"That's being right bright there, buster boy."

He released me and, when we went forward, gathered up Chook from the galley and brought her along to prevent her going to the lounge and releasing Arthur. He wasn't going to make any obvious mistakes. As I went forward, ahead of the gun, I was trying desperately to figure out a problem in compass compensation. The compass that controlled the automatic pilot was set well forward, away from any chance bulk of metal which could put it off, cased in a wooden box in a sort of flat shelf area forward of the forward bilge hatch. I wanted to change the automatic pilot direction from southwest to southeast. Okay, so I had to move magnetic north . . . to the left. And with north behind us that meant I had to put my hunk of metal . . . this side of the compass box and to the left. And it had to be a guess. If I pulled it off too radically, Waxwell would feel the change when we corrected onto the new course. And too small a change would do us no good. And there was nothing down in that hatch that had anything to do with batteries. But I kept a big wrench down there, in a side rack, one too big for the tool box. And there was a switch down there, obsolete but never removed. It had run a separate forward bilge pump before I had put the three of them on the same control. I had to move fast, and in the dark. I yanked the hatch up, told him to hold it, and dropped down. I got the wrench on the first grab and slid it onto the shelf, behind and to the left of the compass box. I reached and found the purposeless switch and changed the blade from up to down. I waited a few moments, pushed the wrench closer to the compass.

"Climb on up out of there, McGee!"

"All done," I said cheerfully. I jumped up and sat on the edge of the hatch, feet dangling, casually examined my knuckle as if I had barked it.

"Come on!" he said impatiently. As I turned to climb out, I found the wrench handle with the side of my foot and pushed it further toward the compass box. I sensed the course change then, stumbled on the edge of the hatch, fell clumsily to create a diversion. He moved cat-quick out of reach, letting the hatch slam, keeping the gun on me.

"Foot's asleep from that wire, Boo," I said apologetically.

"Get on back to your chair, boy."

Back in the lounge, as if in answer to a prayer, I heard a beginning patter of light rain on the deck above. I doubted Waxwell had the training to use the navigation aids aboard to figure a position, but I knew damned well that he could take one glance at the stars and know the heading was way off.

Arthur and I sat on the straight chairs. Waxwell instructed us in how to act if we were intercepted by launch or float plane. He would be below, with the girl tied and a knife at her throat. And if we were boarded, he estimated he had a good chance of taking them.

"Was that the gun you had the silencer on?" I asked him.

"Damn mail order thang," he said. "Too loud. Tried it one more time once I got home that night and it pure blew all to hell."

Chook came shuffling listlessly in with sandwiches and coffee for him. He took the tray on his lap, sat her at his left, held the knife in his left hand close to her ribs, put the gun on the couch at his right, kept his eyes on us as he wolfed the sandwiches. I tried to get some clue or signal from Chook. She sat dull-faced, hands slack in her lap, staring at the floor. The diesels were roaring at high cruise, setting up little sympathetic vibrations, rattlings and jinglings. The Gulf was as flat calm as I've ever seen it, and the gentle rain continued. I knew that sooner or later he would go up top and check the control panel and the compass direction. I knew I had altered it, but I had no way of telling how much. I wanted to delay him. I looked at my watch and saw to my surprise it was nearly ten o'clock.

As he put his empty coffee mug down I said, "Want to hear on the radio how they're about to catch you?"

"Let's have a good laugh, sure thing."

I went over and spun the dial on AM, brought in Key West, and was pleased to hear them give national news first, ten minutes of it. Boo sent Chook to bring him more hot coffee.

"And on the local scene, the big hunt for Everglades killer Boone Waxwell has shifted abruptly to a new area tonight. Just as authorities were beginning to fear that Waxwell had slipped out of the net in the Clark River area, two small boys, skiff fishing in the islands west of Chokoloskee Bay returned home to Everglades City at dusk to report seeing a suspicious acting man in a boat that tallies with the description of Waxwell's boat in which he made his escape from the Caxambas area."

"Swore them little bastards din spot me," Boo said.

"Based on the boys' account of details not released previously, authorities are convinced they saw the fugitive, and all efforts are now being concentrated on sealing the area and conducting a massive search beginning at dawn."

"Well, I just *did* get out of there in time now," Waxwell said.

"But they'll have our name and description from the Rod and Gun," I told him, "and I'll bet you they're trying to raise us on all bands right now. They'll start an air search for us at dawn, Boo baby."

With furrowed brow he held his hand out for the coffee. Chook came slowly toward him, dragging her feet, the mug steaming. She reached as though to put it in his hand, then hurled the contents at his face. He could have seen it only out of the corner of his eye, but quick as she was, he was quicker, reminding me of the way he had almost gotten to me to stomp me before I rolled under his boat. He got his face and eyes out of the way, but a dollop of the boiling brew hit him across the throat and shoulder. With bullroar, he was up off that couch, knife in the left hand, pistol in the right. By then I was in mid-air, launched at his knees. As he spun away from me, he took a flashing slice at Chook, and she evaded it only by the speed of a dancer's

185

reflexes, jumping back, curving her body, sucking her belly away from the very end of the blade. I rolled up onto my heels, squatting. Arthur was trying to edge around behind him, a heavy pottery ashtray poised.

Boo backed away, put the gun on Chook. "In the belly," he said tightly. "That's where the bitch gets it. Lay that down gentle, Arthur boy. Back away, McGee."

I knew from his eyes we were not going to have another chance. Not now.

And then there was a funny hollow thump from up forward, and then a horrible smashing, thudding, grinding, ripping noise, with the bow going up, canting, slowing so abruptly we were all staggered. She is not a fast old lady, but she has thirty-eight tons of momentum. To a boat owner, a noise like that is like hearing the heart torn out of you, and it froze me in place. And Arthur, still staggering, hurled the ashtray at Boone Waxwell. Sensing something coming, Boone whirled to fire. Arthur confessed later he had hoped to hit Boone in the head. The broad dimension of the ashtray hit the hand and the pistol as Boone was swinging it around. The heavy pottery broke into a dozen fragments and the pistol went spinning toward Chook's feet. She pounced on it and came up with it, holding it in both hands straight out in front of her, eyes squinched, head turned slightly away from the expected explosion. It made one hell of a bam in the enclosed space. Boone tried to run to get behind Arthur, but ran right into the chair I threw at him. Another wild bam from the pistol in the hands of the very earnest brunette convinced him, and he ran out onto the after deck. The poor old diesels were still laboring, trying to shove the *Flush* all the way up onto the island. He scurried to the port side and swarmed up the ladderway to the sun deck. I started after him and Chook yelled to me to look out. She braced herself on the tilt of deck and fired up at him. Maybe Waxwell thought to go forward and jump off onto the mangrove island. But the determined girl apparently convinced him he should take to the water. The forward twenty feet of the *Flush* was wedged up into the mangrove tangle. When he ran across the sun deck, I ran across the after deck, nearly knocking Arthur overboard.

I got around the corner in time to see him make his leap into the black water, a dozen feet short of the mangrove roots. He jumped high and wide to clear the narrow side deck, jumped feet first like a kid going off a high board. He

186

hit just where the bright galley lights shone out the port, silvering the water. You expect a great splash. He stopped with a horrid abruptness, the waterline still a few inches below his belt. He remained right there, oddly erect, silent, head thrown back, cords standing out in his neck. I thought he had wedged himself into a shallow mud bottom. But then I saw he seemed to be moving back and forth, a strange sway like a man on a treetop. He reached down to himself, putting his hands under the water, and he made a ghastly sound, like someone trying to yell in a whisper. He turned his head slowly and looked toward the three of us. He held his right hand out toward us, opened his mouth wide and made the same eerie sound once more. Then he bowed slowly to us, laid over gently, face down. Something seemed to nudge at him from below, nudge him and shove him free, and as he floated toward darkness, slowly there reappeared, with a slowness that told of the length of it that went down through black water to the dead root system, just an inch or so showing above water, the dark rotted end of the stub, four or five inches thick, upon which he had burst himself and impaled himself.

Chook was clinging to Arthur and crying as though her heart had broken.

Her arms went around his neck, and the gun slipped from her slack fingers, put a little dent in my rail before plopping into the sea. I sent them inside, got a light and the longest boathook, went to the starboard deck, hooked him most gingerly by the back of his shirt collar, towed him forward and hung him against the small dark shoots of the new mangrove sprouting at the waterline. Only then did I remember my laboring engines and run to turn them off before they burned out. Arthur sat in the lounge in the big chair, Chook in his lap, all arms wrapped tightly and all eyes closed, making no sound and no movement. I crawled the bilge with the big flashlight, looking for some little hole the size of a motorcycle sidecar. Probably some seams were sprung, but she looked sound. Surprisingly sound.

When I went back through, Arthur asked me if he could help. I took him aft and we sounded all around the stern area with boat hooks and found there was plenty of water back there. I sent him forward in the bilge with a light and a little emergency horn on a compressed air can to give me a blast if broken mangrove trunks started to come in.

I tried to back it straight off. I got about a yard with full throttle, thought things over, then tried one forward and one in reverse to swing the stern. It swung, with an unpleasant crackling sound from up forward. I had noticed that the compass put us on a dead easterly heading at the time we hit. It'd gotten more change than I'd hoped for. Figuring time, we couldn't be very far south of Pavilion Key, maybe halfway down to the Chatham River. I backed, gained a little more, swung it the other way, backed again. After the fourth swing, she suddenly came all the way off, making very ugly noises.

I backed clear, turned her, put her on pilot on a due west heading, and at very meager rpms, went scrambling down to the bilges to see how she was. And she was, astonishingly, bone dry sound. Apparently the hull shape had just pushed that springy mangrove aside.

I located our position with the radio loop, close enough for my purposes. I remembered the wrench and got it away from the pilot compass before I ran us aground again.

A Coast Guard chopper circled us a half hour after dawn, making that distinctive whappling noise. He hung off the stern while we all beamed and waved at him, and finally, after he had done everything but throw his hand phone at us, I gave a great gesture of comprehension and ran to my set. He moved a half mile away so I could hear and came in on the Coast Guard frequency. I was astonished we'd been so close to a maniac like Waxwell, yes indeed. Wow. It makes you think. When we broke off, he gave himself a little treat. He came over and took a long appreciative look at Chook. She had come out in a little flimsy shorty nightgown to wave at the pretty helicopter, and the flyer and his buddy up there swung craftily around to put the rising sun behind her. But the instant he was gone, we stopped grinning like maniacs.

"Is it right, Trav," she said. "All those people hunting and hunting?"

"The tide was an hour past high when I snagged him onto the shore. There aren't any branches over him. They ought to find him soon."

I put her on radio watch, monitoring the Coast Guard frequency. At quarter of eight she came up to tell us they had the body and a positive identification. She looked wan and dreary, and we sent her back to bed. But before she went, she gave Arthur a rib-cracking hug, stared into his eyes with her head cocked, and said, "I just thought I'd tell you something. Frankie would not have done what you did. For me. For anyone. Except Frankie."

188

After she sacked out, we went through Waxwell's gear. We deep-sixed it, rifle and all. Except something we found in the box under his dehydrated rations. Carefully folded into saran wrap. Ninety-one brand new hundred dollar bills in serial sequence.

Chook came up for air at three in the afternoon, all soft and blurred and dreamy.

"What do we do," she said, "anchor for four or five or six days, like on the way over, huh?"

"Okay," they said, simultaneously, and it was at that moment I decided the unexpected nine thousand was a wedding present, if my hunch paid off.

SIXTEEN

MY HUNCH paid off, on the Fourth of July, with perhaps the only beach picnic reception of the season serving hamburgers and champagne to about two hundred types, from beach bums to a state senator, from waitresses to a legitimate, by blood, baroness.

And on the afternoon of the Fifth of July, as I was once again making the motions of assembling the delayed cruise over to the islands, a merry voice called me up from the engine room. And there, at my gangplank, slender and graceful as a young birch tree, dressed in a pale high fashion gray, five matched pieces of luggage standing beside her, cab driver hovering in the background, stood Miss Debra Brown, Calvin Stebber's disciplined cigar-lighter and daiquiri mixer, her crystal mint eyes alight with mischief and promise.

"It's all right, driver," she said.

He turned to go and I said, "Hold it, driver."

"But darling," she said, "you don't understand. There was this contest, three words or less, how and where and with whom would you most like to spend your vacation, and you *won*, darling McGee. And here I am!"

I slowly wiped my hands on the greasy rag I had brought up from below. "So Uncle Cal got it in his head I got a very nice piece of Wilma's bundle, and you've cooked up something that might work."

She pouted. "Darling, I hardly blame you. After all. But really, I have just been terribly terribly mopey ever since you

189

visited us. You genuinely intrigued me, dear. And this is a very seldom thing with Debra, believe me. Poor Calvin, he finally got so weary of all my little sighs and hints that he told me to come over and get it out of my system before I came down with the vapors or something. I swear to you, dear McGee, this is an entirely personal affair, and has nothing whatever to do with . . . my professional career."

It was a temptation. She was a convincing elegance. Headwaiters would unhook the velvet rope and bow you in. Elegance with the faintest oversweet odor of decay. Perhaps for any man there can be something very heady about a woman totally amoral, totally without mercy, shame or softness.

But I had to remember her, too vividly, lighting Stebber's cigar.

"Sweetie," I said, "you are a penny from heaven. And you probably know lots and lots of tricks. But every one would remind me that you are a pro, from Wilma's old stable of club fighters. Call me a sentimentalist. The bloom is too far off the rose, sweetie. I'd probably keep leaving money on the bureau. You better peddle it. Thanks but no thanks."

The lips curled back and her face went so tight, I saw what a pretty and delicate little skull she'd make, picked clean, as Wilma's now was, in the dark bottom of Chevelier Bay. Without a word she whirled and went off toward the distant cab. The driver looked at me as if I'd lost my mind. He managed three bags on the first trip, and came after the others at a trot, looking whipped with a salty lash.

I don't know what it is that makes that difference. I don't know now, and maybe I never will. Maybe the people who fit have some forlorn fancy about perfecting themselves in their own image, about living up to some damned thing always a little out of reach. But you try. You reach and slip and fall and get up, and you reach some more.

I went below, slapped a wrench on a nut, put my back into it, and took the hide off the top of three knuckles. I sat down there in the hot gloom like a big petulant baby, sucking on my knuckles, remembering the shape and sway of her in gray, walking away, and thinking some of the blackest thoughts I own.

About the Author

JOHN D. MacDONALD, says *The New York Times,* "is a very good writer, not just a good 'mystery writer.' " His Travis McGee novels have established their hero as a modern-day Sam Spade and, along with MacDonald's more than 500 short stories and other bestselling novels—60 in all, including *Condominium* and *The Green Ripper*—have stamped their author as one of America's best all-round contemporary storytellers.